OUT OF MY MIND

A Collection of Short Stories

By

Tom Maloy

Thomas O. Maloy
4171 Lovingwood Trail
Powder Springs, GA 30127

The characters and events in this book are fictitious. Any similarity to any persons, living or dead is coincidental and not intended by the author.

ISBN-13: 978-0-9964407-0-7
ISBN-10: 0996440704

Printed in the United States of America

For
My Mother, Father
and Sister

Contents:

Introduction

One might say that my friendship with Tom Maloy had as its genesis a shared love of chili dogs from Atlanta's famous Varsity restaurant. I met Tom when he was a vice president at Equifax, the giant information services company, and I was a senior vice president of Manning, Selvage and Lee, Equifax's outside public relations counsel. We began meeting regularly for lunch at Atlanta's world-famous Varsity restaurant. Thus, what began as a business relationship grew into a close friendship. That friendship—along with the tradition of enjoying Varsity chili dogs together—has continued into our retirement years.

Among the things that struck me about Tom from the beginning, two stand out: one, the depth of his knowledge of a variety of subjects, and two, an understanding of the good and the bad of the human condition. It was not until we had retired that I learned Tom was a short-story writer.

Having written and published several books, including four works of fiction, I am often asked by aspiring writers to critique their work. I have learned to be wary of such requests. Experience has taught me that most people who ask my opinion of something they have written really want my approval, not my criticism. Thus, I have found it impolitic to offer *real* criticism, so I simply say something like, "Way to go; keep up the good work" or some equally meaningless platitude.

Tom often asks me to read something he has written, such as the stories in this book. When he does, I know that he really welcomes my opinion, good or bad. He may not accept every suggestion I make—I would be surprised if he did—but I'm confident that he considers them all seriously.

Every writer needs someone he can count on to give criticism. For me, Tom has become that person. When he tells me something, I take it to heart because I'm confident it is sincere and intended to make my work better. It often has.

I have read and criticized every story in this book. I have enjoyed them, some more than others, of course. I flatter myself by thinking that in some small way I have made them all a little better. So, sit back, prop up your feet, and invest a couple of hours in reading some good yarns. You'll be rewarded.

Richard Dowis
Waleska, Ga.

From the Author

Ideas need to be expressed. Neglected, an idea withers and dies, leaving nothing more than a canker on the mind that restricts imagination and denies deeper exploration. Over the years, I have expressed my ideas in writing. Some ideas simply require writing down to satisfy their longing for freedom. Others beg to be developed into a scene, and the scene into a story. For me, an idea can emerge from an experience that may be as subtle as an aroma or as palpable as a gunshot. But once it is implanted, it nags to get out. The seventeen short stories in this book represent just a few of the ideas that, at long last, have made it out of my mind.

Tom Maloy

I

"To one who has faith, no explanation is necessary.
To one without faith, no explanation is possible."
— Thomas Aquinas

Only Love Survives

It was November in northern Indiana. Leaves were still falling from the maple, oak and elm trees that lined the Fort Wayne streets. Large piles, like multi-colored snowdrifts, accentuated the boundaries between street and sidewalk, creating forts, caves and other types of imaginary battlements in which neighborhood kids frolicked. I played here when I was a kid. Those were good times; hiding out under the cover of leaves, the red and yellow colors intensified by the brilliant fall sun filtering through the naked branches overhead. The peaceful beauty of the scene gave no warning of the events that would soon change my life.

Due to the exceptionally mild fall weather, the leaves had held onto the trees an extra-long time, finally falling all at once after a late first frost. In my rear view mirror, multicolored pieces of leaves looked like confetti, rising in the slip stream of my car, then falling back into the piles along the sides of the street. It was a picture that could have been found on a post card in a local pharmacy, but the memories that it conjured were bitter sweet, memories of leaves that I had raked into piles more than four decades ago in order to do my part to support Mom and me, memories of the rough wooden rake handle and the blisters that rose on my hands, the skin weeping, toughening and finally sloughing off until nothing remained but calluses, memories of Mom's gentle hands as she applied a poultice

2

to ease the discomfort—those same gentle hands that paid the rent, put clothes on our backs and groceries on the table while I was growing up.

What a wonderful woman, my mother. Just thinking of her elicits feelings of warmth and security long since erased by the callousness of life. She gave me the courage to leave this Midwestern town to pursue my destiny, and she was the only reason I was returning. She carried me, nurtured me, and from the time I was nine years old, raised me by herself. I always thought she did a damned good job too, given what she had to work with. And work she did, sacrificing her own happiness and well-being to make sure that I was fed, clothed, housed, educated, and above all, loved. Her high school education had taught her typing and shorthand, and that was all she needed to land a secretarial job spanning the few years between her graduation and marriage to my father. She never dreamed she would ever need those skills again. And then my father left us.

Just the thought of him provoked a sudden chill, too cold to be attributed only to the brisk fall air. There was little to think about really. He was a salesman of some sort, so he was gone a lot, and we never got a chance to do those things that father and son are supposed to do together. Then, when I was nine, he left for good. No goodbyes, just left. Mom and I never saw him again, and I vowed to forget about him just as he had forgotten about us. My only feeling for him was rancor, but that was enough to fill the void created by his absence. Mom never knew why he left or where he went. *I knew*, but I never told her. I tried a few times, but didn't have the heart. Perhaps things would have been better if I had.

The police had no interest in the case. After all, they had more important things to do than to track down an errant husband. Mom's daily phone calls to the police department's missing persons section, always elicited the same answer. "If we find anything, we'll let you know." It was finally filed as a simple case of abandonment.

"Mrs. Martin, I'm afraid your husband just ran away. They do that sometimes. Sorry, but we don't have the manpower to keep looking. If he ever shows up, you can have him thrown in jail," they had said.

Mom never accepted the idea that he simply had abandoned us. Her greatest fear was that he may have been somewhere hurt or ill and was suffering. She always told me he would come home if he could, but I knew different. Tomorrow, on her 79th birthday, Mom would still believe he was coming back

When dad drove away, he left us with no insurance and little savings. Mom and I had to work doubly hard just to keep what little we had. Every odd job I had to take was a reminder that my father didn't love me enough to stay. It would have been better if he had died, like Freddie Watson's dad. Freddie seemed inconsolable at his dad's funeral, but within a few days he was back at school playing and cutting up like nothing had happened. At least he knew where his dad was, and the insurance money put his family in pretty good financial shape. As a nine-year-old, I *hated* my father for not dying. Thinking about him as I drove toward Mom's house made me realize that I still did.

Mom pulled us through by typing term papers for the college students from the Purdue and Indiana University extensions and the other colleges in the area. She was good at it and the word got around that Marilyn Martin was the only person to type your term paper. She soon had more business than she could handle. She was making almost as much money as she could have as a secretary, and she could stay home with me to do it. Between Mom's typing and my yard mowing, leaf raking and snow shoveling jobs, we were able to keep the house and buy groceries and necessities. We had no car; Dad took that when he left. I don't remember any more about the car than I do about Dad, but Mom told me it was a black 1954 Cadillac. "He really loved that car," she said once. I believed he loved it more than he did us, since he took it with him.

As I pulled into the driveway that ran alongside the small, clapboard bungalow, I could see Mom standing at the window as if she had been waiting the entire eleven hours it took me to travel from Atlanta. She waved, then disappeared behind the curtain to unlock the side door for me.

She still had on her long white apron, the one she always wore when she baked cookies. As we hugged on the porch, the flour dust transferred itself to my shirt and jeans, causing Mom to apologize.

"Now look what I've done. I got flour all over you."

The aroma of warm chocolate chip cookies greeted me as I entered the kitchen. A pair of bulky oven mitts hung from a hook near the stove. Judging from the scorch marks and the tattered appearance, these could have been the same ones Mom used when I was a kid. It reminded me of other days like this, raking leaves till nearly dark and coming into Mom's kitchen from the chill fall evening, the wonderful smells of baking, a glass of milk on the table, and a little plate of warm cookies waiting for me.

"Why don't you bring your suitcase in and get settled while I finish these cookies?" she said as she donned the oven mitts to extract a pan of delight. "I'm almost done here. Then we can talk."

The bedroom seemed smaller than when I was younger and had considered it *my* room. Facing west, the room was warmed by the setting sun and was the beneficiary of the deep orange glow that turned the walls incandescent, announcing the coming of evening. How comfortable this room had always been when I was a child. My warm bed was a refuge, made even more secure by the glow of light seeping in under the door and the sounds of Mom's typewriter churning out someone's term paper and earning us another ten or twelve bucks.

My reverie was cut short by a crashing sound coming from the kitchen, then a thud.

"Mom, you ok?"

The answer came not as a word, but as a sound too quiet to distinguish. "Uhhh!"

"Mom?"

She was on her knees and trying to pull herself up onto a chair. The look on her face was one of fear and bewilderment. As I rushed to her, cookies that had spilled on the floor crunched under my shoes. By the time I carried her into her bedroom and placed her tiny frame on the comforter, she had lost consciousness. I felt for a pulse. It was there—barely. Her face was pale and drawn.

I watched her chest rise and fall with shallow breaths as I dialed 9-1-1 from the bedside phone. I don't remember talking, just someone saying, "The ambulance is on its way."

Her hands were cold and as I tried to rub the warmth of life back into them, her eyes flickered.

"It's my heart, honey," she said weakly. "I've been having spells and the doctor says it's my heart. I was hoping it wouldn't happen while you were here."

"You should have told me, Mom."

"Didn't want to worry you. I'll be ok. Just need to rest a little."

"The ambulance will be here in a few minutes and we'll get you to the hospital."

"Thanks, honey. I'm sorry to bother you with this . . . and mess up your vacation."

"You're not messing up anything, Mom." She looked so tiny, lying in the center of the double bed—so weak and vulnerable, and my fear for her froze the words in my throat. I finally managed, "and you could never be a bother to me."

"My ring, honey. I had to take it off when I made the dough—on the table—would you get it please?"

"Sure Mom."

It was a small ring. Mom had always worn it. I had never seen it off of her finger. A light coating of flour dust had accentuated what appeared to be an inscription inside, but nearly 60 years of wear had erased all but a few letters. The ring had an unusual shape, not round like most, but square on the outside. A few light machined scratches indicated that it might have been florentined at one time, but that too was nearly worn away.

I placed the ring in Mom's hand. She smiled as she held it, no doubt remembering some distant past. "Richard put this on my finger when we were married, and the only time I ever take it off is when I bake," she said. "Did you see the inscription inside?"

"It's kind of worn, Mom, and I couldn't . . . "

"It says 'Forever me with your love.'"

Dad's love for Mom certainly wasn't forever. The inscription was just a hollow promise that he found too easy to break. I was there when he broke it. The night before he left I heard him talking on the phone, making plans to deceive my mother, whispering over the phone, setting up the meeting with that woman—the woman he went away with. I wonder if he would have had the guts to go through with it if he had known his nine-year-old son was outside his office that night . . . listening.

". . . Of course Marilyn doesn't know, but I think she might be getting suspicious. We've got to be real careful or it'll ruin everything . . . Yes, yes, of course I do. I have to go to Tommy's recital tonight, then I'll see you tomorrow. I told Marilyn I have a sales meeting in Chicago. I'm a pretty good liar when I need to be. If she knew what was going on, she'd kill us . . . Hold on, I think I heard someone in the hallway. I'd better hang up.*

I'll meet you at Cramer's cafe in Wabash and we can go from there. I can't wait. I'll see you tomorrow morning . . . I love you too, Carol. Bye."

The next day, dad was gone, and when he didn't come back, I knew why.

"Forever me with your love?" I questioned. "I don't get it."

7

"It comes from a little poem that Richard gave me when we were going together. I don't know who wrote it, but it just means that after all is said and done; only love survives. And if a man and woman truly love each other they can go on forever, because their love goes on forever. You're proof of that."

Mom was seeing something I couldn't see. It was a memory from before I was born, and that private vision brought a faint smile to her lips.

"Richard and I were married in 1943," she continued, "and the next day he reported for duty in the army. We had to put our life together on hold for three years, but our love was never on hold. We wrote to each other—I more than he—and even when we didn't get a letter, we could still feel each other's love. We talked about it a lot after he came home. He said he nearly froze to death during one of the big winter battles but all of a sudden he felt me there and I kept him warm. To this day, when Richard goes on one of his business trips, he always writes down everything he does and everything he thinks about. He calls it his journal, but they're mostly just letters to me. Just like during the war. Then when he returns home he lets me read his journal. I look forward to it. Of course he always talks about you; he loves you so much and he's so proud of you. When he comes home, it'll be like he never left."

The paramedics arrived and took Mom to the hospital. I rode with her as they tried to get her heart rhythms stabilized.

"When he comes home, it'll be like he never left." Mom's words echoed in my mind. She always believed he would come home and that there was something that was just holding him up, making him late. Today he was nearly forty-five years late. I always wanted Mom to know the truth, but I couldn't bring myself to tell her. I don't think she would have believed me anyway.

When the police stopped looking for my father, Mom took up the search herself. She asked friends, relatives and business acquaintances for any clue they might be able to offer. I knew where he was, or at least where he was going that day. "Why don't you look in Wabash?" I had asked her once. "Maybe he went to a restaurant there . . . or something." As a child, I had no idea where Wabash was, but I heard my father tell his girlfriend he would meet her there.

"Why would Richard go to Wabash?" Mom had replied. I didn't have the heart to tell her, and I never mentioned it again.

Mom was admitted to the hospital and placed in intensive care. I waited outside the ward until her doctor emerged through the large double doors. His grave expression telegraphed his message.

"She's resting now," he said.

"Is she going to be all right?"

The doctor looked at me for a few seconds, sizing me up as if to see just how blunt he could be.

"I'm afraid not," he said. "Your mother's heart has been failing for several months, and quite frankly I'm surprised she lasted this long without a major episode. She probably just wanted to see you one more time."

"How long . . . does she have?" I asked, nearly choking on the words.

The doctor pursed his lips and nodded. "A few days—maybe a few weeks at most. Anything more would be a miracle . . . I'm sorry."

"Can I see her?"

"Sure. She's been asking for you. Just a short visit now; she needs her rest."

"Richard!" she said as I entered the room.

"No mom, it's me, Tom . . . your son."

"Oh, for a moment I thought you were Richard." Then she reached out her hand and grasped mine. Her grip was much stronger than you might imagine for someone as sick as she.

"Darling," she said softly. "I know I'm dying . . ."

"No Mom . . ."

9

"I've known for some time and I know I'll never leave here. Honey, before it's too late, I want you to know how much your father and I love you; how much you mean to us."

Mom was speaking as if my father could come around the corner at any time. What an abiding love she had for this man who left her nearly fifty years ago. At that moment I wanted her to hate him for leaving her to die like this.

"Mom . . . dad abandoned us when I was nine. He never came back. He never will. Mom . . . he's just a bum."

My regret for saying that was immediate. How stupid of me to say that to this sweet woman whose only fault was loving someone too much. Her expression didn't change. She didn't argue with me. For her it wasn't a point for debate.

"I don't think Richard knows I'm sick," she said. "I want to see him again. Honey . . . Find him!"

Those last two words startled me. "What?"

"Find your father and tell him I'm sick. Tell him I want to see him."

"But Mom, I wouldn't even know where to begin looking. He's been gone for forty-five years. He might not even be . . . alive."

"He's your father, Honey. You can find him. I know you can."

"But . . ."

She pulled my hand close to her chest, drawing me to her as she whispered. "Go now, before it's too late. Go out and find your father. Do it for me . . . please."

I held her two tiny hands in mine and brought them to my lips, kissing them so I didn't have to talk. I couldn't talk and I couldn't look at her. I was afraid she would see in my eyes that I could never honor her dying wish. We stayed silent for a time. Then she told me to go.

"Bring your father back to us, Tommy."

The doctor assured me that my staying at the hospital would not be of any help, and that Mom would sleep and be closely monitored.

The floor nurse took all my phone numbers and told me she would call if anything changed.

Driving back to the little house, I went over all the reasons why trying to locate my father was a bad idea. I had spent a lifetime ignoring the fact that I even had a father. Now after all those years I was faced with the prospect of seeing him again. Even if I could locate him, he might not want to see Mom, and he could hurt her even more. Also, finding him in the short time Mom had left might be impossible. But if I didn't at least try, I would be no better than the man who abandoned her. My flesh chilled with that thought and I knew then that I had to do it for Mom's sake and my own. I had to figure out where to begin and I had to do it in a hurry.

As I turned into the narrow driveway, my own words echoed in my mind. *Why don't you look in Wabash?* I stopped the car in the driveway and got the Indiana roadmap from the glove compartment. Wabash looked like about an hour drive from Fort Wayne, and if I started now I could be there before dark.

My mind was flooded with questions, and it was hard to focus on any one thing. *Where in Wabash? What was the name of that damned restaurant? Would it still be there? Who would remember anything after all those years? Am I being stupid? Am I wasting time I could be spending with Mom? If only I could think of the name of that restaurant where Dad went to meet his 'girlfriend' . . . Crawford's . . . Clayton's? It was two words. "Clayton's Diner . . . Clayton's Inn?" No it was something else.*

I was now on the main drag in Wabash. The buildings were not tall enough to shield my eyes from the setting sun, making it difficult to read the names of businesses, especially those on the neon signs. Turning off onto a side street, I looked for a place to park, so I could at least ask directions. I didn't see the sign at first; just the flashing red light that it emitted, as if someone had forgotten to shut off a turn signal. As I exited the car my eyes were drawn to the source of the light and there it was. Cramer's Cafe, it said.

That was it, and it was right there in front of me, the cafe at which Dad and that woman had met. How could I have forgotten that? Could this be the same one? It was designed like a diner out of the '50's, but it didn't look old enough. It was black, white and chrome on the outside, and as I entered I saw that the theme continued faithfully throughout the place. Booths lined the windowed walls. The focal point was a large oval fifty-ish soda fountain where patrons could sit on swivel stools and belly up to their favorite ice cream confection. The place would have been empty had it not been for one customer nursing a gray frothy concoction at one of the booths, and a red-faced middle-aged man tending the soda fountain. I chose a stool on one end of the oval and perched my feet on the chrome rail that ran at its base.

"What can I getcha?" the red-faced man asked.

"Do you have chocolate malts?"

"Sure, how many, ya want?" he laughed.

"Just one."

"Comin' up."

"Has this place been here long?"

"Nah, 'bout four—five years."

My spirits darkened. "Oh . . ." then brightened. "Do you have any other locations around town?"

"Nope. This here's the only one. I'd go bankrupt if I had another one like this."

"Business is that slow, huh?"

"Oh, I guess it's not really that bad. It's just not as good as it was at the old place."

"Old place? There was another Cramer's Cafe?"

"Oh, sure, right across the street where that strip mall is. My old man built it in the fifties. Turns out that the property was worth more than the building, so when Pop died 'bout five years ago, I sold it and built this one. Just doesn't seem to work as well over here for some reason."

"I'm looking for somebody," I said, now regaining a bit more hope in this lost cause. "A man who might have come in here a few times . . . back around 1956. He was a salesman. Drove a kinda flashy car, a black 1954 Cadillac?"

"Can't help you there, friend. I was only about three years old and still tryin' to keep from pissin' my pants. Didn't know much about cars at that age."

I finished my malt and tossed three dollars on the counter top. I was beginning to feel a little foolish. How could I expect anyone to remember a non-event from forty-five years ago? "Well, I guess I'll be heading back to Fort Wayne."

"A '54 Cadillac, huh?" The man in the booth said. "Had the fins, didn't it? I used to know a guy with a car like that. It was black, coulda been a '54. He never drove it though. Just kept it in his garage all covered up. His kid used to come into the old place every now and then. He showed it to me once."

A flash of distant hope brightened my despair. "Is he still around?"

"The kid? Nah, he was kinda retarded; I haven't seen him in years. Never saw his old man. I think he died quite a while ago."

"Do you know where he lived?"

"Well, the old man had a shop over on Euclid Street. He worked on cars. Name was Messman or Messer—something like that. The place might still be there."

After getting directions to Euclid Street and thanking the red-faced man, I left, buoyed by the thought that I may have found someone who was connected to my father. Euclid Street was a few miles across town. It was a short street and the shop wasn't hard to find. It was a low, concrete block building with two single garage doors and several metal framed, multi-pane windows on the front and sides. A faded round metal sign anchored between the two overhead doors proclaimed Messer's Garage—Engine Repair. The small parking area in front of the building was paved with ancient

13

cinders that had been soaked in the oil from the hundreds of crankcases that had been drained there over the years. Oil, grease, anti-freeze and other chemicals that routinely had been dumped out onto the cinders years ago, still emitted a sharp odor that piqued my nostrils.

The doors to the garage were locked and as I strained to see through the dirty windows, I could only make out the rough outline of something large on the far side of the service bay. *Perhaps a side window would offer a better view.* A small stack of cinder blocks beneath the right side window provided enough elevation for me to see in. The long bulky shape could have been a car, but then, it could have been a large sofa or half a hundred other things that might be stored in an old building. The twilight had faded too far for me to make out much of anything inside, but as I turned away from the window, the impending darkness didn't hinder my view of the twin barrels of the shotgun poised only inches from my nose. Regret, not fear, flooded over me. Like a skydiver who suddenly realizes his chute is still in the plane, I regretted that I was not somewhere else. *Did they shoot people for trespassing in Wabash?*

"Who the hell are you and what the hell do you think you're doin'?" spoke the voice behind the shotgun.

"Geeze, don't shoot," I stammered. I'm just looking in the window. I'm not going to steal anything."

"I didn't say you were," the man snapped. "But you are trespassin' and I could shoot ya fer that. Who the hell are you anyway and why are you lookin' in my winda?"

"My name's Tom Martin and it's a long story. Can you aim that gun somewhere else? I'm looking for a car. A black 1954 Cadillac."

"This look like a used car lot to you, mister?"

"No of course not, but the guy at Cramer's Cafe said you might have one."

"I ain't got one, but if I did, it wouldn't be for sale."

14

"It was my dad's. I thought he might have . . . sold it to someone in Wabash . . . some time ago. I know this sounds crazy, but . . ."

The man had been staring at me; squinting at me would be more accurate. "You telling me that you're Dick's kid?" he said lowering the shotgun and intensifying his squint.

"Dick? Uh, yeah, Dick . . . Richard Martin . . . that's my father; do you know him?"

"Nah, I think he was a friend of my ol' man though. I didn't know him that good. I was just a kid. I remember this guy named Dick used to come around every now and then when I was about nine or ten. He'd sell my ol' man some stuff for the shop and sit around talking about the war and stuff. Guess they musta been in the army together or somethin'."

The man walked over to a narrow door in the side of the building, unlocked it and switched on a bare light bulb hanging from a cloth-covered wire. "Come on in here," he said motioning me in.

He walked over to the object that I had seen through the window. It was draped with a large piece of brown canvas that looked like a surplus army tent, the U.S. still readable on one of the flaps. The man gently removed it.

"This what you lookin' for?"

It was exactly what I was looking for, a mint condition 1954 black Cadillac. The wheels had been removed and concrete blocks had been placed under the suspension to keep the brake drums off the ground. Other than that, the car looked as if you could drive it right out of the garage. It was just as Mom had described it. The chrome was still shiny and smooth, not pitted as you would expect from a car of this vintage.

"I thought you said you didn't have this," I said once I regained my composure.

"Well, it ain't mine. It's the one that Dick guy left here back in nineteen fifty-somethin'. My ol' man said he was coming back for it. I always figured he would, but after my ol' man died and I

15

closed up the shop, I just took the wheels off to keep the tires from going bad and put her up on blocks. She's been back here for so long; I almost forgot she was here."

"Do you know where he, uh, 'Dick' went?"

"Nah, only person who might know that would be my big sister and I ain't seen her in years. They took off together one day and never came back. I think they were gonna get married er somethin'. Sis told me a couple of times that she loved him a lot."

"How did they go? I mean . . . he left his car here."

"Oh, they went in my sister's car. Think it was a Studebaker or sumpin' like 'at . . . kind of a yella color. Yeah, I remember that pretty good, 'cause it was the only time I ever saw my ol' man cry. Yeah, I remember that. They were drivin' away in that big ol' yella car. They were a wavin' and he was a cryin'."

"Do you ever hear from your sister?"

"Oh yeah, she sends me money in a envelope every now and then, but she ain't been back here in years.

"Do you have her address?"

"I don't know, I can't read too good, but I s'pose it's on the envelope. I can get one and you can look at it."

The man walked over to the little dirty, gray frame house adjacent to the parking lot. In a few minutes he returned with a handful of envelopes and handed them to me.

"I didn't know which one you wanted to look at so I brung 'em all."

The one on top of the pile had a recent postmark, but most important, it had a return address:

Carol Jones
445 Elm Street
Bloomington, IN

Jones was probably her married name, or it could have been a name my father had assumed after he abandoned Mom and me. It was a long shot.

"Tell me," I asked, not really expecting much of an answer from this poor confused man, "how old is your sister?"

"Dunno; five or ten years older than me, I guess."

That wasn't much help. That meant my dad's crime could range anywhere from polygamy to statutory rape. The thought made me shudder and I began to seriously question my judgment in trying to pursue this. But I had gone too far to stop looking and if I could find him, it might be the last thing I could do to make Mom happy. I thanked the retarded man and walked toward my car.

"Don't you want your daddy's car?" he shouted as I slid behind the wheel.

"No, you keep it. It's yours."

"Oh boy," he said, his glee apparent in his gait as he shuffled back into the garage.

It was now eleven p.m., and according to my map, the trip to Bloomington would take about three hours or so. I could grab a bite to eat, and even if I stopped at a rest stop for a short nap I could be in Bloomington by around breakfast time. Maybe I could catch Carol Jones and my father before they started doing whatever they do during the day. I reached for my cell phone. Now that I had the address, I could call 4-1-1 and get the number. A simple phone call would be much easier than a three-hour drive in the dead of night. My hand stopped before I could press the buttons. No, that would telegraph my punch and if I was going to get Dad to come back with me, I had better confront him face-to-face when he's not expecting me.

The drive to Indianapolis was easy. Highway 31 was a straight shot right in, and a stop at a Big Boy restaurant solved my two most immediate concerns before making the transition to the Interstate that bypassed the city. Bloomington was only an hour or so away, but it was getting increasingly difficult to keep my mind from drawing its drowsy curtain. My need for sleep was beginning to conflict with my need to make every minute count, but sleep was not in the plan for tonight. I turned the volume up on my radio and cringed as the heavy metal band banged from the speakers. *Who could sleep through that?*

My map showed a couple of small county roads that together, appeared to create a nearly straight shot into Bloomington. But only moments after making my turn it was obvious that this road was no longer a high priority with the county. My tires on the rough surface of the worn pavement created a monotonous whirring noise that would have been mesmerizing had it not been for the potholes that jarred my mind to full attention from time to time. There wasn't much of a shoulder, so turning around would be difficult. I turned the volume control on the radio up full to compensate for the road noise and decided to continue. Maybe the next road would be better. It wasn't. At least there wasn't any traffic.

The heavy metal station began to fade as another station heterodyned with it. Soon the heavy metal was replaced with something more familiar and, to my ear, more pleasant. Judging from the strains of *Goodnight Irene*, the new station must have had a nostalgia format. *Not bad, brings back memories, I must have been six or seven when I first heard that one.*

A fog was beginning to form in the woods on either side of the road. There was no moon, and my headlights were having difficulty piercing the dense haze that was settling in the low spots. The absence of the heavy metal music was having an adverse effect on my concentration as I negotiated the curves and hills characteristic of nineteen-thirties road construction. Time and again the music rather than the road became my focus. Now came another song from my childhood, back before my Dad left.

"Tra-la-la, tweedle-dee-dee-dee, it gives me a thrill . . . "

In my tired state it was impossible for my mind to reject the thoughts that this old song inspired; thoughts that I had avoided for forty-five years. I was too tired to separate memories from reality or even to care. I was seeing brilliant colors and sweet smells. The sky was perfectly blue and the air felt as good as it smelled, neither too cold nor too hot. I was a child in a field of wild flowers that seemed to go on forever, and I was running with a handful of the flowers I had picked for the smiling young woman who had her arms outstretched toward me. No, I hadn't picked them at all. Someone else had and had put them in my hand and told me to give them to my Mom. Something in the grass tripped me, but before I could realize the pain in my scraped knees and palms of my hands, I was swept up into the air, and reassured. *"Whoa there, li'l pal; you're ok."* The big hands brushed off the dirt and the big man kissed the hurt from my little knees. It was my Dad, the first fond memory of him I'd ever had.

". . . to wake up in the morning to the mocking bird's trill."

The hill was long and steep and a glance at the speedometer warned me that I was going much too fast for the curve I was about to enter. Shifting my foot quickly from the gas, I tried to resist the temptation to hit the brake too hard. With the wheels squealing on the damp pavement, I tried to use as much of the road as there was, and I found myself wishing for a wider road. Thank God there was no traffic. My car was slightly sideways now, but that was helping to reduce its speed. If I could straighten it out I'd be OK.

"Tra-la-la, tweedle-dee-dee-dee, there's peace and goodwill . . ."

The car straightened out, but I was on the far-left side of the road and about to go into another curve. At the reduced speed, I might be able to make it. As I crossed back over toward the right side of the road, a set of headlights split the fog.

"Another car on this road? Dammit!"

He was too close. He went for the shoulder, not realizing that I too was heading in that direction. The two cars slid sideways into each other and left the road joined together, flying through the air as they went over the steep embankment.

". . . you're welcome as the flowers up on Mockingbird Hill."

I don't know how long I was unconscious, or if I was unconscious at all. I felt the way people do when they fall asleep on a transatlantic flight and wake up in an unfamiliar airport, several time zones from where they began. Everything seemed slightly out of sync. The windshield of my car had fallen like crushed ice into the front seat, and I was thankful that the now deflated airbag had kept it out of my face. I was not dead or even badly injured. At least that seemed to be the case. One of my headlights was still operating, but the head-on collision with a large oak tree had skewed it inward, giving my car a cross-eyed appearance. The radio was still working, filling the night with the sounds of *Shrimp Boats is a Comin'*.

Standing up now on solid ground, I was better able to assess my condition. I seemed to be all right. Wondering if the other driver had fared as well, I looked around to see where he ended up. The steep embankment continued on for several hundred feet and was covered with a thicket of vines and tall weeds, which would have obscured anything that lay down there. I couldn't see the other car, but I assumed it might not have hit a tree as my car had and probably had plummeted further down the hill. At that moment, I wasn't sure if that was good or bad. A voice coming from further down the hill caught my attention. "Hello," it said. "Is anyone out there? I seem to be stuck. I can't get out of this darn car."

20

I worked my way toward the voice. It was coming from the other car, which was nearly buried in heavy brambles and vines. The front of the car was badly smashed as if it had hit the ground nose first. Remarkably, the windshield was still in place although badly shattered. I could see a face staring out at me through the cracked windshield. I pulled back some of the vines in order to reach the driver-side door. It was jammed, but the window was open. The driver was pinned behind the wheel of the vintage car, the steering column pressing into his chest.

"Can you help me?" he asked, in a tone more like that of a man looking for a part in a hardware store than one trapped in a wrecked car.

I reached into the car and tried to pull the steering wheel away from the man.

"No son," he said, "You can't do that. I've tried and it won't budge." He raised his right hand, which was resting on the passenger seat and pointed to the glove compartment. In there . . . a pen . . . get it for me please . . . put it in my hand."

"But . . ."

"I'm a dead man, boy; I need to tell my family goodbye . . . while I can."

I went around to the passenger side of the car and reached in through the open window and retrieved the pen from the glove compartment. I placed it in his right hand.

"Thanks," he said.

There was a black leather-bound book on the passenger seat. He flipped it open to a clean page and began writing. I told him to hang on while I went for help and then started back up the embankment.

Reaching my car, I remembered my cell phone in the glove compartment. As I sat again in the driver's seat, exhaustion overcame me and my body refused to move, demanding that I rest just a few minutes. Finally, I gathered up my cell phone and pushed on the door but it wouldn't budge. The smell of gasoline and a hint of smoke now made my exit from the vehicle a more urgent matter. The driver-side door seemed jammed and the only other escape route was through the gap left by the shattered windshield. After crawling across the hood of the car, I made my way up the embankment to the road and dialed the emergency number.

My 9-1-1 call went through and I gave the best directions I could to my location. They said a unit was on its way. Leaning on a jagged piece of broken guardrail at the top of the hill, I peered into the moonlit darkness toward my mangled car. It had come to rest about fifty feet from where I was standing, hitting the only tree on the embankment. I could still hear my radio, heavy metal again blaring from its speakers. There was no sign of the other car. Not having a tree to stop it, it had gone further down. I tried to see the path that it might have taken, but the strange shadows cast by the brilliant moonlight made that impossible. My harsh ride down the embankment was now slowly evoking a realization of pain that began to creep through my body as if I were being dipped headfirst into ice water. The sharp pain that stabbed at my lungs with each deep breath was only slightly worse than the throbbing in my head. My bloody hands still held fragments of the shattered glass that I had picked up upon escaping across the hood of my wrecked car. Lowering myself to the ground, I leaned back against the broken guardrail and allowed myself to pass out until the police car pulled up in front of me, its lights flashing. As I struggled against the pain in my side to get to my feet, a short, rather chunky police officer ran toward me.

"You OK, sir?" he asked, shining a black handled flashlight in my eyes.

"I guess I'll live . . . Might have hurt some ribs though."

"An ambulance is on its way," the officer said; "be here in a minute."

I gestured down the hill. "Don't know about the other guy though."

"Where's he; Still in the car?"

"Yeah. The other car went on down the hill. The brush is pretty thick. I talked to him. He's in pretty bad shape."

"Hey bud," the officer called to his partner who was making his way down the hill toward my car. "He says there's another car down there somewhere."

"Yeah, I'm lookin'," came the reply.

The chubby officer led me over to the police car and let me sit in the back seat as he questioned me about the accident. The details were not as clear in my mind as they were only a few minutes earlier. "I dunno," I said trying to remember the sequence of events. "I was coming into this curve and this guy just cut in front of me."

"The other car?"

"Yeah . . . I seemed to be on the wrong side of the road," I rambled on. "I don't know why . . . I was on the wrong side of the road. Seems like I was going sideways down that hill."

"Sideways? You mean like you were in a skid?"

"Yeah . . . I was skidding sideways, coming down the hill, but I brought it back . . . almost, and then this other car . . ."

"Sir, what hill are you talking about?" the chubby officer asked, pointing down the embankment toward my car. "That hill?"

"No," I said, pointing up the road. "That hill."

"What hill?"

I peered around the doorframe of the car toward where I had pointed. The road was completely flat for as far as I could see.

"Ain't no other car down here," the chubby officer's partner shouted.

"You sure you saw another car, sir?" the officer asked.

"Yeah, I'm sure. He cut right in front of me. We crashed together. I talked with him. I gave him a pen"

"You gave him a pen?"

"Yeah." I realized how ridiculous that sounded. "Yeah, he asked for a pen . . . to write a note . . . to his family."

23

"Sir," The chubby officer gave me one of those phony compassionate looks that say, *I think you're crazy, but I'm going to give you a way to get off the hook.* "Do you think you might have fallen asleep and just dreamed you saw another car?"

I rankled at his condescending tone. "No, I saw what I saw."

"Well sir, you also said you came down a hill and as you can see, there is no hill back up the road, and you said you were skidding and there ain't no skid marks. You just went straight through the guardrail. You didn't even hit the brakes."

The chubby officer's partner began shouting from somewhere deep in the thicket of the embankment. "Hey, I found the car."

Chubby ran to the edge of the embankment and started toward his partner's voice. I followed painfully behind.

The partner was pulling brush away from a dark object about a hundred feet further down the hill from my car. The pre-dawn light was changing the texture of the whole scene and some colors were becoming visible. The car was a rusty brown, but some gold paint was still distinguishable.

"Man, this thing really buried itself, the partner said, tearing away more brush. "Man, this thing is a piece of jun . . ."

The partner stopped short and squinted through the cracked windshield. Then he retreated, tripping and falling backward away from the car.

"Holy shit," he said

"Is he dead?" chubby asked.

"Yeah, damn right."

I had finally made my way down the embankment to where the two officers were now leaning over the car and peering through the dirty windshield.

"I told you there was another car," I said, feeling relieved that I hadn't imagined it.

"Is this the guy you talked to?" chubby asked as he stood back to give me some room to look.

24

The skeleton was sitting up straight in the driver's seat. It had no choice. The steering column was pressed against its shattered sternum. The skull was turned to the right and tilted down as if looking at the leather-bound book on the passenger's seat. The right hand of the skeleton was on the book and there was a pen that had rolled into the crack of the seat from what used to be a person's hand. The left hand was clutching what remained of the bent steering wheel in a futile attempt to relieve the crushing effects of the wayward column.

No one but me noticed the glint of gold that wrapped a bony finger on that hand, giving color to a predominantly colorless scene. I moved to the driver side of the car where the window was open to get a better look.

Chubby went back to the car to call for a wrecker and some forensic backup. Partner continued pulling the brush back from around the car.

"Wow," partner said. "You don't see these babies every day . . . a Studebaker Golden Hawk."

I removed the square shaped wedding band, taking care not to disturb the skeletal human remains. The nearly perfect Florentine made the ring look new. I looked inside the band, knowing already what I would find.

Forever me with your love.

My two broken ribs were not enough to keep me in the hospital for more than a few hours and I was soon back in Fort Wayne at another hospital where Mom was still holding on to life.

As I entered her room, she tried to raise her head, but the strength wasn't there and her head sank back into the pillow.

"Did you find him?" She asked. "Did you find Richard?"

25

"Yes Mom, I found him, but . . ." I felt the gold ring in my pocket, retrieved it and slowly extended it toward Mom. "I brought you this, Mom. Dad wanted you to have it."

She clutched the ring tightly in her small fist, brought it to her lips and kissed it. Still clutching the ring she smiled at me, tears glistening in her sweet dark eyes.

"I understand," she said.

"I have something else, Mom," I said as I produced the tattered leather bound book. "I found this with Dad."

Her eyes brightened. "His letters to me. Oh . . . read them to me, honey"

I hadn't the chance to read any part of the book yet and I was afraid of what it might reveal to Mom about the man who had left us so many years ago. But after reading a few pages, I was surprised that it was simply a series of notes to a woman about everything that had happened to her husband while he was away from her. Little seemed to be left out and the writer did not hesitate to bare his deep love for the woman.

4 January, 56
My Darling Marilyn,

I'm so sorry to have had to leave you again so soon after the holidays. I was hoping I could steal a little more time with you, but as we know, sales is a demanding profession and I can't stay away from my customers too long and still keep my job. I'll bring Tommy a souvenir from Chicago. I'll see you in four days. I love you both.

5 January, 56
My Darling Marilyn,

What a day. The conference this year is even more boring than usual. This morning, during one of the sessions, Joe Paladino, the guy from Boston, got sick and threw up all over the guy in the seat in front of him. I guess he had too much to drink last night at the reception. I'm glad I left the reception early and didn't drink much. I wish I was back home with you and little Tommy. I'll be there soon. I love you."

6 January, 56
My Dearest Darling Marilyn,

Lord, I'm so lonesome for you. The only thing good about these trips is that they remind me of how much I love you and how lucky I am to be your husband and Tommy's daddy. Today we had some interesting speakers and the marketing department demonstrated two new products. They look pretty good and I think I can do a good job selling them. Our lunch today was decent. It was roast beef again, but at least it wasn't tough like yesterday's. Dinner was dismal. I think it was chicken, but it might have been pork. I sure could go for some of your wonderful fried chicken. The best I've ever tasted. No doubt about it. Mostly, honey, I sure could go for you. Just to touch you, to hold you, to watch you breathe when you sleep and see your eyelashes flutter when you're having a dream. God, I love you and I can't wait to kiss you when I get home tomorrow.

The notes continued, skipping only those days when Dad was not traveling, which were very few. Each series of notes mentioned me, how much my father loved me and how proud of me he was. I don't remember his ever telling me those things. Some of the notes to Mom were very personal, others were just conversational, but each exuded a love that did not diminish with time and distance, a love that was the reason for this man's existence. The depth of emotion displayed in some of the notes was embarrassing at times; the innocence and vulnerability of this man almost hokey. I was reading about someone I had never known, even though I had lived with him for the first nine years of my life.

As my mother listened, she wore a slight smile and her eyes were closed tight as if she were asleep, perhaps dreaming of the man who had penned these simple words of love to her so long ago.

Occasionally, I would stop reading to see if she wanted to get some rest. But she would always tell me to continue. Her expression did not change, nor did the fervent love that permeated each note. The book was a chronology of thoughts that my Dad entertained about his wife and son and the love grew more intense with each day. It was increasingly obvious that we were the focus of his life. There were only a few pages left and there had been nothing that would indicate that Dad was going to leave his family.

1 November, 57
Darling Marilyn,

Here it is November already and I don't even have your birthday present yet. I have something in mind that I think you will like, but of course, you'll think we can't afford it. It will be worth any price just to watch the look on your beautiful face when you see it. I haven't made any sales yet today, but I have two good leads over in Wabash. I'll call you tonight to let you know I'm going to be a day later than I thought. I sure am proud of Tommy for getting the gold star in reading. I love you.

2 November, 57
My Dearest Marilyn,

This has been a great day. I made two sales today. My commission from just these two will make my month. Maybe I can stay home and work on my prospect list for a few weeks. It's kind of late so I think I'll stay the night here in Wabash. I'll call you from the pay phone at Cramer's Cafe. It sure gets lonely out here on the road, but I just think of you and the loneliness goes away. It's strange how just the mere thought of you makes everything warmer and more friendly. I am such a lucky man. I'll be so glad to see you and Tommy when I get home tomorrow. I love you both so much.

8 November, 57
My Darling Sweetheart,
 Well, the best laid plans and all that. Here I am on the road again after only five days with you and Tommy. I didn't know my prospecting would be so successful. I guess that's good, but I sure hate being away from you and Tommy. I'm going to be in Indianapolis today and tomorrow, then Peru the next. I'm going to swing back by Wabash to check on some things and I might stay overnight with a friend there. I'll be home on the twelfth. I'll be there in time for Tommy's recital. I'm looking forward to that. Who knows, he might turn out to be a musician instead of a salesman like his old man. Wouldn't that be great? I love you both.

The recital! I had forgotten about that. Dad had left us the day after the recital. From then on we had to be more concerned about paying for groceries than piano lessons. As I continued reading, I feared what might come next.

17 November, 57
My Dearest Marilyn,
 I hope you can forgive me for lying to you. I really didn't have a meeting in Chicago. I'm in Wabash at Messer's garage. You remember old Bob Messer, the mechanic I met during the war. We do a lot of business together. He has a daughter, Carol. She and I have gotten to know each other quite well over the years. Today Carol and I are taking off to Bloomington. She has a job there in her aunt's dress shop and Bob asked me to drive her there since she doesn't have a car . . . anymore. I just bought it from her and now it's your birthday present. Surprise! I'll be bringing the car back with me tonight, so by the time you read this you will have

already seen it. It's the Studebaker Golden Hawk you like so much and it's only a few months old. Bob bought it for Carol, but couldn't keep up the payments, so I talked him into selling it to me. I told Carol that you'd probably kill me for buying it, but don't worry; with the new business I've been bringing in, we can afford it. I'll really be glad to get Carol down to her aunt's. It seems she's developed quite a teenage crush on me and it gets kind of embarrassing sometime when Bob and I are trying to do business. Even Bob has noticed it. Maybe with all the college guys around the University, she'll find someone more her age to fall in love with.

I'm going to leave the Cadillac here and drive the Studie to Bloomington. It sure looks fast. We can come back for the Cadillac next weekend. Tommy will be excited about it too.

I love you both.

17 November, 57 – 10:30 p.m.
Darling Marilyn,

Just dropped Carol off at her aunt's house. There are a couple of college guys rooming there too and she was already making goo-goo eyes at them. Looks like I just lost a girlfriend. Too bad. The trip took longer than I thought. It's 10:30 p.m., so I should be home by 2 o'clock at the latest. I can't wait to give you your birthday kiss. I love you.

17 November, 57
My Dearest Darling Marilyn,

Things didn't go as I had planned. I'm afraid I just wrecked your birthday present. I'm so sorry. I guess I was in too much of a hurry to get home. I've been pinned in the car for about an hour and I have been blowing the horn, but no one has heard me. I hope someone comes by and finds me soon. I don't want to be late for your birthday. I love you and Tommy.

18 November

 Battery is dead. I heard some trucks on the road above, but no one saw my car. I have a lot of pain in my chest and I can't feel anything in my legs. I think it must be around one o'clock in the morning. At least the moon is out so I can see to write this.

 More cars above, but no one stops. I may never be found down here. I'm not so afraid of dying here as I am of never seeing you and Tommy again. I hope he doesn't hate me for leaving him while he's so young?

 The pain isn't so bad anymore, but I think I might be bleeding inside. I'm getting weak and I'm having a hard time focusing. I feel so alone. I miss you and Tommy so much.

 Sun's coming up. I must have dozed off. Dreamed about Tommy. Thought I talked with him, but he was all grown up. It seemed so real. I can feel you close to me now and I don't feel so alone. I love you. Please don't forget me.

This was the last entry. My mother's eyes were closed, never to open again, and it didn't matter that she hadn't heard her husband's dying thoughts. She was once again with her beloved Richard. My tears were not so much for her, as for the man I had judged so badly—for whom I had never shed a tear before this day.

The police report says that I had fallen asleep at the wheel and my ending up so close to where my Dad's accident occurred forty-five years earlier was nothing but coincidence. They said I had dreamed I spoke to the man in the car. I don't believe it was a coincidence and whether I was dreaming is irrelevant. Whatever happened, my father and I were there together, we forgave each other and I finally felt the full force of my Dad's love for me . . . something I had not felt in so many years.

I buried my mother and father side by side on a hillside in a small cemetery just outside of town. I don't get back to Fort Wayne much anymore, but when I do I visit Mom and Dad on their hillside. The grave marker tells nothing of their lives together or of my mother's life-long devotion to the man who left her so many years ago. It says nothing about the man whose love for his wife and son transcended time so he could say his goodbyes to them. But for me, the marker speaks volumes:

Richard Martin 1920 - 1957 & Marilyn Martin 1923- 2002
Forever me with your love

Marsha Blaine

The state prison had been Marsha Blaine's home for twenty years and it would continue to be for possibly 30 or 40 more or until her life sentence had run its course. Yes, she did kill Bob Blaine, her husband, but it was an accident, or so she claimed. Her defense was that she thought her husband, who came home a day early from a sales trip, was a burglar, and as she and her three-year-old son cowered in the darkened bedroom, she put nine .45 caliber slugs into her husband when he came through the bedroom door. It was a simple case of mistaken identity and near-paralyzing fear; it was self-defense. That was how her lawyer tried to make his case. Unfortunately for Marsha, the prosecutor was a twenty-five-year veteran who made a much stronger case for conviction. His experience plus some damning evidence and a witnesses who claimed she had heard Mrs. Blaine threatening to kill her husband only a few days earlier, won the jury over, and Marsha went to jail.

Prison wasn't so bad. After all, she didn't have a life anymore. She had lived for her family, and now that was gone. Her husband was dead by her own hand, and her son, who she thought she was protecting that fatal night had been taken away by the Department of Family and Children's Services (DFACS). Since neither she nor Bob had any living relatives, the three year old was offered for adoption. She had no resources left to stop it. It was all her fault, she reasoned; prison was probably where she belonged. Only she knew the truth, but after twenty years, even she had become skeptical of her motive.

The terror of that night and the tragic aftermath, coupled with lingering pangs of guilt kept Marsha from appealing her conviction. An automatic appeal filed by her lawyer within a year of the trial was denied and she refused to pursue any further action. She felt that someone had to be punished for the tragedy and believed that she was the most logical candidate.

Marsha was a model prisoner from the start. Despite having been convicted of a terrible crime the warden and guards liked her, and due to her kind-hearted and gentle ways, she was known as "Mom" among her fellow prisoners. As a trusty, she was in charge of the prison library, a job for which she was well suited, given her occupation as librarian prior to her marriage to Bob.

As Marsha was checking in some of the returned magazines, she was approached by Frank Strong, one of the guards.

"Marsha, the warden wants to talk with you. Want to drop what you're doing and come with me?"

"Sure Frank; what's it all about?"

"Dunno. I think he wants you to talk with somebody from the outside."

Oh crap, Marsha thought. *Not another shrink.* She had talked with a battery of psychiatrists, psychologists and crime writers over the past two decades, all trying to turn her story into a thesis, book or a made-for-television thriller. She hoped that chapter was finished.

Being a trusty, she was allowed to walk without an escort to the small interview room where such activities were usually conducted, but this time the guard told her to come with him—that they were going to the warden's office.

Warden, Paul Samuelson told Marsha to take a seat as he introduced the two other people in the room. The older man he introduced as Dr. Clarence Whittier, dean of the law department at State University. The other, a man in his mid-twenties, was Benjamin Ashkenaze, a law student at the university. Samuelson then nodded toward the dean and said, "Dr. Whittier, tell Ms. Blaine what this is all about."

"Ms. Blaine . . . can I call you Marsha?" Marsha gave an affirmative nod.

"Marsha, the University, in cooperation with the state corrections department, is initiating an experimental program to provide our law students with real-life experience with the appellate process of our justice system. Having been a librarian, you've probably heard of moot court, in which students can practice oral arguments based upon actual cases. Moot court, while an excellent educational experience, only goes so far. Our new program takes it to the next level and gives our students the opportunity to work directly with people who have been convicted of a crime. To put it simply, it will provide the law student with a deeper understanding of how an actual verdict correlates with applicable law." Whittier was leaning forward in his chair, his enthusiasm for the new program evident in his broad, wide-eyed grin.

"I don't want an appeal," Marsha said. "I shot Bob nine times . . . he's dead and I'm where I deserve to be."

"No, Marsha," Whittier replied. This won't go to an actual appeal. In fact, Ben here, who we've assigned to your case, may find that there is no basis for an oral argument. But the fact that you have only one previous appeal gives him a clean slate on which to work."

Ben now spoke. "Mrs. Blaine, most of my work will be in researching court transcripts and evidentiary materials. I would like your permission to do so, and I would like to interview you to hear your account directly. I promise that I will terminate the interview immediately if you begin to feel uncomfortable. If you agree, it shouldn't take more than an hour or two of your time."

"I'm not worried about the time," she said. "I've got plenty of that." Marsha looked down at her hands. Her slight smile had been replaced by a look of hopelessness. "I just don't want to think about that night."

"Your cooperation would be very helpful, Marsha," Samuelson said. "It would get the program started off on the right foot and that could be a great benefit to a lot of students. The governor is fully on board with this."

As a librarian, Marsha had had the opportunity to help numerous students ranging from primary school to college; she had gotten a lot of satisfaction from it, and the young law student, Benjamin seemed nice. She felt she could trust him, even though they had just met.

"OK," she said at last, "I'll do it."

———

The interview took place a week later in the small, grey, cinder-block room at the prison. Ben had already read through the court transcripts and looked at the evidence presented at the trial. He even had located one of the prosecution's witnesses, Marsha's former neighbor, and interviewed her. This had been somewhat out of the program's parameters, but Ben was nothing if not thorough.

"Marsha," Ashkenaze began, "How do you feel today?"

"OK, I guess."

"Good. I know this may be a little painful for you, but would you tell me exactly what happened the night of the incident? Perhaps you could start earlier in that day . . . some of the events leading up to the shooting."

Marsha was sketchy with the details of events up until about 1:00 a.m. when she had heard someone "jiggling" the front door latch. She was in bed, her three year old son beside her. That, she explained, was a pretty common occurrence when her little son had a bad cold and needed some TLC.

"What's your son's name?" the law student asked.

Marsha looked away and stared at the gray enameled cinder block wall. "Flag," she said quietly as if her son were in the room with her.

"Flag? That's an unusual name."

"Yeah, it's a family name . . . Flagler, my maiden name. Since I have no living relatives, Bob and I thought it would be nice to carry on the name that way. Flagler Benson Blaine . . . we just called him Flag." She looked down again at her hands, which were folded on the table.

Marsha went through the details of how she came to shoot her husband nine times. Her story didn't deviate at all from the court transcript.

When she finished Ben said, "According to the court transcript, two witnesses testified that you and Bob were having some pretty loud arguments around that time. Do you remember what they were about?"

"Sure, I remember exactly what those arguments were about. We were arguing about the gun."

"The gun? You mean the one you shot Bob with?" Why were you arguing about that?"

"I didn't want the gun in the house . . . you know, around a very rambunctious little boy. I thought it was dangerous. Bob bought it the month before he was . . . before I shot him. He said he was going to get a gun safe for it, but kept putting it off. We argued about that."

"Where did he keep it?"

"In the top drawer of the bureau where Flag couldn't reach it. He kept the clip and the bullets in a different drawer away from the gun. At least that's where he was supposed to keep it, but he didn't always do it that way. When he got careless like that, well, that's when the arguments would start."

"Who showed you how to shoot it?"

"Nobody. I didn't have any idea how to shoot it."

"The evidence sheet shows it as a Colt model 1911 .45 caliber semi-automatic pistol, a pretty powerful handgun and not necessarily a point-and-shoot weapon. You would have to insert a loaded clip, pull back the slide, take off the safety, aim and pull the trigger. Did you know how to do that?"

"No, Bob wanted me to go to the range with him the weekend before the shooting, but I refused. So he went alone. I guess he got careless again and didn't take the clip out. Bob's trip was supposed to be three days, but he came back a day early. He wasn't supposed to be back from his trip that night, so when I heard the noise of somebody trying to get in, I got frightened. I thought if I had the gun, I might be able to scare whoever was breaking in and they would leave. So I got it out of the top drawer and told Flag to get under the bed. I had no idea that Bob had left the clip in it. I guess he left the safety off, too. When Bob opened the door, I must have pulled the trigger . . . I was so frightened, I don't remember doing it. The gun wasn't supposed to be loaded. When it went off it startled me and I couldn't stop pulling the trigger. I guess I shot it until it was empty."

"Why did Bob buy the gun in the first place?"

"He said it was for my protection. That's why he wanted me to go to the range, so he could teach me how to use it."

"I drove through your old neighborhood. It seems like a nice place to raise a family, quiet and safe. It's not in a high-crime area. Why did Bob think you needed a gun for protection?"

Marsha broke eye contact with Ashkenaze, and again turned her head toward the cinder-block wall. "I dunno," she said tersely. Then in a near whisper, "I don't think, I want to talk anymore."

"OK, Marsha. You've been very helpful. I won't press this any farther than you want to go, but if you can think of anything else to tell me, please give me a call." He handed her a card.

As the guard opened the door to let Ashkenaze out, Marsha said. "You can come back tomorrow if you want—if you have any other questions."

"That would be good; I'll tell the warden I will be here about the same time."

Marsha Blaine liked the young law student; she felt more comfortable around him than she had with anyone since that tragic evening. He had a gentle wisdom beyond his age, but she wondered if he was "mean" enough to be a really good lawyer. She waited most of the day for his visit. Finally the guard came by and said that the warden asked him to relay the message that Ashkenaze had a conflict, and had to postpone the interview until the next day. Marsha could not fathom the reason why she felt such utter disappointment.

Ashkenaze showed up the next day and picked up the interview where they had left off.

"OK, Marsha, can you remember why Bob felt that you needed a gun to protect you?"

"Well, he was out of town a lot."

"Yes, but that was also true during the entire five years of your marriage and during the three years after your son was born. Had he always wanted to get a gun?"

"No, he just came home with it one day."

"Did he say why?"

"He said so I wouldn't be so frightened when he went away."

"Had you always been frightened when he left?"

"No."

"What changed, Marsha? Why all of a sudden were you frightened?" The law student knew he was moving into territory that had little bearing on the oral argument that he would present to the panel of law professor "judges" in two weeks, but Marsha's story was compelling and the deeper into it he went, the deeper he wanted to go.

Marsha turned back toward the gray wall; Ben couldn't see her morose expression or the tears glistening in her eyes. "I don't want to talk about that," she said finally.

"That's OK. Let's go back to the neighbor's testimony. The transcript states that she heard you say you were going to shoot your husband. Did you say that?"

"I don't think so . . . no, I would never have said anything like that. I remember that I worried that he might accidently kill himself or somebody else, but I would never have talked about shooting anyone, especially my own family. I hate guns."

"I believe you. I was able to talk with your former neighbor on the phone and she said she couldn't remember exactly what you said, but she thought it was something about killing somebody. I also checked the weather for the night she said she heard your argument. There was a pretty powerful thunderstorm occurring about the same time. I doubt she could have heard anything accurately. I wonder why your attorney didn't bring that up. Perhaps there was a little incompetence going on there. Could be grounds for an appeal."

"I told you, I don't want to appeal."

"Don't worry Marsha, There will be no appeal. This is just an exercise so I can present a cogent oral argument. I'm just trying to think like an attorney.

"Marsha, I need to ask you, did you love your husband?"

"Yes, of course I did . . . Bob was the only family I had . . . he and Flag."

"Did Bob ever . . . hit you?"

"What?"

"Your neighbor had said at the trial that about a month or so before the incident, she saw you with two black eyes and bruises on your face and arms. Did Bob do that?"

"No. Bob was gentle; he couldn't hurt me or anyone. He loved me . . . and I loved him."

"Where did the bruises come from then?"

Marsha turned away. She was silent for a time. Her shoulders shook slightly and Ben thought she might be crying. When she turned back, the redness in her eyes confirmed this notion.

"I guess I might as well tell you. It makes no difference now anyway." She paused to gather her thoughts.

"I used to help out at the day-care center a couple of nights a week when Ben was in town. The day-care took care of kids whose parents had to work evenings. It was just two blocks from our house and I could walk there and back. I loved working with the kids and it brought in a little extra money. Bob was glad to stay home and take care of little Flag. One evening about six weeks before the incident, two men grabbed me as I was walking home. They pulled me into their van, beat and raped me. Then they threw me out and I somehow managed to walk home. When Bob saw me he wanted to call the police, but I said no. I had heard about what they do to rape victims. I had been battered enough, I didn't want to have to relive the experience and be questioned as if I was somehow responsible for the crime.

"After a couple of weeks I had come to my senses, but by then it was too late to report it. I guess I was just grateful that I wasn't pregnant and hadn't contracted some disease. I got checked out by a doctor friend of mine and he promised not to report it. If anyone knew about that, he'd probably be in a lot of trouble." She paused again; her sullen gaze told Ben that she was reliving that terrible event in her mind.

"Physically I was fine, but I couldn't shake the fear. I no longer felt safe, even in my own home and when Bob traveled, it got much worse. Bob hated to leave me, but he had to. That's why he bought the gun. He thought he could teach me to use it and that would help me through my fear. It only made things between us worse . . . and of course we all know how it turned out."

Ashkenaze could see that Marsha had gone farther into the details than she had wanted, so he brought the interview to a close, saying that he still had a few more questions, and asking her to let him come back the next day. She agreed.

The following day Ben was back. Marsha seemed uncharacteristically buoyant, even joking with him a little about his finally being on time. Ben hoped Marsha's openness the previous day had been cathartic.

Ashkenaze began: "Now there's one piece of evidence that I am having trouble with. You claimed that you thought Bob wasn't coming home until the next night, yet the police found a message on your answering machine from Bob, saying that his meeting ran short and he would be home around midnight that night. Did you get that message?"

"No, I had no idea he would be home early."

"Well, according to the transcript, the answering machine playback had been activated that day and the message had been played by someone. Officers at the scene said that the red message light was not blinking when they first looked at the phone, but when they played back the messages, there it was; it had come in at 3:15 in the afternoon. Were you the only one in the house?"

"Yes, me and little Flag; we were the only ones there. *No, actually we weren't there.* That's right; I had to take Flag to the doctor because his cold had gotten worse. The appointment was around three o'clock, so we would not have been there when Bob called."

"Did you check your messages?"

"I probably put Flag's medicine away first, but then if I did check the messages, I would have seen the message light blinking, so maybe I forgot to check; or maybe Flag pushed the button and played it back . . . he liked to play with the phone."

"I need to see that phone," Ben said, not really knowing what he would discover if he did.

When the interview ended, Ashkenaze went directly to the police evidence locker to see if the phone was still there after twenty years. It was. It was nothing unusual—a phone with a digital answering machine built in. The playback button was the largest button on the base unit. He knew that somehow that phone was the key to his oral argument.

Ben didn't sleep that night. He visualized the phone, the message coming in, the light blinking, and little Flag seeing the blinking red light and inadvertently pressing the playback button, after which the light stopped blinking, leaving no indication that a new message was on the machine. It was very possible that Marsha didn't know her husband would be home and there was every reason to believe that she thought she and her son were about to be attacked when she heard the sound of someone coming into the house, but there was no way to prove it.

Why were they not home when the message came in? They went to the doctor. Why did they go to the doctor? Flag had a cold.

"Flag had a cold!" he shouted out loud.

After a quick breakfast, Ben called the prison and asked Samuelson's assistant if he could speak with Marsha. The assistant had been told to cooperate as much as possible with the young law student in matters regarding Marsha Blaine, so Marsha was called to the warden's office and allowed to use that phone to speak with Ashkenaze.

"Marsha," Ben said. "Flag's cold, was it pretty messy, you know, runny nose and like that?"

"I guess so; I remember he was coughing a lot. "I guess he had a runny nose."

"Ben ended the conversation and made two more calls, one with a very special request that was expedited by virtue of the governor's interest in Dr. Whittier's law school program. The other call was to DFACS. He was lucky to get a meeting with the department head early that afternoon.

Claire Davisson's answer to Ben's request to see Flagler Blaine's file was a flat "no." Davisson was only an assistant department head when Flag was adopted, but she knew the case and also knew the rules. Now, as department head, she was going to enforce them.

"I'm sorry. Adoption files are not public information," she said.

After fifteen minutes of unsuccessful cajoling and everything short of an overt bribe, Ben finally asked, "Can you at least look to see if you still have a file? I need to talk with Flagler Blaine. Perhaps you could call him and ask him to call me."

"I can tell you if I have a file, but I can't tell you what's in it." Davisson went to her computer and hit a few keys. "Yes, there is a file, but I . . . wait a minute. Your name is Benjamin Ashkenaze?

"Yes."

"What are your parents' names?"

"Joe and Wanda. Why? What does that have to do with anything?"

"If you can show me a couple pieces of ID, I think you might be allowed to see this file."

———

Marsha hadn't heard from Ben in more than three weeks. She decided that he had gotten enough to write his oral argument for presentation to the panel of law professors, and that she would probably never hear from him again. It was a pity, she thought. She really liked the young law student and felt that he kind of liked her, too. She felt that they had developed a special bond, but then she realized that it was just her loneliness talking.

It was Wednesday after lunch and she had a visitor. It was Ben.

"I'm sorry I haven't been in contact with you in a while, Marsha, but I had to go back to see my parents. While I was there, I did a lot of research. I found out a lot of things that would warrant an appeal, but I didn't present my oral argument regarding the appeal to the panel of professors."

"You didn't? I'm so sorry. So all of that time you spent on research was wasted?"

"Not exactly; I took it to the Governor instead."

Ben reached across the table and grasped Marsha's hands. "First of all, let me assure you that none of this was your fault. The rape and beating that started this mess, the arguments with Bob, the gun in the house and the shooting—especially the shooting—none of it was your fault. You were frightened out of your wits by that attack. Bob saw that and did the only thing he could think of to make you feel safe; he bought a gun. Bob was careless and left the clip in the gun after he returned from the range, and he hadn't made the gun safe. He broke nearly every safety rule there is."

Ben squeezed Marsha's hands tighter and she could feel that he was trembling.

"You could not have known that Bob was coming home that night, because the message had been played back before you had a chance to even check the answering machine. You couldn't have known there was a message on it. After 20 years the phone was still in the evidence locker, so I had it tested for DNA. Modern testing can get a match on minute amounts of DNA even after decades, and I figured there may be traces of it from you and Bob around the mouthpiece. Since little Flag had such a bad cold there might be some on the playback button if he had touched it after wiping his nose with his hands as toddlers do. So the lab matched any DNA that we found on the phone against the DNA of everyone living in the house at that time—anyone who may have touched the phone.

"I don't get it," Marsha said. "I know they had DNA samples from me and Bob in case they needed them in the investigation, but they didn't get any from Flag, so how could they match it against his?"

45

"I read Flag's adoption records and I talked with his parents."
Ben smiled. "They said that they didn't like the name Flagler so
they changed it. They figured at only three years old, he would
never remember his birth name, and they were right. He didn't
know he was adopted until now. We got a cheek swab from him
and compared the three DNA samples with the DNA on the phone's
playback button. We got a perfect match."

"So whose DNA was on the playback button?"

Benjamin Ashkenaze smiled broadly as he held Marsha's hands.
"It was mine . . . Mom," he said.

Headline in the Morning News: Governor Pardons Marsha
Blaine.

The Question

Her answer to his question didn't come as quickly as he had
hoped . . .

Maybe it was all a mistake. Why did he chance ruining
everything by asking anyway? He could feel his face reddening as
his heart began to pump emergency supplies of adrenaline to his
muscles. That was the system his body had set up. He had a choice
now; fight or get the hell out of Dodge. His body provided the extra
chemicals to do either, but the choice was still his. He certainly
wasn't going to fight; there wasn't anything to fight about. Defend
perhaps. But he could run away—as he usually did in similar
situations—before she could show her offense at his asking the
question.

My god, not with her, he thought. *I thought this would be
different.* It had been, different that is, ever since she came along
and sat on his bench.

Sweat that had begun pooling beneath his skin was now ready to
spring from his pores. His shortness of breath, dizziness and dry
mouth were all too familiar, having occurred hundreds, perhaps
thousands, of times during his life. He felt faint. *Oh no, not in front
of her.*

The last time this happened was five weeks ago when his boss
had called him into his office, he assumed to chew him out for

something. He didn't know what, but he could imagine any number of things. He sat in front of his supervisor's desk, head down. He knew he couldn't make eye contact. Even the medication he had taken that morning wasn't that effective.

"Good morning, Tim," the supervisor began. Tim winced at the sound of his name being spoken aloud and he prepared for the scolding he would receive for . . . whatever. "Tim, somebody upstairs was pretty impressed with that software patch you developed for the HT 700. I've got to admit, I was too. And you know, Carl resigned last week to take that job at Oracle. That leaves the department manager's job open, and . . ."

Tim knew what was coming. *No, not that. Chew me out, but don't make me be a manager.* All those people . . . He couldn't possibly . . . He was getting dizzy.

"No!" Tim wheeled from the chair and bolted from the office. The supervisor sat in startled surprise and never again mentioned the promotion to Tim.

Now it was happening again, only this time his body was preparing him to flee from a place he didn't want to leave, his park bench . . . and her.

He had seen her every day for the past month. He didn't notice immediately that she was beautiful. In fact it had taken three or four occasions before he noticed her at all. Oh sure, he knew someone was there, sitting next to him on his park bench, but he never really looked. Making eye contact would have been embarrassing. It would have brought on the panic again, the sweat, the blushing, the staccato breathing and the resulting hyperventilation. That would have ruined everything, and he could never have sat on his bench again.

She was different. She sat so gently on the opposite end of the bench; she didn't crowd him. She never looked at him, just at her sandwich, which she ate slowly, in tiny bites. He watched her out of the corner of his eye, pretending to concentrate on his lunch. This seemed perverse to him, something he had never done before.

He watched in this fashion for three weeks, focusing on the tiny bites that passed between her lovely moist lips. He found himself becoming aroused by the dainty way she held the sandwich with both of her hands, bringing it carefully to her mouth. He watched as she chewed, his eyes occasionally following a crumb as it tumbled from the sandwich onto her blouse. He noticed her breasts pushing out beneath that blouse, sweetly, demurely. They were lovely as well. He also noticed that she seemed to sit closer to him each day.

Until she came to his bench, lunchtime had always been an unwelcome event. He would have much preferred eating his sandwich at his terminal and creating code while he ate. Company policy prohibited employees from eating at their terminals, so they ate in the cafeteria or outside in the little park. He disliked the park, but not so much as he hated the cafeteria. In the cafeteria, someone might sit at his table and want to talk. He never knew what to say and panic would set in again. He was safe in the park as long as he avoided eye contact.

He had never meant to make eye contact with her. His eyes just happened to be focused on a particular point in space and she just happened to walk into that exact point of focus. Then he saw that she was indeed beautiful. Her auburn hair framed a flawless complexion and her large, dark eyes seared into his soul when their eyes met that one time. They didn't speak. She sat on her end of the park bench as she had on each previous occasion, and he sat silently on the opposite end, tossing small portions of bread from his sandwich out to the pigeons.

The only place on earth where his body could let down its defenses and allow him to relax was in his small apartment. It was his refuge. But while securing him from the daily anxiety that plagued his existence, this solitary environment left a hole in his being that was filled to overflowing with loneliness—loneliness that

49

before she came along had been like a muted background, something there, but ill defined. Now this woman provided the contrast that brought his loneliness into sharp focus and increasingly made it the dominant feature of his previously featureless existence. His apartment could no longer offer asylum from his thoughts of her. Even his dreams allowed no respite, and in them he explored every facet of a relationship with her.

He was in love with her, and for the first time in his life he felt driven by something stronger than fear.

He knew he had to speak before she did. He had to have the upper hand in this, something he had never had in his life. If he could say the first words, she would have to reply, and this would put him at an advantage. What could he say? Probably a question would be best. That way she would have to respond. It shouldn't be trivial—*How do you like this weather?*—or too personal. He didn't feel comfortable asking her name; he didn't feel comfortable asking her anything, but he had to. He would think of the perfect question to ask, even if it took all night. Then somehow he would muster the courage to ask her when she sat on his bench tomorrow. Yes, it had to be tomorrow or he'd go crazy.

Tomorrow didn't arrive quickly. He had not slept; instead, he weighed every question he could think of. *My god, what if I offend her? I could lose her.* "I could lose her," he repeated aloud at 3:30 in the morning. It was a novel thought. He was actually more concerned about losing her than embarrassing himself. This was uncharted territory and that, he knew, was good.

He was half finished with his breakfast cereal when he thought of it. It was the perfect question and it was something he had wondered about all these weeks. It had haunted him daily and had recurred in his dreams. It was a good question. He would ask her today and that would be the beginning of everything about which he had fantasized for so long.

Lunchtime came and he raced through the lobby of the building to get out to the park. Now his heart was racing too as he felt her sit beside him. His timing had to be just right. He waited until she had opened the small brown bag. He waited until she had unwrapped the sandwich. He waited until she had taken that first dainty bite. The time had come, and with his heart in his throat, he asked the question.

"Is that chicken salad or tuna?"

Her answer to his question didn't come as quickly as he had hoped.

"Why, it's chicken salad," she finally replied. "Would you like some?" Her words formed less of an invitation than those spoken by her fervent, enchanting eyes.

Her warm voice melted away thirty years of fear, and he knew his life had just begun.

Father Kelly's Thanksgiving

Father Patrick Kelly sat at his small desk, hunched over the glowing screen of his laptop computer. The room was in total darkness with the exception of the light emanating from the screen, which made the lines in the priest's face appear deeper; perhaps they were made deeper by the stress of writing another one of his all too boring homilies. Of all the things he had to do as a priest, writing the sermon that he would give at Sunday Mass was by far his most dreaded task. He was not a good speaker and, as he approached his sixtieth birthday, he had finally and somewhat painfully reached the conclusion that he wasn't a very good writer either. The mere thought of speaking in public had always made him sweat, and the unrelenting glare of the blank computer screen made him sick to his stomach.

There were so many things he needed to tell the parishioners of Saint Stephens Catholic Church, but in his twenty years as pastor, his words never seemed to hit the mark. Problems abounded in his economically and ethnically mixed parish, and the fact that he knew about them primarily through the sacrament of Confession made it difficult for him to address them directly in his weekly sermon. Of course he always got an earful from Mrs. Sanchez, the cleaning woman who came in once a week to tidy things up. Juanita Sanchez was a forty-five year old widow who cleaned several houses in the neighborhoods surrounding the church, and the dirt she picked up went well beyond that in her vacuum. Every week she regaled Father Kelly with the latest gossip. Occasionally, it included the Turners, a young newlywed couple who just couldn't get along. "They fight all the time and I don't think they're even sleeping in the same bed," reported Mrs. Sanchez. "I'd bet a dollar to a donut they're divorced within six months."

But that wasn't the worst of the gossip. There was Mike Flynn, father of eight, who couldn't stay sober long enough to get a job, let alone hold one. Then came the weekly update on Maggie Jackson, a married woman, who was having an affair with . . . "You know, what's his name, the guy from Jamaica."

Today the big news was Sally Munson, the banker's teenaged daughter, who every boy in the parish knew was good for a romp in the hay. "That gal's gotta be stopped," Juanita said. "I hear she's knocked up and going to get an abortion. And that banker dad of hers . . . I think he's skimmin'."

Father Kelly hoped that part about Sally being pregnant wasn't true, but it was likely, based upon what Sally had admitted to in the confessional over the past few years. It didn't take long for a priest to recognize the voices of regular customers, and Sally's light wispy voice was very recognizable. To the kind old priest the confessional was a gauge of his effectiveness, and based on that measure he felt he had fallen far short. Spousal abuse, child molesting, thievery, fighting, infidelity, lying, cheating, fraud, drunkenness, drugs abuse, every manner of depravity—even attempted murder—had been confessed to Father Kelly over the years by members of his parish. Same sins, same people committing them, and nothing the good father had said over the years had reversed the trend. The sins of his flock weighed on his soul like an anchor, dragging him down till he felt he would drown. The litany of sins he heard every Saturday in the confessional had become his great burden, and due to his inability to change the hearts of the sinners it was an unwelcome mantle he had to wear. He knew his sermons were dull and his words ineffective, but worse still, no one seemed to care about anything he said. They just sat there in the pews, staring, probably thinking about the NFL or golf, the bank examiner's visit, the beer in the fridge, or Mary Callahan's cleavage.

This week Father Kelly had a new challenge. Someone had broken into the steel box containing the special collection for Ebola victims in West Africa. The entire $1,856.37 was missing and he hoped he could think of something to say that might shame the thief into returning it.

There Kelly sat with his elbows straddling the keyboard and his two hands cupping the bald spot on top of his head. He stared at the screen and the screen stared back, giving him no clue about what to write. *So many problems*, he thought. *These people need so much help and I can't think of one word that might help them.* "Oh my God," he said aloud in his growing despair. "I can't do this. Please help me, Father; please help me."

God had always helped him for as long as he could remember. He was only six when he discovered his father's body behind the candy counter of the little family pharmacy, the victim of a robbery gone terribly wrong. Little Patrick prayed, and God comforted him and his mother. Having no insurance, they would have been destitute had it not been for the secretarial job that his mother had said was a gift from God. When his older brother Sean's F-4 Phantom was shot down over Vietnam, God brought him through the five years during which Sean was missing in action. Then when Sean's remains were found, Pat sought comfort again and received it. He wasn't a good student at seminary, and he always believed it was prayer that got him through. When his mother died of cancer, his faith was tested again and he felt that even God couldn't ease his pain, but even that was mitigated through prayer and a renewed focus on his studies.

But this was different; he had always believed that he could speak to God through prayer, and God would respond, but Father Kelly had failed to teach his flock that they could do the same. Now, as he sat before the unyielding computer screen, he couldn't help but wonder why God had allowed him to fail at such an important task. Was God teaching him a lesson about his becoming complacent— too comfortable? Or was it something worse? Had God just given up on him and his troubled flock? Perhaps God had never really answered his prayers at all, and the comfort and guidance he had received was just a figment of his imagination.

The very idea that he, of all people, could harbor such doubts startled him. But the reality that his sheep had gone so far astray and he seemed incapable of retrieving them was overpowering. That his prayers had not helped had rendered the situation hopeless. Kelly recognized that he was not a charismatic leader whose sermons could lift an entire congregation out of the mire, so he knew that prayer was all he had left.

Just one, Lord, Father Kelly prayed. *If you could help just one; if it's only to stop Juanita from gossiping, then I would know for sure.*

"If I could just get started," he mumbled to the screen, "perhaps more words will come." After a moment of reflection, he began typing the first thing that popped into his mind, and printed it out. After looking at what he had printed, he tossed it on the stack of administrative stuff that always cluttered his desk. Then he began again at the top of another blank page.

He awoke Sunday morning to the tolling of the bells from the steeple of the old gothic style church. His face bore the imprint of the computer keyboard where, totally exhausted, he had rested his head, *just for a minute.*

"Oh heck, I'm late!" he said as he rushed to the rectory window and saw people walking into the church for seven o'clock Mass. He quickly put on the appropriate vestment for the day, grabbed the stack of papers from his desk and ran across the parking lot to the back door of the church. Kelly handed the papers to the altar boy and told him to place them on the elevated pulpit. The altar boy gazed at the material quizzically, then did as he was told.

Following recitation of the specific prayer for today's Mass, Father Kelly ascended the four steps that led to the pulpit where he read the Epistle and the Gospel for the day. He was one of the few priests who still used the pulpit for this part of the Mass, but he was old school. Then it was time for his homily. It would be a long one. There was a lot to cover and he was grateful that it was written down, as his memory wasn't what it used to be. He was surprisingly relaxed. His words flowed, his voice steady, and for the first time in 20 years he was making eye contact with many of the people scattered throughout the large church. But beyond that, they seemed to be paying attention.

He saw Amie Turner sitting in the south nave. Her husband Bob was seated in the north. They both looked morose. Maggie Jackson was sitting alone, seemingly mesmerized by the priest's words as she wiped tears from her eyes. Sally Munson, in the front row with her parents, was smiling, her eyes wide as if she had just come to some happy conclusion. Her dad, Frank, had removed his glasses and would not make eye contact with Father Kelly. Mary Callahan was tugging at the bodice of her low cut dress to better conceal her ample bosom. Juanita Sanchez was staring at the floor and fidgeting. Mike Flynn was attempting to sit up straight after his usual Saturday night binge.

After Father Kelly had proclaimed "Go, the Mass has ended," he walked down the center aisle, through the large gothic doors and stood at the top of the concrete steps, as he had been doing for twenty years. This was a force of habit, because he seldom received more than a few hand waves, or a nod. Most Sundays he was just ignored by people anxious to get on with their day as quickly as possible. But today people weren't rushing away. They were smiling and talking with each other as they walked across the parking lot. Some came over and thanked him for his sermon or wished him a "happy Sunday."

He was startled by a light voice behind him. "Father Kelly?" He turned to see Sally Munson.

"Father, I just wanted to tell you that . . . that your sermon touched me." Sally was smiling broadly while tears streamed on her cheeks. "No one knows this, but I'm pregnant." She paused as if to gather herself. "I . . . I was going to do something terrible, but after what you said today, I want my baby; I already love her. I don't care what anyone thinks." Sally gave the priest a hug. "Thank you," she said. He hadn't been hugged since his mother died so many years ago.

Frank Munson, still not making eye contact, stammered, "Yes, thank you Father." And as Sally skipped joyfully toward her dad's Limo, he said, "Uh, Father, when will you be hearing Confessions again. I've had some, uh, 'dealings'. Nothing illegal mind you, but they may not sit too well with . . . you know . . . the big guy upstairs." Frank pointed to the sky to illustrate his reference. "I'd like your advice and maybe some . . . forgiveness."

"No need to wait till next Saturday, Frank," Father Kelly said, maintaining a confidential tone. "You can stop by the rectory this afternoon or evening if you like."

Before Munson could respond, Bob Turner, who had just emerged from the north nave door interrupted. "Father, have you seen Amie?"

Turner's appearance betrayed his emotional state, and his panicked expression provided ample exoneration for his rude behavior. He looked as if he was lost, or indeed that he had lost something most special to him.

"Yes, as a matter of fact, she was on the opposite side of the church from you."

Bob ran toward the south entrance.

"Father Kelly, have you seen Bob?"   It was Amie; she was crying.

"Well, he just went back in looking for you."

As she turned to run toward the entrance, the priest grabbed her shoulder. "Wait, he'll be back."

And within seconds, he was.

"Father, I . . .," they both started at once. Amie looked up at Bob, "You first."

"Father, what you said in there was right on." He held Amie by the shoulders and looked her up and down. "I love this woman, but I've been such a fool."

"No, I was wrong," Amie said. "Oh Bob, I love you so much. How could we let such petty things come between us?" She turned to the priest. "Father, we don't have big problems, but sometimes they just pile up".

"Of course, but when you see that happening, I'd be happy to help you two work things out.   In fact I have some time next Tuesday . . . say around 7:00 pm?"

"Oh, Bob, can we?"

"Sure, sweetie," Bob replied.

As they walked away hand in hand, Father Kelly couldn't suppress a broad grin of self-satisfaction that was developing on his handsomely craggy face, but when he turned around to return to the church, he nearly buried his smug smile in the chest of a very big black man.

"You Kelly?" the man asked, pointing his finger down toward Kelly's nose.

"Yes, I'm Father Kelly," he said emphasizing the 'Father' part. "What can I do for you, young man?"

The man proceeded in a thick Jamaican accent. "I was supposed to pick up my Maggie here at de church and take her home wid me to Jamaica, but she say you tole her she could not go. Why did you

58

do that terrible ting?" The man was poking Kelly in the chest as he spoke. "Now she say she want ta stay wid her stupid husband. My heart is broken and I would like to kill you, but I won't 'cause . . . well, you being a priest and all."

Thank God, I've got that going for me, Kelly thought, his smug grin now completely wiped from his face.

"Now you seem to be a nice young man," the priest said. "By any chance would you be Catholic?"

"Nah! I am Rasta. I believe that Haile Selassie was the incarnation of God.

"Ah yes, a Rastafarian." Kelly was totally intimidated by the man's size and build and wanted to get away from him as quickly as possible. "I believe you also believe in Jesus as another of God's incarnations, so any time you feel the need to learn more about Jesus Christ, please feel free to come back to our church, perhaps some other time. Now I must get back to the rectory. It has been nice meeting you, Mr. ah . . . ah . . . well it's been nice meeting you."

Well, that was a humbling experience, Kelly thought as he skirted away from the Jamaican. *Thank you, Lord, for bringing me back to Earth.* When he looked across the parking lot and saw Maggie Jackson entering a green Ford pickup and sliding across the seat to sit close to her husband Earl, his grin returned.

As he reentered the church to retrieve his printed sermon, Kelly tried to remember exactly what it was he had said that had elicited such a positive response from so many of his parishioners. He couldn't come up with the first thing. Asking the altar boy, who was extinguishing candles, to bring him the materials that he left on the pulpit, he spotted Mike Flynn sitting in one of the pews and gazing straight forward as if he were deep in thought.

"Hey, Mike," Kelly said. "How's it goin'? Nice to see you back in church again."

"Man, Father, you were talking right at me," Mike said, shaking off his reverie. "I'm so ashamed. I been living my life in a bottle. Lost my family and until now I wasn't sober enough to care. I came in here drunk, but I ain't drunk now and I ain't gonna be drunk tomorrow. And when I get to where I'm sure of myself, I'm gonna go get my family back. It was all on account of what you said up there on that pulpit." He said the word as if it were hyphenated, "pull-pit." Mike continued, "And when I'm completely sober, I'll have you to thank for devotin' that whole sermon to me and my problem. Thank you so much."

Just before Mike began to slobber, the altar boy brought the papers. "Here you go Father," he said, handing him the material. "That was a super sermon; by the way, you're a little late paying the water bill. See ya."

As Kelly walked across the parking lot to the old red brick rectory building, he wondered what the boy meant by that remark. Perhaps it was a new catch phrase the kids were using these days.

In its heyday, the rectory housed three priests, but now with the Catholic population shrinking in this part of town only Father Kelly remained to shepherd his dwindling flock. Upon entering his cluttered office, he saw that Juanita was already there, but she wasn't cleaning, just sitting in the chair. When she saw Father Kelly, she dropped to her knees; "Bless me Father for I have sinned. It's been one day since my last confession."

"But Juanita, what could you have done in only one day that would require you to confess again?"

She tilted her tear-stained cheeks up toward Kelly. "It's what I didn't confess," she said.

"Go on."

"You may not have noticed, but I'm a terrible gossip." I love getting the scoop on people and then telling everyone."

"Yes?"

"Sometimes I embellish it a little—you know, to make it juicier."

"Ok, and . . .?"

"That's it. I'm a gossip; a malicious gossip like you said in your sermon. I'm a horrible person. The Bible says so."

"But I . . ." Kelly didn't recall mentioning gossips in his sermon.

"I know you were talking about me," she cried. "I don't want to be a horrible person. Can you forgive me? Will God ever forgive me?"

"Juanita, my good friend, God has already forgiven you," Father Kelly said as he reached out to hug the distraught woman. "And you're not a horrible person. But just to make sure you don't *become* a horrible person, I will stop you if I detect the first drop of gossip falling from your lips. OK?"

As Kelly led the contrite house maid to the door, he passed one of the teenaged ushers at the reception desk counting out the money from the collection baskets.

"Father, I think we won the lottery today," the young boy said. "Look at this haul. Somebody dropped a whole wad of bills in one of the baskets. They were all rolled up with a rubber band around 'em. It must have been after Mass 'cause I woulda noticed it when we took up the collection. I counted it; $1,856."

"Was there any change in there with it?"

The boy looked into the basket. "Yeah, 37 cents."

Praise God! Kelly thought. *I must have written one heck of a sermon.* He was anxious to read again the wonderful homily that brought such conviction to so many of his parishioners; the sermon that he sweated over nearly all night and finally, with his own hand, had typed and printed out just in time for Sunday Mass. With little ado, he politely dismissed the two people who were keeping him from reading the masterpiece of a sermon that he had delivered less than an hour ago.

Kelly sat in the overstuffed chair in the corner of the room, switched on the antique table lamp, and looked down at the papers he had been holding since the altar boy had brought them to him.

The cover sheet was blank, so he flipped it over and placed it on the lamp table. He was surprised to see that the second sheet was actually the water bill for the church compound. It was 30 days past due. The next ten pages were not any part of a sermon, but an email printout of the bishop's strategic plan for the Diocese.

Then he was staring at the final page. His hands trembled as he read the one thought that he had written down the previous night in his moment of great despair, *just to get himself started*. Suddenly he realized that it was the *only* thing he had written. The words of the Apostle Paul that always had been a source of solace throughout his life.

"Do not be anxious about anything, but in everything, by prayer and petition, with thanksgiving, present your requests to God. And the peace of God, which transcends all understanding, will guard your hearts and your minds in Christ Jesus."

The priest's mind echoed with the admonishment of the Christ, "O you of little faith."

A thankful and more humble Father Patrick Kelly fell to his knees and wept.

II

"*Science cannot solve the ultimate mystery of nature. And that is because, in the last analysis, we ourselves are a part of the mystery that we are trying to solve.*"
— *Max Planck*

Four Light Years from Home

Dr. Joseph Lanham watched nervously as the three bodies were loaded onto the ship. Each had been placed in a separate sarcophagus and frozen solid for preservation during the journey. The cold titanium cylinders appeared ominous, as if they were capable of unleashing some nightmarish horror if it were not for the webs of multicolored cables and liquid nitrogen-filled tubing that constrained them. Only the steadily blinking green lights on the containers' control panels gave the impression of calm. Fifty-seven years after the crash, this ordeal was almost over and he was glad to see them go, but he knew in his gut that this was only the beginning.

Those years had gone by quickly although he would have preferred at times that they had moved even faster. At first it was an exciting challenge, dismantling the crashed space craft, deciphering the system diagrams and performing the prodigious task of reverse engineering that led up to this historic moment. But from the beginning, there was always the vague fear that his work could backfire on him with catastrophic consequences. As Lanham had learned more about these beings and their magnificent technology, this vague fear came into sharper focus and he began to realize that his fear was not for himself alone, but for all mankind. Perhaps it

64

was the secrecy surrounding the project that produced a dismal mood of extreme paranoia in everyone who had worked on it. He prayed that the maiden voyage of this magnificent craft and its carefully selected crew would somehow end the secrecy once and for all. Then there was his own secret, the stress from which had killed the only woman he had ever loved, a secret, which when revealed, could save the human race or destroy it.

Lanham followed the last of the titanium containers into the hold of the ship where each was being secured to the bulkhead with metal straps. He observed every move of the technicians as they disconnected the containers from the portable refrigeration units and attached them to the onboard support system that would maintain a temperature cold enough to preserve the bodies. The men making the connections were career military, although their white clean-suits gave no indication of this. They had spent much of their careers on the project and had been selected by virtue of the low security risks they presented: None had families. For them the job had become routine and Lanham was now looking at the result of the kind of work produced when the extraordinary becomes mundane.

One of the large cables from the ship's back-up power supply was not connected properly. It was of no immediate concern, but if the back-up system needed to be activated, it could cause a fire. The risk of this happening was extremely low, but too much was riding on this mission to overlook any potential hazard. With so much at stake, he felt compelled to inspect the three and a half million electrical connections and one hundred thousand plumbing components that were incorporated in this, the greatest engineering feat in human history. He couldn't, of course, but he did make sure he had been present during the critical moments in the birth of this unique craft. It had paid off too; he had discovered dozens of errors as the ship was being built, several of which could have had serious consequences. This one didn't appear that serious, but needed attention just as well.

"Sergeant, get someone in here to fix this," Lanham said, pointing to the bad connection. "And tell your men to be more careful. This thing has got to hold together for at least ten years."

"Yessir," Sergeant Garrison snapped back. Garrison tucked his head into his left shoulder and spoke into a miniature microphone, "Beckman, you there?"

"Yeah, Sarge," came the reply, somewhat muffled by the half meatball sandwich Beckman had just stuffed into his mouth.

"Get your ass back in here and check the back-up power connections on number four—and while you're here, might as well double check all of 'em."

"What's wrong with 'em?" Beckman asked bolting down the last large bite of the sandwich.

"Bad connection, I guess." Garrison replied, then in more of a whisper, "It's Lanham again."

"Shit," Beckman spat as he wiped the sandwich juice on his clean-suit. "That son of a bitch is a pain in the butt; damned civilian."

Beckman saw the problem immediately. The "quik-clik" connector that had been hastily developed expressly for this project was broken. One of the Kevlar tabs was missing and the only thing left to hold the two ends together was friction between the pins and the socket.

"Shit," Beckman said, in a volume too low for anyone to hear. "This damned thing's got twenty-four wires and a fiber optic. I'll have to re-do the whole friggin' thing." He went into his tool box for the snips and saw the silver backed tape.

"Shit, this'll work," Beckman told himself as he wrapped a short piece of the tape around the connector. "Better than new."

"All fixed, Sarge," he said as he passed Garrison in the companionway. Outside the ship, Beckman gave a half-hearted

66

wave toward Dr. Lanham, who was standing a few hundred feet off. Lanham, nearly mesmerized by the sight of the enormous machine, was too deep in thought to even notice. Beckman shrugged, "friggin' egghead," he muttered, and went back to his unfinished potato chips.

Lanham squinted at the strange looking craft and marveled that anything that large could even get off the ground. He understood the physics behind it of course, but the sheer size of it, the awkward shape, seemed to defy all laws of aerodynamics that until now had to be obeyed if something was to fly. Of course, this thing wouldn't really "fly"—not in the true sense of the word. And he knew that aerodynamics had nothing to do with why, just a few hours from now, this object would leave the earth and begin a journey to a place that couldn't even be seen on the most powerful earth-based telescopes. Even though this thing was the largest and, by far, the heaviest object ever designed by humans for space travel, he knew that weight was not a consideration with this unique machine either. The fact that it also wasn't designed by humans didn't escape him, and no single person on Earth understood everything about how this thing worked.

Now, looking up at this magnificent craft, its dull, ultra-black skin appearing more like a gigantic hole in the desert sky, than any kind of a recognizable object, Lanham began to feel the weariness that comes upon completion of a high-energy project. It seemed to press down on him, pushing him back until he rested against an aluminum light pole at the edge of the concrete pad. It was a weariness that had always been denied and was now finally surfacing after more than half a century of battling with this project. *My God*, he thought, *had it been that long?* It had. It was the centerpiece of his entire career; the "Project" *was* his career. A profound emptiness seeped into his body as he began to realize that at the moment of launch, his career would be over, and for the first time in his life he was feeling old.

Lanham's old legs did not want to support the weight of his body and, using the pole as a backrest, he allowed himself to slide toward the ground until he was sitting at its base. Still staring up at the ship, he tried to reconstruct the events that brought him to this place, the fantastic discoveries, the days, nights, weeks, months, years that blended together so tightly that he now had little sense of chronology:

1947

The war had been over for nearly two years, and the only country left for Americans to worry about was the Soviet Union. No one worried too much though because we had "the bomb"; they didn't. Few Americans had ever heard of Arzamas-16, but those insiders who had, knew that it was the postal code for a top-secret project that was accelerating the Soviets toward their first fission reaction. We couldn't stop it, but we could stay ahead. There were a few laboratories around the country and a handful of scientists to make sure that we did.

Joe Lanham was one of those. Somewhat of a prodigy, he had entered MIT at 16, and had received a Ph.D. in physics by the time he had turned 22. Hired upon graduation by the Federal government, he was now doing what he had dreamed of doing for so long. He was working on a cutting edge project—it was *the* project, the Atomic bomb—at its birthplace, Los Alamos National Laboratory. *It couldn't get any more interesting than this*, he thought, but fate would soon prove him wrong.

Katie Lanham didn't care much for New Mexico; she was born and raised in Atlanta and had been the belle of the debutante season during her eighteenth year. She lived for the southern social scene. But when she married Joe, she simply followed wherever his career took them.

She was the perfect foil for Joe. Having attended Smith in North Hampton, Massachusetts, she met Joe by accident at a mixer in Worcester, the convenient halfway point between MIT and Smith. She taught Joe to dance when he was still an undergrad. It was one of the few social skills at which he became proficient. When he held Katie in his arms, he held her especially close because he knew she enjoyed it. She responded to his every move keeping their bodies so tight together that their clothing provided little barrier between their skins.

Katie had graduated only nine months earlier and was very relieved to have gotten a bachelor of arts degree after nearly flunking out of her math and science prerequisites. If it hadn't been for Joe's diligent tutoring, she would have had to go back to Atlanta and listen to her parents' fabricated excuses for her failure. They were married a few months before Joe received his Ph.D.

After the government moved them to Los Alamos, there was little to keep Katie occupied, so she spent most of her time trying to decorate the small frame house that their federal employer had provided. She was thankful for the Friday evening dances, where many of the scientists and their wives would gather, dance, and drink too much. Katie was always the loveliest woman there. She charmed the other women and beguiled the men, but mostly she danced with Joe, and smiled in anticipation of going home to their bed were they would try joyfully to conceive their first child.

Katie had almost finished making the rounds at the dance, inching her way closer to where Joe was talking with two of his associates, Dr. Phil Roberts and Professor David Keelor. They were deep in a theoretical discussion when she arrived at Joe's side.

"Hello, Doctors," she said overdoing her best southern belle accent, "can I borrow this cute li'l ol' boy for a dance?" She wrapped her arm around Joe's and led him to the dance floor, anxious to be encircled by his strong arms.

When they reached the dance floor, the band had already played the first few bars of Benny Goodman's *Memories of You*. Katie nestled her head against Joe's shoulder and, feeling safe and content in his arms, she awaited the kiss that she knew would be coming next. Feeling the warmth of his lips on her forehead, she wondered if this might be the night that their child would be conceived. They had been trying now for six months, and she was beginning to worry.

It was a magical evening and neither Joe nor Katie noticed the soldier walking toward them until he tapped Joe on the shoulder.

"Sorry my friend, no cutting in tonight," Joe said, his eyes closed as he absorbed the bliss of the moment.

"Beg pardon, sir," the sergeant said. "General Hampton wants to see you."

Joe moved his hand slightly away from Katie's waist and gave a dismissing wave. "Tell the general I'll stop by first thing in the morning. I'm kinda busy right now."

The seasoned non-com didn't move, fixing a hard gaze on Dr. Lanham.

"Go on," Lanham said, "Whatever it is, I'm sure it'll wait till tomorrow."

The sergeant stood firm. He didn't care much for civilians and these young eggheads seemed to have the run of the place. Stiffening his back, he towered over most of the dancing couples; then, speaking at a volume loud enough to turn the heads of several other dancers, "NOW . . . SIR!"

Lanham stopped dancing and turned to give the soldier a piece of his mind. That was the first he noticed the man's uniform. Stiffly starched khakis and knife-edge creases in the trousers suggested that he was part of the commanding officer's staff. The stripes on his sleeves—three up and three down—gave notice, even to a civilian, that he was probably the ranking non-com on staff. *What would warrant sending Mr. Spit 'n Polish here to do a corporal's job,* Lanham wondered. *Perhaps whatever it is* can't *wait till morning.*

"I'll be right with you, Master Sergeant," Lanham said, addressing him with the correct rank in an attempt to avoid the civilian stereotype. He kissed Katie on the forehead. "Guess I gotta go, Sweetheart. You can catch a ride home with Dave Keelor."

"I'm sorry sir, Dr. Keelor will be going with us," the soldier said, nodding toward the door where Keelor and Roberts were both waiting. "We will make sure Mrs. Lanham and Mrs. Keelor get home."

Lanham knew immediately when the brown Ford staff car made the turn out of the parking lot that they were not heading toward the General's quarters. They were heading southeast and away from Los Alamos.

"I thought we were going to see General Hampton," Lanham said.

"We are," the sergeant said matter-of-factly.

"Where?" Lanham, Keelor and Roberts asked almost simultaneously.

"I'm sorry, sirs, that is classified information. You'll be told everything when we get there."

The car sped on in silence for more than an hour until the driver switched on the radio. The announcer had just declared that it was eleven o'clock and time for the KROS news. There was the sound of a teletype machine in the background.

"Earlier this evening, more than thirty local citizens reported seeing strange red and white lights in the sky," the announcer began. "Many are speculating that the army is testing a new airplane or a rocket. Jimmy Doermeyer, a mechanic at the Franklin Garage, said he had never seen anything like it and in his view, it wasn't anything the army could build. Doermeyer said the lights were just going too fast and speculated that they may have been from outer space. Other witnesses agreed that . . ."

The master sergeant reached over and switched off the radio, eliciting a frown from the driver. The sergeant nodded toward lights in the road ahead. "Road block," he said. "Pull alongside that Jeep. I'll talk to 'em."

A black-and-white sawhorse barricade, punctuated by an army Jeep on one side and a deuce-and-a-half truck on the other, obstructed the roadway. Two soldiers with M-1 rifles were standing at port arms in front of the barricade. As the staff car approached, a sergeant wearing a white M.P. sleeve band walked out toward it.

"You have business down this road, sergeant?" the M.P. asked.

The master sergeant held out an I.D. card. "General Hamilton's chief of staff," he said. I'm bringing in some V.I.P.s . . . by order of the general."

"Hold on a minute," the M.P. said, walking back to the Jeep and picking up a field telephone. He returned thirty seconds later. "OK, give my regards to the general. Take it easy, lotta military traffic on the road tonight."

The two soldiers slung their weapons on their shoulders, and, each grabbing an end of the barricade, swung it to the side to open a lane wide enough for the staff car. There was indeed a great deal of traffic on the narrow country road. As they proceeded, Lanham counted five deuce-and-a-half army trucks, three larger ones, a flatbed truck, and a tank crane heading in the opposite direction then turning off somewhere behind them to go off-road toward a hazy bluish light in the distance. There were also a number of open Jeeps and a field ambulance that seemed to be in a hurry to get somewhere.

Lanham wondered if a military plane might have crashed. That might explain why Phil Roberts was in the car. He was a medical doctor as well as a physicist and his job at Los Alamos was to study the effects of radiation on living tissue. *Keelor maybe*, Lanham thought, *He's a biophysicist and he knows anatomy, But why me? No, probably not a plane crash. Maybe a weapons test that went sour. Hardly—not in this location—too close to the civilian population. Perhaps a rocket from White Sands went haywire.*

The staff car stopped at the entrance to a large corrugated steel Quonset hut. Several other vehicles were parked close by and it was apparent from the excited voices coming from inside the building that Lanham and his associates weren't the first to arrive.

Inside, Lt. General Hamilton was standing next to an area map and speaking loudly to a Lt. Colonel and a Major.

" . . . I want that area swept so clean that your mommas couldn't find anything. Is that clear? And I don't want to read about this in the papers. You tell your men not to let any of those reporter sons-a-bitches anywhere near that site. If anyone leaks this to the press, I'll personally nail his hide to the shithouse wall. Clear?"

"Yessir," the two lower ranking officers snapped in unison.

"OK, now get back out there and make sure every one of your troops understands that this operation is top secret."

The two got up and as they passed the master sergeant and the three civilian scientists, flashed a look of relief and fear.

"Come in men, sit down" the general commanded, half-heartedly returning the master sergeant's salute. "Has Sergeant Corley filled you in on what's happened?"

"No sir, he said it was classified and we'd get the details from you," Roberts said, being the only one of the three who wasn't at all intimidated by the general's demeanor.

"Good. He's right. This . . ." the general searched for the right word, ". . . event is classified and will remain so until we figure out just what it is we have here." The general stopped talking and re-lit the cigar stub that had been neglected on the corner of a glass ashtray.

"What *do* we have here, General?" Roberts asked.

Hamilton took a few puffs, rotating the burned down Churchill over his match to get an even light. "What we got, gentlemen, is a hell of a large craft of unknown origin that augered into the desert

73

about five miles from here." The general began pointing to some pencil markings on the map. "We got a very large piece of that craft here, and parts strewn across a four square mile area . . . right about here." Hamilton indicated an area on the map with a circular motion of his hand. "We got something else, too, gentlemen," he said, bowing his head toward his cigar and looking at the three scientists out of the corner of his eye as he took another puff. He wanted to watch their reaction when he finished his next statement. "We got three bodies."

The scientists had been looking at the map where Hamilton's hand had been previously. Suddenly they were focused on Hamilton as he continued. ". . . and they don't seem to be from here."

"Russians?" Keelor asked, knowing that the Soviet Union was more than mildly interested in the U.S. military's activities in this part of New Mexico.

"Too early to tell where they're from, but I think we can be pretty sure they aren't from the Soviet Union. We'll go out to the site tomorrow at first light and maybe you guys can tell me where it came from." Smirking, Hamilton added, "I haven't a clue." Then turning toward the sergeant, "Show these men to their quarters. Get some sleep, gentlemen. Breakfast is at oh-four-hundred and we'll be on site by sunup."

The three were led to a small frame barrack about a hundred feet from the Quonset hut. There were three bunks and some army blankets to fend off the desert chill. A kerosene lantern hung from a ceiling rafter.

"What do you think?" Lanham asked the other two after the sergeant had gone.

"Got me," Keelor said.

"Like the general said, I haven't a clue," Roberts chimed in.

Each was thinking the same thing, but dared not articulate it. Each felt the excitement of an impending discovery but wasn't sure exactly what it was or if the others felt the same thing. Each wondered if he was being childish and feared making a fool of himself in front of his peers. The electricity that seemed to permeate the air kept the three scientists from sleeping. It was already after one a.m. Oh-four-hundred would be here soon, but not soon enough.

After breakfast, General Hamilton took Roberts, Keelor and Lanham to the plateau overlooking the main site. From here the men could get a good view of what was left of the craft and the four mile long trench it had plowed out of the desert floor.

Robert's reaction: "My god!"

Keelor's reaction: "Jeezus!"

Lanham's reaction: Wide eyed silence.

Looming before them was a huge black object, a third of which appeared to be buried in the desert sand, stuck there like a Ritz cracker in a bowl of soft cheese. At first glance it looked like a disk, but upon further observation it took on the appearance of a sphere. From yet another perspective, it appeared to be elongated. It had left a crater-like footprint where it had initially hit the ground, skipped then hit again, its enormous weight ejecting thousands of tons of sand and creating a cut in the earth that was quite possibly visible from the moon.

The top edge of the object stood higher than the top of the plateau and the pure blackness of its skin absorbed the rays of the rising sun so completely that no features were visible on its surface. The black arc that it formed looked like the entrance of a huge cave where light could enter and not escape. Anything that may have been attached to the outside of it had been ripped off in the violent crash and strewn across the landscape. Large black pipe-like objects stood out from the ejected sand like straws in a furrow. Other indistinguishable pieces created a debris field that seemed to stretch endlessly across the barren landscape. The main body of the object appeared intact, save for a relatively small irregular hole in the center of the arc.

"That, believe it or not, is some sort of hatch," Hamilton said, pointing toward the hole. "We found two of the bodies very near there. The other one we found farther on inside. There could be more of 'em: It's a huge thing and we haven't gotten all the way through it yet."

———

Lanham had no reason other than curiosity to be in the area where the autopsies would be performed. He was a nuclear physicist working at the testing range at Alamogordo when he got the call to accompany Doctor Roberts and Professor Keelor, to investigate the crash. His task was to determine what kind of propulsion system the ship used to reach that spot near Roswell, New Mexico from somewhere in deep space. His business was in the huge, rapidly-constructed hangar where the badly damaged object awaited him. The autopsies were being conducted in a small cinder block room in the rear of the hanger.

Lanham suppressed a smile when he first saw the creature on the table. Even in death, the alien was beautiful. While emulating a human shape, the lines of its body were smooth and flowing, appearing more like a fine sculpture than a once living thing. Lanham noted that the alien appeared to be about the size of an average human and was obviously male. The body was thin, but muscular, not sinewy. The only things disturbing the soft contours of the body were the traumatic injuries resulting from the crash. The alien's skin was pale, transparent looking. The alien's face looked almost human, but had symmetry not seen in the countenance of mankind. As Lanham viewed the alien he found it difficult to look away, as someone might find it difficult to casually stroll passed Michelangelo's Pietà. Had it not been for the injuries, the alien's external appearance would have been flawless.

A light aroma permeated the air around the examination table; fresh, like some variety of springtime flower. Lanham breathed in deeply.

"Nice smell," Lanham said. "New after shave, doctor?"

"No, that's coming from our friend here," one of the attendants said. "They all smell like that."

"Are they all so . . . attractive?" Lanham asked trying to find the right word, and knowing his word choice fell far short.

"Yes," Roberts said. "It's not like they all look alike either. They're clearly individuals—different features—but all extremely beautiful."

"And they smell real nice," the attendant added.

By the time Lanham returned to his car in the lot behind the hangar, it was past ten o'clock. It was the weekend, and he would have to rush to get all the way back to Los Alamos before Katie went to bed. It was not until Lanham had cleared all the checkpoints that he realized he was not alone.

———

1985

When he suggested that a ship duplicating the alien craft could be built, Lanham had not anticipated that anyone would want its maiden voyage to be to the planet of the alien visitors.

"We know everything we need to know about the technology, but after nearly 40 years, we know very little about these beings," Lanham reasoned when he met with the President and a select congressional group. "We know something about their physiology, but we don't know how they think; we have no idea what motivates them. Diplomacy would be impossible. We don't know if they came here to befriend us or to conquer us. Lord knows they have the technology to do either on a whim. We humans can't get along with each other, and *we* have common ancestors. How can we expect to get along with an alien race that may have nothing in common with us and is significantly more advanced?" Lanham pleaded.

"Nonsense," the senator from Massachusetts replied. "They look pretty much like us. I'll even allow that they look better. They're obviously not monsters from some science fiction movie. What motivates them is probably the same thing that drives us, curiosity, the thrill of adventure, wealth, power, sex.

"I just don't think we're ready to . . ."

"Dr. Lanham," the senator continued, "this is an opportunity to finally make contact with beings from another world. It will be recorded as the most important event in human history. Would you pass up such an opportunity because of some primeval fear? They may be more advanced, but we're not cavemen after all. Dr. Lanham, our society has prospered on diversity. We have all colors, shapes and sizes in our world and we have been able to make that work for us." The Senator was now standing, leaning over the table and gesturing broadly. "Don't you think we can accept and be tolerant of these obviously intelligent people, even though they may look a little different?"

"Senator, how they look has nothing to do with it," Lanham protested.

"I think it does," chimed in the congresswoman from California. "I think your pre-conceived notions of what people should look like are clouding your judgment. Diversity, doctor—diversity is the key word. If we go to them with a friendly hand outstretched, and show them that we can accept them into our diverse global—uh, interstellar—community, why, we might find all sorts of things in common and possibly avoid a conflict in the future. I think the esteemed senator from Massachusetts is absolutely correct."

"Damn right," agreed the senator from Texas, I'll bet we can even set up some sort of trade with 'em. Don't matter if they are prettier than we are."

"I propose," said the Massachusetts senator, "that we build a ship using the science that we have gleaned from the alien craft, and assemble a crew of Americans that represents Earth's diverse people. Then we will send our glorious, courageous, and multi-cultural crewpersons to the alien's planet, and when they see how well we all get along, well, they'll want to be our friends too . . . and as a further gesture of friendship, we will return the bodies of their fallen comrades so they can give them a decent burial." The senator finished with a flourish and graciously accepted the applause from the President and the select group in the room.

"Senator, what do we tell our own people?" Lanham inquired. We've kept this from them for decades because we didn't want our enemies to know we had access to such advanced technology. We've stonewalled and lied to them. We'll have to ask Congress for an appropriation to build the thing—perhaps trillions of dollars—and it will take years. How do we explain it to the public?"

"National security," the President offered. "And it would be the truth; we couldn't tell them because it could have compromised national security."

"That won't be necessary," the Massachusetts senator said. "It still can be built in secret. With the cost amortized over the years that it will take to build this thing, the annual costs might be small enough to hide in the military budget."

———

2005

Indeed, Lanham thought as the loading of the containers continued, *the aliens are the most beautiful creatures he had ever encountered.* And he knew that their beauty extended beyond their external features, however; he couldn't help feeling that the impending launch was premature.

The ship's four-person human crew had been frozen too, albeit not so solid that they couldn't be thawed out in time to make the necessary preparations for landing on the dead aliens' home planet.

Such a distant planet would have been impossible to locate had it not been for the detailed charts recorded in the crashed ship's computer memory. There were also schematics, and diagrams, which allowed the new ship to be built in a shorter time span than at first thought. It was smaller than the alien's ship, but still large enough to transport all seven—three dead aliens and four living humans—to the alien solar system.

Unceremoniously, the launch clock counted down to zero and the huge craft began a slow ascent from the wide concrete stage that NASA had constructed in the desert not far from where the original ship had crashed. There was no thunder as with past NASA launches, no billowing clouds, no acrid smell of hydrazine and other chemicals. The ship simply rose, its motion accompanied by a deep humming sound and a sudden pressure as if someone had slammed a door in a very small room. It ascended thus for twenty thousand feet. Then with another burst of pressure it vanished. Two seconds later, it was 150,000 miles beyond the faint crescent moon that was still visible in the morning sky.

For the next forty-two months the ship was on its own, its speed preventing communication with Earth. The progress of the ship could be tracked from Earth however, not as an object in space, but as something that simply wasn't there and moving away at a velocity greater than that of light itself. The ship was an attentive nursemaid, adjusting temperatures, oxygen flow, and nutrients to the frozen humans, and regulating their body functions. Simultaneously it conducted speed adjustments, course corrections, and internal monitoring. It performed flawlessly.

The awakening process was pre-programmed. Air Force Captain Derek Blake, a nuclear physicist from Lanham's team, was first. Blake, from Montana, could have been the poster boy for the Helena

Chamber of Commerce. The rigors of ranch life in his adolescence had provided square-jawed character that complemented his athletic body. Tall, fair-complexioned, blond and blue-eyed, he was handsome by anyone's standards, even with his wavy hair plastered to his head by the freezing gel in which he had been submerged for three and a half years.

Sitting up in his container, he looked about the compartment, not the least bit groggy, not the least bit disoriented. He watched as the lids of his shipmates' containers popped open one at a time. Second to rise was Dr. Zuri Eshe, who served a double role as chief engineer and physician. Immediately alert, she stood, stretching to her full six feet, her lovely mahogany skin still glistening from the gel that had preserved her cells these long months. It was an unexpected treat for Blake since, to this point, he had only wondered what she looked like naked. He wasn't disappointed.

Lee Wang Ha and Anna Shelikhov sat up almost simultaneously. Lee was short and thin, his Asian skin stretched tightly over his sinewy body. He was a seasoned diplomat who had learned the alien's language from their computer voice tracks. Shelikhov, a Siberian by birth, was about the same height as Lee, but outweighed him by twenty pounds. Her training in astronomy and astrophysics led to her assignment as navigator. All four had been chosen because of their backgrounds and diverse physical features. They were all Americans, but they were the perfect showcase for ethnic diversity on Earth.

The four were now standing—shivering, as the compartment was too chilly to be comfortable for a wet naked body.

"Check your monitors," Blake commanded, pressing the function button on his body monitor. "Let's get into some clothes; it's cold as hell in here."

Warm showers eased the chill and their blue jumpsuits kept it from returning. Each of the four went to an assigned work station and began fine tuning the ship in preparation for entry into a new solar system and landing on a planet whose atmosphere, scientists back home agreed, should be much like Earth's.

"I saw you looking at me," Zuri said, her soft East African accent rounding her words in a way that delighted Blake's ear.

"Oh? When was that?"

"When we were awakened."

"Uh, yeah. Just wanted to make sure you were all right."

"Well? What do you think? Am I?" She said flashing a mischievous smile.

"Well, yeah . . . you're fine," Blake said, not knowing exactly what answer Zuri was looking for.

"My body . . . is it . . . all right?"

"Doctor Eshe, you have one of the loveliest bodies I have ever seen," Blake answered sincerely. "In fact, if we weren't, four light years from my apartment, I'd let you know in a much more convincing fashion," he joked.

Zuri, lowered her head and smiled, her dark skin hiding the blush rising in her beautiful face. When they were in training, Blake seemed aloof, almost an automaton. Today he showed her he was a man after all, much to her pleasure.

——

The landing procedures began nine billion miles from the alien's planet, with reversal of the gravity drive slowing the ship at a rate that would have crushed the crew had it not been for the ship's gravity compensation system. As it was, the crew continued to have little sense that the craft was moving at all. It would take nearly six months to traverse the relatively short distance from the solar system's ecliptic plane to the planet itself and there was little to do but monitor the automatic systems and try to tune into any radio signals that might emanate from the planet.

Lieutenant Shelikhov busied herself with her charts, calculating the craft's linear deceleration to make sure the ship's velocity was being reduced enough to accommodate a proper orbit by the time it reached the planet's gravitational field. Lee Wang Ha listened to voice tapes from the alien ship, trying to pick up on subtleties he might have missed during the hundreds of hours of listening to and speaking the fluid alien language. Blake spent most of his time before a small computer console, checking the ships systems and rehearsing emergency procedures in his head. Even though the ship was nearly fully automatic with double or triple system redundancies, Blake didn't completely trust them and thought of himself as the ultimate backup system. *Anyway*, he thought, *it's something to do.* He looked over occasionally at Zuri, who was reading a book from the ship's small library. It was fiction and Blake was surprised to see that it was a love story.

She is beautiful, he thought, letting his mind return to the day they came out of their frozen sleep. He felt himself warming as he recalled the sight of her sleek, lovely body. Closing his eyes, he let his thoughts continue the scene, only this time embellishing it with new dialogue and a much more satisfying ending. In his mind he filed, *I will get to know this woman sometime . . . when we get home.*

Blake's reverie was snapped by the master alarm buzzer. Three of the lights on the system panel went from green to yellow then to red and began to flash. Within seconds the buzzer silenced and the lights all went back to green.

"Ok," Blake said. "We had an electrical power failure. No problem; the ship automatically switched to backup. Dr. Eshe, see if you can locate the source of the problem and get us back on primary."

Eshe quickly traversed the few steps between her seat and the elevator that connected the two decks and went to the electrical switching room on B-deck where the failure had occurred. After running a series of diagnostic tests she reported back. "Everything looks OK here."

Blake checked his display, toggling the power switch between primary and backup. Suddenly, a different warning light began to flash in unison with a pulsating buzzer.

"Zuri, get out of the power module. I've got a fire indicator light on my panel. The Halon will fire up in 30 seconds."

Halon, the fire-extinguishing agent, had a proven record against electrical fires. It simply depleted the oxygen in a room and suffocated the fire almost instantaneously. To contain the Halon, the air tight hatch door would automatically lock in thirty seconds and would not unlock until the Halon had been pumped out of the module. The de-oxygenated environment would kill not only the fire, but any living thing present.

"I don't see a fire," Eshe said. "Override the Halon and let me see what's going on here."

"There's no override on the Halon. Get out now, Doctor. You have 15 seconds."

"Wait, I think I see . . ." Zuri's sentence was cut short by the thud of the hatch lock engaging.

She turned and threw her full weight against the hatch lever. The hatch lock held. Then she heard the hiss of the Halon. She knew her oxygen would soon be gone and the lock would not be released for another fifteen minutes when all possibility of a fire had passed. Zuri peered through the small triple pane hatch window. Blake was on the other side hammering at the hatch lock control box with the handle of a large wrench. He was shouting back toward the bridge.

"Override the locks!"

"We can't!" came the reply. "We didn't engage the master override; the ship still thinks we're asleep." It's trying to handle the emergency for us."

Blake looked up and saw Zuri's desperate face through the window. He watched as her eyes closed slowly and she disappeared from his view. A torrent of emotion welled within him. It was his fault. He had not ordered the master override to be engaged; now it couldn't be until this emergency had run its course. His mistake was going to kill this woman who had been his friend through months of rigorous training and who he had grown to admire and respect for her intelligence, drive and compassion. At that moment he realized that his feelings for her went far beyond respect, and that she meant much more to him than just another member of the crew.

Blake kicked the box cover furiously until it yielded, ripping away from the bulkhead, exposing the wires to the solenoid that was holding Zuri captive. Releasing the lock, he pulled the hatch open; fresh oxygen rushed into the room. Zuri was lying in the hatchway, not breathing. Blake began applying CPR, breathing for her until Shelikhov brought a small tank of oxygen and a mask, which was applied as Blake carried Lieutenant Eshe to her bunk.

Blake looked down at Zuri and knew the oxygen had come too late.

"Captain, I found the source of the fire." It was Lee who had just entered the space. The anguish on Blake's face stopped him in mid-sentence.

"What was it?" Shelikhov asked.

"It was one of those damned cheap-ass connectors on the backup panel. Someone tried to fix a broken one with duct tape."

Zuri's body was placed back in the refrigerated support unit that had kept her alive during the 23-trillion-mile journey. The life support monitors would not need to be attached for her journey back.

———

After several dozen recon orbits, Shelikhov remarked that she was finding it difficult to find a space large enough to land the ship.

"Looks like Disney World down there," she said. "Islands of what appear to be cities surrounded by vast forests and one huge ocean. No place to sit down."

"Any movement on the ground?" Blake asked

"Nothing that I can see, nothing in the air either."

"Ok then, descend to 5,000 feet. Maybe we can find a clearing at that level."

The ship assumed that altitude and slowly traversed a lavish jungle that ran to the coast of the large central continent.

"My god!" Shelikhov exclaimed. "We're not in Kansas anymore; looks like we just found the Emerald City."

The large viewing screen reinforced her comment. Thrusting up from the lush jungle was a city of magnificent crystalline structures. Soaring hundreds of feet in the air, the monoliths had a translucent appearance and seemed to radiate light of varying color, at times reflecting the color of the jungle, at other times that of the azure blue sky, and again the pure white of the puffy clouds overhead.

"Are those buildings?" Lee wondered aloud.

"Must be; they don't look like they were created by nature," Shelikhov said.

Suddenly a white disk about a fourth the size of their own craft dropped down from above and settled in directly in front of them. Two more came up alongside, and radar detected one to the rear as well.

"Well, who do we have here?" Blake said, a note of tension in his voice.

The lead vehicle then began tipping from side to side as if to say, "Follow me."

"I think we're getting valet service," Lee said.

"Let's see where they want us to go," said Blake.

They came to a spot near the center of the large grouping of crystalline buildings. About a quarter of a mile in diameter, the clearing appeared to be the perfect—perhaps the only—spot to set the ship down. As it settled to the solid floor, the four smaller white discs disappeared from view.

Shelikhov checked the computer analysis of the outside environment and pronounced that the atmosphere, pressure, gravity, temperature, and radiation were similar to those of Earth.

"What now, captain?" Lee inquired.

"Well, I guess we get out and look around," Blake replied. Lee, you come with me. Shelikhov, stay with the ship until we know for sure what's out there."

The alien guide was waiting for them as they stepped down from the hatch. As beautiful as the ones in the titanium coffins and emitting the same fresh spring-like fragrance, the guide led Blake and Lee into one of the larger of the crystalline structures. Inside, the structure was similar to an Earthly office building with a magnificent atrium of glittering crystal and what appeared to be rooms and hallways surrounding it. The guide took them into one of the rooms where five more aliens were seated in comfortable chairs around a large bright metallic table. The guide took a seat at the table and motioned toward the two remaining chairs. Up to this point, not a sound had been uttered by anyone.

"Please, be seated," one of the aliens said in perfect English. "We have been expecting you."

"You speak English?" Blake said, his tone revealing his astonishment. "My name is Captain Derek Blake and this is Lee Wang Ha. We are from the planet Earth, where one of your ships crashed many years ago.

"I am Dorn," the alien said. He did not give any title or rank, but appeared to be in charge.

"Yes, all in this room speak English. You see when our expedition was lost on your planet Earth, we knew you would eventually replicate our ship, and there was a high probability that you would come here. About a thousand of us learned to speak every major language spoken on Earth so we could communicate with whoever came. We assumed it would be English, but with all the turmoil on your planet, we couldn't be sure.

There was a silence and the aliens looked at the two visitors as if expecting them to say something.

Lee spoke first. "We have come here on a peaceful mission to return the bodies of your people who died in the crash. On board our ship you will find containers that have preserved their bodies so you can perform whatever ceremonies you wish."

"Of course," the alien said, matter-of-factly. "It is appreciated. We will retrieve them for reconstituting. But I am sure that you didn't come here just to return our expedition crew. We know you are very inquisitive people and must have many questions."

Blake spoke up. His mind was full of questions, but his first was the one that struck him as they were searching for a landing spot. "Where are your people? I see many of your beautiful structures, but the people to inhabit them seem to be missing."

"Our people are many," the alien answered. "They are spread far and wide. This is but one of thousands of planets that we inhabit. There are millions more habitable planets in the Universe that we can reach, so you see we have no problem with overcrowding."

"Did you come to Earth to establish another colony?" Lee asked.

"No. We have always avoided Earth. Our expedition was searching out habitable planets not inhabited planets, but unfortunately the ship became damaged and Earth was the only planet where it could crash-land with any possibility of crew survival." The alien looked down at the table. "Unfortunately, it didn't work out that way."

"Why didn't you send another ship to rescue or recover them?" Blake asked.

"As I said, until then, we had always avoided Earth. You have shown yourselves to be a violent, deceitful, vicious people. You have been since you first walked upright on your planet. In that regard, Earth appears to be unique among all the inhabited planets in the Universe. There has not been a time of peace on Earth since mankind rose from the mud. On the other hand, we and all the other civilizations in the Universe are peaceful. Sentient life began on our planet at about the same time as it did on yours, yet we have never had a war. Hatred, murder and perversion don't exist here. We compete, yes—but graciously. Our kind of competition has made us better. Yours has made you worse. Our civilizations are of equal age, yet ours has evolved well beyond yours.

"We avoid Earth," Dorn continued, "not because we dislike you, but because we fear that once your people expand beyond your Galaxy, and discover us, your inherent avarice will compel you to wage war against us and force us to destroy you. The mere thought of such savagery is repugnant. We can only hope that you will come to your senses before that happens.

The alien's lecture put Lee on the defensive and he immediately launched into his well-rehearsed diplomatic rhetoric.

"We are a good people," Lee insisted. "We enjoy great diversity and we get along well. We have many religions and are a God-fearing people who . . ." Lee stopped himself. He had no idea if these people had any concept of a supreme being. As a diplomat, he knew it was a mistake to introduce an extraneous concept that needed additional explanation. The reference to God was simply a practiced reflex for use with specific audiences; this was not one of them. Lee's feeling toward religion was ambivalent, but this slip-up resurrected questions that he thought his agnosticism previously had laid to rest. This was an opportunity to put them to bed for good.

"Do you understand the concept of God?" he asked.

The alien smiled. "Of course, God is the creator, the Beginning and the End. He is with all of us at all times, and we love and worship him."

Lee hesitated before asking the next obvious question.

"Many of our people believe in Jesus Christ. Do you also believe in him?"

"Again, yes. He is God."

"How do you know that? Did he come to your planet to . . . save you?" Lee said with a note of derision.

"There was no need for him to come here as a savior; it never was required. Unlike humans, we have had a continuous relationship with the God of the Universe that has never been broken. We know him for who he is. We also know that he came to the people of Earth, as a man named Jesus, with a message of peace to restore your relationship with God . . . and we know that you have ignored it," Dorn continued. You have piled war upon war until your people are on the brink of self-destruction. And that's why we avoid Earth."

Blake asked, "If the ship that crashed in Roswell was the only one to visit Earth, how can you know that?"

"As I said, our relationship with God has never been broken. Let's just say that we get whatever information we need, when we need it." Dorn replied.

As he finished his answer, two aliens came into the room with Shelikhov following behind. One of them spoke to Dorn in the alien's language. Blake asked Lee for a translation.

"They said that they have removed the containers from our ship," Lee whispered; "and something else about the bodies being processed. I suppose they mean for burial."

Blake nodded.

Dorn said something in the alien language and the two aliens left the room.

"Come sit with us, Anna," Dorn said as one of the other aliens stood, offering her the chair.

Blake jerked his head toward Dorn. "We've never mentioned Anna's name. How did you . . ."

"How do you think, Captain? We also know that you had a crew of four and that one of your crew members was killed during your journey."

"Yes, but . . ."

"I sense that you cared very much for her, and she for you." With that Dorn nodded toward the door as three aliens entered the room. "These are the ones from our ship that you returned to us. We've been able to reconstitute them. They would like to thank you."

The three of them bowed toward Blake, Lee and Shelikhov, and said something in their language which Lee translated as, "We are most appreciative for your mercy and kindness."

The three Earth travelers were incredulous. "Alive after more than 50 years?" Blake said.

Dorn smiled and once again nodded toward the group of three alien travelers as another figure emerged from behind them. "And she is alive as well," Dorn said.

Her motions were tentative, as if she did not fully understand where she was or what had happened. Her puzzled expression turned to one of joy as she began to recognize her three companions at the table.

"Captain Blake!" Zuri Eshe said, still in a state of confusion.

Blake, who had held Zuri's lifeless body in his arms weeks before, now rushed to embrace her, Lee and Shelikhov close behind.

"Zuri, Zuri, you were dead. How. . ." A tearful Blake looked toward Dorn for an answer.

"Yes, Captain, death can be reversed. If you people would only open your eyes you would know that."

"You mean your people don't die?" Lee said.

"Of course we do, but only when it's our time to die. Premature deaths can always be reversed."

"How can we thank you," A bleary-eyed Derek Blake asked, still holding Zuri tightly.

"If you feel obligated to thank us, you may do so by willingly staying with us. You see, we cannot allow you to return to Earth. You will tell others about us and they will come too. They will tell us that it is to establish commerce—to set up trade, but our observations of your civilization have shown us where that leads.

Let me assure you, you have nothing we want, but we have everything you want. If we allowed such a relationship to develop, you would soon want to dominate us. You would force us to fight you, in order to preserve our way of life, and although we would be victorious, you would make us killers. It would be against everything God created us to be. So you must stay; you will be very comfortable here." Dorn turned to the tall dark woman in Blake's arms. "Zuri Eshe, your name in the Swahili language means 'beautiful life'; that's what you will have here on our planet."

"No!" Blake shouted. "Anna, get back to the ship and prepare for lift off."

"There is no ship," Dorn said. "It has been removed to a museum of unusual items where it will be disabled, so you have no choice but to continue to be our guests."

Blake was pleading. "Look, we can teach our civilization what we've learned here. We can make them understand. We can change our world if you just let us go back."

"That has already been taken care of by a higher power than you." Dorn said. "Your world will most certainly change. You see, while we are grateful to you for returning our three explorers to us, the ship that crashed in Roswell, New Mexico, carried a crew complement of *not three*, but four.

2015

Dr. Joseph Lanham returned to his house near Los Alamos. He had been visiting Katie's grave, a weekly pilgrimage that he made every Sunday since her death of a stress related heart attack some thirty years earlier. Those visits no longer left him sad, because he knew he would be joining her soon. Everyone told him to sell the house, but he held on to it. His friends thought it was because so much of Katie was there. To a great degree that was true, but he knew there was another, more compelling reason.

As he entered the darkened living room, a shadowy figure moved on the couch.

"You OK, Joe?" the figure said.

"Fine . . . just a little melancholy."

The man on the couch stood into the shard of light streaming between the partially open curtains. His smooth, youthful features looked almost human, and even though he was much more beautiful, he had been passing for one for several years.

"Well, it's been ten years since the ship was launched toward my planet," the figure said. "I think we can safely assume that they're not coming back."

"Yes," Lanham said, appearing even more tired than usual, "given the loss of the ship and crew and the rotten economy I doubt there will be any strong sentiment in government to send another one. It was my life's work. I hate to see it end this way, and I'm sorry that we can't provide you with a ride home. Looks like you're stuck here."

"I'm not sorry, Joe. You and Katie were very kind and I'm nothing but grateful to you for rescuing me after the crash and keeping my existence a secret all these years."

"We had no choice, really," Lanham said. There was no telling what the government would have done to you back then when I found you hiding in the backseat of my car; the paranoia after the war was so extreme. If you had survived their inquisition, you would have been paraded around like a carnival freak for the rest of your life. When I brought you home, it was Katie who insisted that we hide you, until it would be safe. She guarded your secret jealously. For her—and for me—you became the child we never had." As Lanham spoke, he noticed something sad in the man's demeanor.

"Yes Joe, you both were here for me when I needed you, and when Katie died, I was here for you, because you needed me." The man approached closer to Lanham and gripped his hand. "Now, it's time to move on. I have a new, greater mission now, one that perhaps finally may bring peace to your troubled people. The crash of my ship was no accident, nor was my survival, and I now know why I was brought here. It is to be a messenger . . . a messenger of peace . . . perhaps the last one your people will get. So it's time for us to leave.

Lanham looked at the man inquisitively, "Us? Am I going with you?"

"No, Joe. You're going to be with Katie. I will miss you my good friend, but I have a lot of work to do."

Blues Legacy

Tom was grateful for the slow tune the little six piece combo had begun to play. It meant that he could keep up with the chord changes. A slow rock song . . . three changes basically, C, F, and G chords, and no guitar solo. Compared with the other guys in the band, Tom wasn't a very good musician; in fact he was pretty bad, but the other musicians were his friends and wanted him in the group and he tried not to let them down. His lack of ability applied to most of the things that Tom tried to do. Theatre—he couldn't act. Sports—he threw a ball like a girl. Speaking of girls, he wasn't very good with them either.

When the song wound down with a soft tom-tom and cymbal flourish by Dave, the drummer, John, the trombone player, whispered the next set. "A-6 through 12," he said. "The crowd is starting to get bored."

"Shit," Tom said under his breath. The "A" set comprised the fast Dixieland stuff, none in the easy key of C, lots of chord changes and worst of all A-12 featured a guitar solo that Tom could barely get through even on his best day. It was the last set of the evening to close out the Central High Senior Prom. *Oh boy! What a way to go out*, Tom thought.

Following John's announcement of the last dance, Bob, the cornet player, reached over and cranked up the volume on Tom's amp.

Crap, Tom thought as he looked for a way to escape another embarrassing screw up at full volume. He looked at the clock. It wasn't quite midnight, which meant they had time to fit that song in before the chaperones shut the dance down. Little beads of sweat formed on Tom's forehead, and his fingers seemed to swell in anticipation of what he knew would be a disastrous solo. *Maybe a little less volume,* he thought, *and fewer people will notice the mistakes.* As he grabbed the volume knob, a spark arced from the amp. The mild electrical shock was more startling than harmful. Tom stood there shaking his head as if to remove the remnants of electrical energy that had just coursed through his body.

"You ok?" Bob asked.

"Yeah, must be a short or something," Tom replied with a bewildered smile. "My regular amp blew a tube and I had to borrow this one till I could get it fixed. This thing's pretty beat up."

As the band launched into A-12, Tom felt a sense of relief that in 4 minutes and 15 seconds his torment would be over and the 1959 senior prom would come to a close.

Then it was over. John went to collect their $300 fee from the class secretary as the rest of the group, with the exception of Sally, the piano player, packed up their instruments. Kurt was wiping down his tenor sax with a soft cloth as Tom uncabled his Gibson L-5 from the ancient amplifier.

"Great solo tonight," Kurt said. "You must be putting in some extra practice. You sounded like a regular Johnny Boyd."

"Johnny who?" Tom asked, stuffing the guitar cord into the base of the old amp.

"Johnny Boyd," Kurt answered, "Some old guy my dad used to listen to; dad had a lot of his old 78 records. He played some cool guitar. Never used a pick, but man could he wail."

"Yeah, well I got a shock off my amp and accidentally dropped my pick. I had to just use my fingers . . . so . . . you know . . . Johnny Boyd," Tom replied, suddenly realizing that his solo was definitely the best he'd ever done. "Yeah, I've been practicing," he lied.

John, tall, dark-haired, handsome and undoubtedly the best musician in the group, returned with the money and something else . . . the senior class secretary. "Guys, this is Loraine. She says she loves our music."

The doe-eyed look on Loraine's face as she smiled at John revealed that her interests leaned more toward the musician than the music. Everyone just smiled and said in unison, "Hi, Loraine." It was seldom that John was seen without the prettiest girl in the room on his arm.

While the band packed up, Sally, with nothing else to do, had decided to take a recon tour of the hotel and had just arrived back with the news that there was a blues singer performing in the lounge.

"He's really good," she said and grabbed Bob's hand. She and Bob had been an item for about a week and it was hard to tell which one of them was the more smitten. "Do you want to go?"

"We're only seventeen," Dave insisted. "I don't want to get tossed in the slammer for underage drinking. My dad would kill me."

Kurt, who had been flirting with the pretty coat-check girl, ten years his senior, said, "We'll go."

Miss Coat Check gave Kurt a sexy smile and said "Yeah!"

John looked at Loraine, who gave a nod. "Count us in," he said.

"I gotta go home," Dave grumbled, shaking his head. "You guys are gonna get in trouble."

"I'm in," Tom said, even though he would be the only one without a date.

"What're you going to do with your instruments?" Dave asked.

"You can take 'em," Bob said.

"Screw you," Dave snapped, "I'm not lugging those things around in my dad's car. You can take them to the lounge. Maybe you can jam with the singer."

"Hey, good idea," John said.

The only light in the lounge emanated from several wall sconces that glowed Cobalt blue, and small candles on each round white-clothed table. One spotlight illuminated the lone blues guitarist on stage. He was a large black man. His body appeared to envelop the old Martin acoustical guitar as his fat fingers danced effortlessly on the strings. He was really good. The blues was in him and poured from him on a voice that sounded like crushed velvet on a gravel road. As he sang, small droplets ran down his cheeks and it was impossible to tell if they were sweat or tears.

Tom was mesmerized. He had never heard blues played or sung like that. He began to hum along, his eyes closed. Soon the humming became words and the words became a song. It flowed from him as if some internal dam had just opened and he couldn't stop the torrent of emotion that streamed from somewhere in his body. He had not noticed that the music on stage had stopped and everyone in the place was looking in his direction.

A sudden tug on his sleeve brought him out of his trance and he opened his eyes to see the huge black singer standing in front of him with a strange look on his face.

"Young man, are you a musician?" asked the blues singer.

"Uh, yeah . . . I mean, no."

"Well then what the hell is that thing in that box," he asked, pointing to the Gibson "California Girl" guitar case next to his chair.

"Well yeah, that's my guitar, but I'm not a musician; not like you."

"Well you sho do sing pretty. Tell you what, why don't you bring that fancy guitar up here on my stage and play us a tune and sing some blues wif me."

"No, I couldn't. I'm no good," Tom protested.

"No good! Son, you jus' belted out some o' the prettiest blues I'd ever heard."

"You know, it's an electric guitar and I'd have to set up my amp and all."

"No problem; we can wait, the black man said. Come wif me, brother."

With that the big man put his enormous arm around Tom's body and gently lifted him out of the chair and up to the stage. Tom never felt his feet touch the floor.

"You know the chord progression in G?" the big man asked.

"Yeah, I think so."

"Jus' follow me then." And the big man started a lilting blues progression that by the fourth measure had Tom playing along.

"I never heard Tom play like that," Bob said.

"Wow! I guess he has been practicing," said Kurt.

"I guess we need to play more blues," commented Sally.

John said, "We've never played *any* blues."

"Maybe you should," said the coat-check girl as she stared dreamily at the two musicians on stage. "Maybe you should."

Tom's eyes were closed as he played. He began to hum; at first it was a low guttural counterpoint to the chord progression the two were working around. His voice had taken on a different character. It was an octave lower than his normal Irish tenor, gritty, tortured.

John's jaw dropped, "Did you know he could sing?"

Kurt, his expression similar to John's, replied in amazement, "I had no idea."

Bob just shook his head. "Lord, where's that coming from?"

The hum became a wail as if pressure had been building, pressure that at long last could be released. Then the words came. They were beautiful, sad and wrenching as if coming from a million souls crying for their lost loves and lost lives.

The musicians at the table couldn't believe this was their Tom; the same one that less than an hour ago cringed at having to play a simple solo in front of a group of teenagers. If it *was* Tom, he had changed, transformed into someone wiser and definitely older. His fingers danced on the strings. His words were far beyond his age and experience; the quality of his voice was transfixing.

The big black man had stopped playing, rose from his chair, walked from the spotlight and stood staring at Tom, relinquishing the stage to him as in a gesture of respect.

After twenty minutes the song ended. Tom stood, packed up his guitar and amp and walked back to the table. The blues singer looked at the guitar, then looked toward Tom as he walked away.

"God amighty," he said under his breath, "you can wail, man."

The room was silent as Tom walked past the tables back to his friends. Then the nearly 100 people in the lounge stood, applauding loudly.

"Let's go," Tom said, his words slurred as if just awakening from a deep sleep. The other four musicians, the class secretary and the coat-check girl followed him out of the room amid applause, whistles, and shouts. As they passed by the other tables, several young girls put napkins with their phone numbers on them in Tom's hand; they were crying. Men wanted to shake his hand; some of them were crying too.

No one in the group spoke. Then John said, "We definitely need to play more blues."

"Oh yeah," said Kurt, "We definitely do."

The old black blues singer shouted from the stage, "Hey, man. Come on back up here, I gots ta talk with you."

"You guys go on," Tom said to the group. "I need to see what this guy wants."

"Hey man," the old black man said as Tom mounted the stage, carrying his guitar and the borrowed amp. "Where'd a white-bread cracker like you learn to play the blues like that?"

Tom was at a loss to answer. "Don't know. It just came out."

"Don't shit me, boy. They's only one person I'd ever heard that could do what you done up here tonight and that's ol' Johnny Boyd—best blues man ever. You know ol' Johnny?"

"Nah; never heard of him."

Well every good blues man in the country know Johnny; he was the first to play blues on an electric guitar, way back in '32 even befo' ol' T-bone Walker did it in '34. I learnt everything I know from Johnny Boyd and we used to play together a lot . . . him with his electric and me with my ol' acoustic. We got to be good friends. A few years back Johnny got real sick. He been in a nursing home for some time.

"It's a damned shame though, as good as Johnny was, in his whole career he never got the recognition he deserved. Far as I know he only got one award for all his contributions to the blues, and I was on the committee that got it for him. He cherished that award above just about everything. He figured that when he died, his soul would just stay in that thing, and now after tonight, I believe he was right."

"What was it . . . the award I mean?"

The old blues singer nodded toward the old amp that Tom had borrowed. "Take a close look at that old amp, Mr. Blues Man," he said.

Tom hadn't paid any attention to the tarnished brass plaque riveted to the back of the beat-up old amp until now, and he had to strain to see the engraved inscription that read: Presented to Johnny Boyd by The South Side Blues Assn., Chicago, Il.

The old blues singer, turned away from Tom to hide his tears. "While you were up here playin' tonight I got a call from Johnny's sister. She said that around midnight, ol' Johnny upped and died."

101

Trial Fail

The experiment to determine the viability of the promising Alzheimer's treatment had been running for a full six days—today was the seventh day—and there had been no change in the little transgenic mouse. But then no one expected a change to occur in this, the control part of the trial, since the mouse had yet to receive the drug. Once again the little mouse was placed at the beginning of the complicated maze and a piece of cheese at the other end just as before. Today's test yielded similar results to the previous six. After expending the full 30 minutes allotted for the test, the mouse came no closer to the cheese than before and it was noted that the test subject, with no drug treatment, could not negotiate the maze under any circumstance. It was quite obvious that the mouse was suffering from the induced Alzheimer's and had no memory of the previous six days of trying to run the maze; in fact, the mouse probably had no thoughts at all.

The following day, the research chemist's big gloved hands reached into the small cage and extracted the little mouse. This time, before placing him at the beginning of the maze, the hands inserted a super-fine needle into the mouse's shoulder and injected something. The mouse felt a sharp twinge, the memory of which faded immediately. When he was placed at the beginning of the maze, he repeated his actions of the past week, bounding straight ahead to the dead end, then turning back and taking the first turn to the left. At that dead end he turned to the right and ran ahead. After fifteen minutes, the mouse began taking different routes that got him closer to the cheese, but when the test concluded, he still had not reached his reward.

The tests continued for the rest of the week and it was noted that with each daily injection the mouse seemed to be learning the maze, but had yet to reach the cheese within thirty minutes. On the fifteenth day, the mouse not only reached the cheese, but accomplished the feat in a mere twelve and a half minutes. With the injections continuing over the next thirty days, the mouse piled success upon success, reducing the length of time until he could navigate the maze in less than ten seconds with no mistakes in the process.

The chemist's big gloved hands carried the little mouse back to the cage.

"You are now a very smart mouse," the chemist said; "the only one of the test subjects that has made it this far. I think we're going to be famous."

The tests continued; each day the little mouse was injected and each day the memory of the pain lingered a little longer in the little mouse's brain. Another fifteen days passed with the mouse consistently running the maze in ten seconds, about as fast as the mouse could run.

As the mouse was being replaced in the cage after another successful run, the chemist said. "Do your best tomorrow, little fellow. We're going to perform for the head of the department and the chancellor of the University. When they see what you can do, compared to the video of what you did in the control phase, they're going to let us take the show to all the pharma companies in the country to get funding. That'll keep us going for at least a year. The chemist didn't notice the slight shudder that went through the test subject as he placed him into the cage. The little mouse bounded over to the corner under the long plastic feeding tray and closed his eyes, but he didn't sleep.

Another day, another injection. With the department head and the chancellor looking on, the chemist placed the mouse at the beginning of the maze. But instead of making an unhesitating dash through the course, the little mouse paused, looking from side to side, as if he were trying to remember. He gave an imperceptible shudder and ran straight ahead to the dead end; then, apparently confused, he turned around and took the first left, then a right. Each turn took him farther from the cheese. The department head looked embarrassed and angry. The chancellor just laughed.

"Yeah that's some brilliant mouse," he said. "I doubt the board will want to fund this thing past the end of the month. Let us know if anything changes."

"Wait," the chemist pleaded, "He's been running the maze in ten seconds, I swear. I don't know what happened. He's gone into some kind of regression. Maybe I need to adjust the dose. Let me try it again."

As the two men walked to the door, the department head said, "You have five days. Please don't bother us unless you have something of value to show." He left, shaking his head.

The research chemist grabbed the mouse roughly and tossed him into the cage.

"Maybe I should increase the dosage until it kills you," the irate research chemist said as if the mouse could actually understand. Then in a calmer tone, "Yes, that might work. I'll increase the dosage each day until the mouse can run the maze again. If it kills him, so what; he's just a mouse. What have I got to lose?"

The little mouse quickly hopped to his corner under the feeding tray and closed his eyes.

When the chemist left the room, the mouse opened his eyes and looked at his surroundings, sniffing all the objects within his reach . . . the old towel in the corner where he slept, glass water bowl and the plastic feeding tray. Beyond the cage he could see the entire room. It was dark and there was something he had never noticed before, a bright light coming from beneath the lab door highlighting a two-inch crack that led to the outer hallway. He wondered what was on the other side of that door. He looked around the cage again, trying to find something . . . then there it was. It had been there all the time, but only now did he realize how he could use it to his greatest advantage.

He quickly ran to the plastic feeding tray and with his sharp teeth began etching along the very top edge of its four-inch length. When he got to the end of the tray, he etched the other way, never biting down hard enough to crack the plastic, but just enough so that with every pass, the etch marks got deeper. After several passes in each direction, he began wiggling the narrow edge until it snapped off. The long thin piece of plastic fell to the bottom of the cage. The little mouse sniffed it then picked it up in his teeth, positioning it so he could hold it between his two front paws.

Now standing on his hind legs, he carefully squeezed his paws with the long plastic stick through the cage wires and began bumping the latch upward. It was difficult because he couldn't actually see the end of the stick or the latch. It all had to be done by feel and memory.

After several attempts, the little mouse succeeded in moving the latch high enough to allow the cage door to swing open.

The mouse climbed up the cage wire to the lip of the open entrance. There he paused, contemplating the implications of his next move, and what might be waiting on the other side of the door.

He began to feel a strange new sensation that he did not like. Had he been human, he would have called it guilt.

Perhaps I should stay and complete the experiment, he thought. *After all, those injections did help me a lot. On the other hand, if I stay, the chemist may just kill me for playing dumb in front of the chancellor and causing him to lose funding.*

The little mouse had learned some words such as "kill" by associating them with the strong emotions that he felt coming from the chemist's hands when he used such words. Words like "injection" and "cheese" he learned by connecting them with sensations of pain or pleasure. The rest of his mental vocabulary he learned by just hearing words repeated when the chemist, working alone in the lab, absentmindedly talked to himself. He even learned to read some words as he watched the chemist type them into the laptop next to his cage on the desk.

He could not remember any thoughts from before he started receiving the drug, so he was pretty certain that his new awareness started with the first shot and grew with each injection. The thought of not getting them anymore, frightened him. He also knew that he was the only test subject left and realized intuitively that failure of this initial trial would doom the drug so that no one else would ever benefit from it.

It could certainly help a lot of other mice, he thought. He swiveled his head around to look back into the cage. The towel in the corner looked warm and comfortable. There was ample water and some cheese was on the floor of the cage where it had fallen when he had torn up his food tray. *Would there be any cheese out there beyond the door?* he wondered. Then he remembered the chemist's anger when he used the word "kill", and had felt his desperation.

No! I'm sticking with the plan, he decided.

With his mind made up, the little mouse jumped onto the desk and scampered across the top of the desk, first knocking over a leather pencil holder, then bounding onto the computer keyboard. He was startled by the sudden glow that emanated from the now awakened laptop computer.

He stared at a screen full of words and recognized only two of them in a large bold face font, but that was enough for him to know that his decision was the correct one.

TRIAL: FAIL

Time for me to go. With that, the brilliant little mouse hopped off the desk, toward the light under the door . . . and freedom.

Revenge of Ol' Stumpy

Alan Ransom was having a bad day. His aging BMW had broken down, and the desolate location rendered his cell phone useless. As he trudged back down the narrow asphalt road toward a service station, the dampness of the dismal day seeped into his soul like a depressing drug, poisoning his mood with each drop of cold rain that splashed on his bald head.

"Why would anyone build the headquarters of an international corporation in a place like this?" he asked aloud, knowing no one could hear him. For the past two hours, he had seen only empty pastures and dead trees, and he was still five miles from Argon, the little town that was the namesake of his new employer.

I never should have taken this job, he admonished himself. *I could have headed up public relations at a lot of companies. Why didn't I hold out longer?* But he knew the answer. Of the 225 resumes he'd sent out, this had been the only offer.

"Damn, I gotta get outta this rain before I catch pneumonia," he said, shivering and pulling the lapel of his suit jacket tightly across his chest.

Allen carefully stepped over a low spot in the hog-wire fence that bordered the road, and jogged toward a large, solitary tree in the center of an ancient cemetery, arriving at the broad trunk just as nature opened her floodgates. The tree had no leaves to channel the rain away— it was dead like most of the others he had seen on his trip—but there was a cleft in the hollow trunk large enough for him to squeeze inside for some protection. The interior of the tree was warm and dark, and as his eyes were still adjusting, Allen extended his arms almost fully to gauge the size of the natural shelter. *That would be four—five feet*, he surmised. *This is a big friggin' tree.* An ambrosial aroma permeated the air inside. *Lilacs*, he thought. *No, too musky, perhaps some kind of mushroom.* The comforting scent perfected his fatigue—*It feels like Mom's house in here*, he thought—and he decided to sit out the rain, perhaps even take a short nap.

Crouching down, Allen cautiously surveyed the ground with his hands, hoping not to touch anything slimy or with teeth. The floor of his shelter was soft and warm—log dirt from the decaying old tree. He closed his eyes and sniffed the sweet, warm air as he lowered himself onto the soft material. In the next instant, Alan Ransom felt the ground give way beneath him and he knew that his bad day had just gotten worse.

———

"Dammit to hell," Clem Forster screeched, slamming the morning newspaper to the bare pine floor in his office. "Where do these bastards get off accusing us? You'd think Argon Chemical was the cause of every environmental problem in the world."

"No, just in the immediate area," Bradley Peet replied, picking up the front page of the paper that was emblazoned with the headline, **"Argon is killing us."**

"Jesus, Peet, you sound like one of them. If you don't get your loyalties straight, you'll be looking for another job."

"That's your prerogative, Clem, you're the CEO; I'm just a vice president. You know my loyalties are with the company. I'm just giving you their slant."

"Well, maybe we oughta put you in charge of PR," Forster groused, pacing back and forth behind his gray metal desk. "Where is that new PR guy anyway? Shouldn't he be handling this?"

"Ransom was due here yesterday but he never showed up. We're trying to locate him."

Forster jerked the paper from Peet's hand. Well when he gets here, fire him." Then stabbing his finger several times into the picture on the front page, ". . . and what the hell is with this damned tree. Every time the Sierra Club wants publicity they take a new picture of it, plaster it all over the media and claim we killed it."

"What? You mean ol' Stumpy? Well, it is the oldest tree in the county. It's dead, and we probably *did* kill it."

"There you go again," the red faced CEO shouted, throwing his hands up in disgust. "We did no such thing. We haven't had a major spill in thirty years."

"Not one that we've reported. We still haven't installed the poly-liner in the reclamation pond and that crap's probably been poisoning the groundwater for years. Then there're the smokestack scrubbers that don't work . . ."

"I want this friggin' tree cut down today," Forster interrupted. "If we don't own the property, buy it."

"It's a cemetery," Peet said in quiet frustration. "You want me to buy a cemetery?"

"If that tree isn't gone by tomorrow, I'll cut the damned thing down myself," Forster blustered.

———

The red F-100 pickup slammed to an abrupt stop beneath the bare gray limbs of the craggy old tree. A thousand uneven loads had softened the truck's springs, causing it to list precipitously under the

110

275 pound bulk of big Ed Fowler, its driver and part owner of Ed and Bob's tree service. Bob Doyle snored in the passenger's seat.

"There she is," Fowler said to his awakening partner. "Ol' Stumpy."

"Thought you said she was dead," Bob replied, pointing toward a large pink and yellow flower on the side of the tree.

"Must be a vine growin' on it or somethin'. Ol' Stumpy's been dead fer more'n ten years."

"You sure? That blossom looks like it's growin' right outta the tree."

"Sure I'm sure. Look, you clear away some of them dead branches at the base while I put the long bar on the saw. That sucker's bigger'n I remember it."

"Ok," Bob complied as Fowler ducked behind the passenger seat to retrieve the long bar for the chainsaw. "Hey, looky here." Bob remarked, seeing the cleft in the old tree. "This thing's hollow . . . Man, it sure smells good in here."

"What's that you say?" Big Ed asked, peering over the top of the cab toward the tree. "Wha'd ya say, Bob . . . Bob?"

———

Clem Forster tramped through the dead grass toward the red pickup; the thick coating of dew on the windshield told him it had been there all night, and he could see that his orders hadn't been carried out. "Where the hell are those lazy bastards," he mumbled. "When I find 'em, I'll fire 'em."

A smell reminiscent of fresh sweet rolls drew him to the cleft in the tree bedecked in pink and yellow flowers. He stepped inside, expecting to startle the two workers sleeping off an all-night binge. The ground moved quickly as if it were a muscle that had been waiting a long time to flex.

"What th . . ."

Forster plummeted downward, landing about twenty feet below. Whatever broke his fall ruptured, covering him with a gooey liquid and a sickening stench. Something slimy fell on his head and oozed down over his forehead and into his eyes. Instinctively, he looked up.

Panic gripped Forster in its icy fist as he watched the ceiling, through which he had fallen, close like the iris of a camera, pitching the chamber into total blackness. Fighting waves of fear, he fumbled in his pockets, finally extracting his cigar lighter. The reason the floor felt spongy became horribly apparent as the flickering yellow flame of the lighter revealed the decomposing body of a large man. Worse yet, he was kneeling inside the belly of another corpse, the thing that had cushioned his fall. As his breakfast rushed back into his throat, Forster knew he had located his tree cutters.

Forster's flesh began to blister from the encapsulating slime. He gulped the acrid air in a futile attempt to scream, but managed only a horrified squeak bespeaking desperate terror.

Forster's heart pounded at a rib-cracking tempo as the terrifying truth revealed itself. Ol' Stumpy no longer needed leaves to make food. She had evolved a digestive system and Argon's chemical soup was the catalyst. The corrosive slime seeped into the hole that once was Forster's mouth, granting him only a few desperate last words.

"Oh God, it's digesting me!"

———

Drifts of pink and yellow blossoms blanketed the cemetery where the tow-truck operators labored to drag the F-100 pickup from the forest of colorful seedlings.

"Looks like somebody finally fertilized this place," one said to the other.

"Yeah, this all used to be dead," the other said. Now lookit, a whole field of them little trees."

"I might dig me out a couple for my yard. Wonder what kind of fertilizer I should use."

If they had stopped long enough to hear the wind resonating past the cleft in the largest of the pink and yellow trees they would have gotten the answer.

"Huuuumans!"

III

"The most painful thing is losing yourself in the process of loving someone too much, and forgetting that you are special too."
— Ernest Hemingway

Heroic Hearts

The B-24 made a low graceful pass, swooping in less than 500 feet above the rain forest. There were people down there, but the crew of the converted bomber couldn't see them. The inhabitants of the tiny village made no effort to hide, secure under the thick canopy that sheltered them from the peering eyes of the American advisers. Through the Plexiglas bubble in the nose of the old plane, Gerry Hurd watched the flashes, like lightning bugs as they sparkled among the trees. They were worrisome at first, but after ten or so missions, fright became amusement and finally, boredom.

"Hey Gerry, you getting those flashes?" It was the voice of Captain Len Marrs from the flight deck above Gerry's head.

"Yeah. Probably some of the locals airing out their pea shooters," Gerry replied. Might better call it in though; could be some N.V. regulars. I heard they might be down this far. "I got it on film. The spooks might see something I didn't. "

Lieutenant Brandon Lewis in the right seat thumbed the mike switch. "Hey Tarzan, you there? This is Jane."

"Yeah Jane," came back the Brooklyn accent of Buddy Lorenzo of the CIA. "You got somethin'?"

"Just some small arms fire at our last check-in. Might want to take a look-see; could be some regulars."

"Roger that. You got movies?"

"Yeah. Gerry's shootin' 'em right now."

"OK. Bring 'em home and we'll watch 'em over some tea and crumpets."

"If you're referring to that mud you call coffee, I'll pass," Captain Marrs cut in.

"Up yours, Captain Sir," Lorenzo replied. "I do the best with what I got. I make good coffee; it's the ingredients that are for shit. I made all the coffee in my Uncle Joe's deli and nobody . . ."

"Yeah, yeah, and nobody complained," Marrs interjected. Ever wonder why nobody ever came back?"

"Ahhh, just get your asses back here with that film . . . OUT."

"You know, one of these days you're gonna really piss him off," Lieutenant Lewis said.

"Nah. He loves me."

The old bomber made a good platform for the cameras. It could fly slow and low and it was tough enough to take hits from the small caliber weapons fire that primarily came from the Vietnamese locals who wanted both sides to stay away from their villages. From his perch in the nose of the plane, Gerry occasionally could see muzzle flashes resulting from the fire. He and the crew called them lightning bugs. The camera equipment that replaced the .50-cal. machine guns in this vestige of a past war left little room for the human operator, and were it not for the vibration of the four large engines, even a short mission could numb the extremities. Only the slight anxiety caused by the "lightning bugs" kept Gerry from falling asleep on most of the missions.

"What the hell am I doing here?" Gerry said aloud, forgetting about his open mike.

"Say again, Gerry?" Captain Marrs asked.

"Sorry, I forgot about the mike. I was just talking to myself."

117

"You keep that up and you'll be section eight back to the States," Lewis said and they all laughed.

"I'll take it," Gerry replied. "I'd take a bullet if it would get me back to the States."

"Oh yeah, I forgot," Lewis said, "You're gonna be a daddy. What's the ETA on that kid anyhow? You gonna get home in time?"

"Doesn't look like it. Doctor says about mid-August. I don't rotate back till September."

"Not bad. You'll be back for the World Series at least."

"Big deal," Marrs said. "It's going to be another Yankee rout anyway."

"You kiddin'? The Dodgers'll take 'em in four," Lewis shot back.

"They got to win the pennant first and I think the Cards have a lock on it."

"The Dodgers are just takin' a breather. Koufax'll pitch 'em outta this slump. You'll see."

"Well if he does, he's going to have to pitch around Mantle and Maris in the Series, and that's not going to happen."

"OK, chump," Lewis chided, "put your money where your mouth is. I say the Dodgers are going to be the 1963 world champeens and the Yanks go away in four."

"Not a chance. Nobody will ever sweep the Yankees."

A flash of light from the ground caught Gerry's eye. It was just a glint from the side as if off a metal object. He craned his head around in front of the starboard film magazine, but it obstructed his view of that part of the landscape. The dual film magazines on each side of Gerry's head obstructed his view on both sides, an engineering necessity that Gerry had loudly lamented—until now.

Thwack! The noise resounded through the small space. "Jesus!" Gerry shouted into his mike.

"Dammit!"

"Say again, Gerry?" Captain Marrs came back.

"Don't know, but I think I just took a hit in the starboard magazine. Nearly got me in my ear. Camera's jammed; might as well go home."

"Roger that," Marrs replied, putting the large plane into a steep bank. "Whoops . . . What the hell . . . shit!"

"What's goin' on?" Gerry asked.

"Aw, we musta taken one in the wing. We're losing fuel . . . wait one!" Gerry detected increased urgency in the pilot's voice. "We got a fire in number two."

"Feathering number two," Lewis said, excitement rising in his voice.

The starboard engine closest to the fuselage sputtered to a halt as oily, black smoke trailed behind. Captain Marrs moved the throttle ahead on the number three engine and eased back on one and four to bring the plane back in balance. Lieutenant Lewis had already activated the fire extinguisher under the cowl of the burning engine, but the black smoke indicated that the fire was not yet under control.

"Cut fuel to number two," Marrs commanded.

"I already have," Lewis said. "Something else is feedin' it"

"Shit! We've gotta get some altitude." Marrs pushed the three active throttles forward to the stops and eased back on the yoke to bring the nose up. At the same time he was jamming down hard on the left rudder to compensate for the big plane's tendency to turn right. "How's the fire?"

Lewis couldn't tell if the tension in the captain's voice was from fear or the strain of fighting to hold the plane on course. He hoped it was the latter. "Still burning," Lewis said, toggling the fire extinguisher switch in a futile effort to squeeze more retardant onto the flames.

"Call base and report our position."

"Tarzan this is Jane. We've been hit and lost an engine. We have a fire in number two. Don't know if we can make it back." The anxiety in Lewis' voice increased as he gave Tarzan the coordinates.

The plane had been flying slow over a suspected North Vietnamese ammo route. Now the Pilot was struggling just to keep it above stall speed. The added drag from the number two engine kept the lumbering aircraft from responding quickly enough to the increased power of the remaining motors. Now at treetop level, they couldn't afford to lose any more altitude. Marrs and Lewis watched helplessly as the airspeed increased in painfully small increments and with the pilot gently nudging the yoke back, the nose of the plane slowly began to rise. Finally pointing in the right direction, the B-24 began a slow, almost imperceptible climb away from the jungle—200 feet, 210, 250, 400, 500—the plane was flying once more and the two men on the flight deck began to breathe again.

"Number two's still on fire," Lewis reported. "We gotta get it out before the fire gets to the tank."

Craning his head around the starboard film magazine for a better look, Gerry could barely see the flames, which were being whipped back across wing's surface by the increasing air speed of the plane. Suddenly, the section of the wing outboard of the number two engine gave way in a large explosion. The plane rolled hard to the right, smashing Gerry's face rudely against the starboard camera magazine, knocking him unconscious.

In an instant the jungle was ablaze as the plane slammed into the ground, the fuel in the other wing released upon impact. The resulting aerosol of fuel ignited into a huge orange fireball.

———

It would have been a difficult labor even if Julie hadn't been mourning the death of the newborn's father.

Julie Hurd was a beautiful mother, as all new mothers are beautiful, but today her beauty was obscured by the ordeal of the Caesarean birth and concern for her baby girl who was struggling for life in the neonatal intensive-care unit of Kettering Memorial Hospital. Little Danielle Louise Herd wasn't due for three more weeks, but severe pains had warned her mother that something was frightfully wrong and the unborn baby's erratic heartbeat confirmed for the doctor what the mother had feared. The baby was in severe distress and had to be taken immediately. The baby's heart had stopped by the time the doctor had reached inside the incision in Julie's body and lifted her out. There was an air of controlled panic as the delivery room personnel initiated procedures that would bring life back into the little girl. It was not easy, but the procedures worked and Danielle Louise took her first breath on her own.

The prognosis would remain guarded for several days and it was all Julie could do to keep from crying for the little baby that she and Gerry had so desperately wanted. Julie had not fared so well either, but her strong constitution and previous good health greatly improved her chances for a rather quick recovery.

"You're too bullheaded to keep in bed too long," the doctor told her, in answer to her query about when she could leave the hospital with her baby. "You should be strong enough to go home the day after tomorrow, but unfortunately Danielle will need to stay for a few more days until her breathing and bilirubin become more stable."

"Bullheaded" was one of the milder adjectives associated with this fiery beauty from Lexington, Kentucky. Her father, who appreciated fire in the animals he bred on his small horse ranch called her "spirited." Her mother called her "willful and strong-headed." Her teachers referred to her as "persistent and dedicated," and except for Gerry, the boys who took her out called her untouchable.

Now it was Sergeant Barbara Waldron's turn to find out what Julie Hurd was made of.

"Yes ma'am, how can I help you?" Sergeant Waldron greeted.

"I would like to speak with General Dolan. Tell him Mrs. Hurd is here to see him."

"Do you have an appointment?"

"No, sergeant. You may recall you told me on the phone that the general was too busy to see me."

"Then, I'm sorry, Mrs. Hurd, you'll have to wait till the general has an opening on his calendar," Waldron said too politely. She stared at Julie, expecting her to leave.

"Sergeant, I have called eight times over the past three weeks. Are you telling me that the general hasn't had fifteen minutes available during that time?"

"Mrs. Hurd, you must understand, the general's busy. I'm sure he has had many more . . ."

"I don't think *you* understand, sergeant," Julie said, leaning across the small desk and lowering her voice instead of raising it, as her father taught her to do in order to make people listen more intently. "I'm Gerald Hurd's wife. He was killed on June 15th in Vietnam. It was the general who brought the news to me in person. The general told me that his door was always open and that if I needed anything, to come to him in person." Julie's face was only inches from the sergeant's and her voice contained the hiss of a rattlesnake just before striking its prey. "Now I need something; I need to bury my husband, so you'd better tell him I'm here."

Sergeant Waldron sat motionless, staring into the eyes of a very angry and determined woman. Perhaps she could find a way to fit Mrs. Hurd into the general's schedule.

———

The Vietnamese liaison officer smiled across the table at John Higgins. *He's up to something*, Higgins thought. *This guy never smiles.* As special U.S. Envoy, Higgins was tasked with meeting with Vietnamese officials periodically to get a status report on American MIAs and bring back any GI remains the Vietnamese found. It was a frustrating job—more political than practical—and he found himself just going through the motions, hoping to be reassigned to a "real" job in the State Department.

Lee Xuan found it hard to repress the glee that he felt today. After months of trying to get more open trade with the United States, he finally held the ace, and it was dealt him just in time for the American election. Played correctly, it could win him the whole pot.

"I must tell you, John," Xuan said, "we have been working very hard to locate your missing soldiers. But after thirty years it is very difficult to make any progress. So . . ." Xuan tilted his head to one side and shrugged. "Perhaps there is nothing more we can do."

"We know you've been working hard, Lee," Higgins lied. "But, with all due respect, we also know there are still nearly two thousand American soldiers who left their wives and mothers thirty years ago and never returned. Now they've got to be someplace here in Vietnam, because this is where we left them. If you could help us locate their remains, the United States would be very grateful . . . The President would be grateful."

"Grateful enough, perhaps to sign a new trade agreement?"

"You know I can't promise anything, Lee, but the State Department would certainly make the recommendation. But you just said that you couldn't locate any . . . "

"I said we have been working very hard, John. Speaking only hypothetically now, let's say we locate one of them after all that work. Would that be worth a trade agreement?"

"If you release the remains to us and we can prove he's one of ours, I would make a very strong recommendation . . ."

"Let's say—and this is still hypothetical—let's say the soldier we locate is . . . alive.

123

"Lee, are you telling me you found one of our guys alive?"

"I was just speaking hypothetically, but what if we did?" A crooked smirk spread across Xuan's face. "Would your recommendation carry more weight?"

"Yeah, I supposed it would. Lee, I'd say that if you could pull that off, the President himself would lobby Congress for a trade agreement. Hell, so would I." Higgins leaned across the table. "Of course, you were just speaking hypothetically, weren't you?"

"Of course."

Alone at dinner, Higgins thought about the report he would write. He could probably change the date on the last one and resubmit it, for all it mattered. The results were the same—the results were always the same. No progress. Xuan was probably right; there probably wasn't anything left to locate. Even the MIA families didn't believe their husbands, fathers or sons could still be alive. Yet Xuan's hypothetical question would have to go into the report that John would write tomorrow during his plane ride back to the States.

The thought that any of America's missing soldiers could still be alive and possibly suffering in this unforgiving country burned like acid in Higgins's mind, preventing any semblance of a restful sleep that night. He lay awake thinking about those young guys who didn't come back, and what a sham his job seemed to be. He had met numerous times with Lee Xuan over the past three years. He knew it was just eyewash for the press, a charade to placate those remaining MIA families. John Higgins felt useless and worst of all he felt guilty for being part of a ruse that doled out false hope in portions equal to the pressure placed on the White House.

The ringing phone was a gratifying noise, signaling the end of his restless thoughts. It was his six a.m. wake-up call. That the clock said five-thirty didn't upset him. The mistake of the front desk just meant he would spend less time with his morbid bedtime thoughts and more time in the shower.

He picked up the phone. "Yes?" he said, expecting the broken English of the desk clerk.

"Mr. Higgins?"

"Yes."

"This is Dr. Xuan's assistant. Dr. Xuan asked me to tell you that he has something important for you. He requests that you meet him at his office at seven o'clock this morning. Can I tell him you will be there?"

"Yes, of course . . . I'll just take a later flight."

"Thank you, Mr. Higgins. You will not regret it."

———

The man, stooped by years of toil, was led into the brightly-lighted, basement room, a Vietnamese soldier on either side of him. He was told in Vietnamese to sit on one of the steel chairs in the center of the room. He obeyed, lowering his thin frame to the edge of the chair. He had no idea where he was or why he was here. His long dull gray hair concealed the man's dark, leathery features, which were ravaged by scars, the origin of which he chose not to remember. The brilliant light in the room, in contrast to the dim corridor through which he had been brought, caused him to squint, accentuating the deep crevasses around his liquid blue eyes. A door on the other side of the room opened and two men entered, a large man in a dark brown suit and a smaller man in a gray tunic. The man in the brown suit spoke, but in a language that was only vaguely familiar to the old man. Gesturing toward the old man, the brown suit spoke again, a bit louder. Then, translating into Vietnamese, the man in the tunic asked, "Are you Gerald Hurd?"

It was a familiar name and the question was worthy of consideration. *Am I Gerald Hurd?* He stared at the brown-suited man for nearly a minute then nodded his head slowly, affirmatively.

"What are you trying to pull, Lee," John Higgins asked. "This man isn't Airman Hurd. He can't even understand English."

"He hasn't heard or spoken it in nearly 40 years," Lee Xuan replied. He most likely has forgotten it. Time can erase many things, John, but time can also bring them back. I assure you this is Airman Gerald Hurd."

"Time can't erase fingerprints, so let's start with those. If they check out, we'll go on from there. According to our records Hurd was killed in 1963, one of the first American casualties of the war. Are you telling me that he somehow escaped a crash that totally destroyed his plane, then managed to survive in a hostile environment for 40 years and now you just found him, just like that?"

"The assumption of your government may have been a little premature," Xuan said. Check his fingerprints and anything else you like. I'm sure you will be satisfied this is Airman Hurd."

"By the way, Lee, where have you been keeping him all these years and why are you dropping him in our laps at this time?"

"We didn't know of him until a few weeks ago. He was taken prisoner by the National Liberation Front after they shot down his plane and he was placed in a prisoner of war camp. For his own protection from your country's incessant bombing, he was moved several times until our victory in 1975. We lost track of many prisoners around that time. Many were retrained and put to work in the rice paddies or factories. It is rumored that some were sent to camps in the Soviet Union. We had records on Hurd, but we didn't know where he was until two weeks ago after investigating reports of a blue-eyed rice farmer. We couldn't have 'dropped him in your lap' sooner because we didn't *have* him sooner."

Higgins shrugged. That he didn't believe Xuan didn't matter. He had a guy who may have been missing in action for 38 years, and that did matter. If his fingerprints checked out, Gerry Hurd soon would be on a U.S. Air Force transport back to his family in the States and John Higgins would be on his way to a long deserved promotion.

"One more thing, Lee; if you knew about this two weeks ago, why didn't you tell me about it at our meeting yesterday?"

"My superior wanted to know just how grateful your President would be," Xuan said, his uncharacteristic candor surprising Higgins, "and I couldn't tell you anything until I told him of your President's interest. You know how bureaucracies work, John."

Yes, Higgins thought, *unfortunately I do.*

———

The two men sat silently for the first six hours of the flight. Higgins used the time to finish his report and catch up on his sleep, the first time he had really slept since leaving the States.

"My wife . . . Julie . . . how is she?" Hurd finally said almost too softly for Higgins to hear.

It was the first time Higgins had heard Gerry speak English, and although the words were recognizable, the idiom was decidedly Vietnamese.

Higgins had been given instructions to answer all of Gerry's questions if he could.

"Mrs. Hurd was told that you were dead, Gerry, but she didn't give up. For ten years she badgered nearly everyone in the chain of command—all the way to the President—just to find your body so she could give you a decent funeral. I think she finally accepted the idea that you were never coming back. She remarried about twenty-five years ago. I'm sorry, Gerry."

"She was pregnant when I left . . .the baby . . . is it OK?"

"Your daughter is also married and has a family. Two boys and a girl, I believe. So you're a grandpa, Gerry."

There was a celebration at the capitol. Gerry received a medal from the President, who in November had been told overwhelmingly by the electorate that his services were no longer desired. The government furnished Gerry with a nice apartment in D.C., paid him 38 years of back military wages, gave him full retirement benefits, and provided a "shrink," who Gerry could visit as needed to aid his adjustment.

Dr. Leonard Schwimmer had treated numerous cases of post-traumatic-stress disorder, but he never had a case like Gerry's. It would be good, he said, for Gerry to talk about what had happened to him. "Just start at the beginning and tell me everything," Schwimmer said. "Some of it may be painful."

It was. Gerry had survived his ordeal day after day by blocking each preceding day from his memory. The pain of his injuries from the crash, the excruciating interrogations and the daily beatings at the hands of his captors were stored somewhere safe in a dark crevasse of Gerry's mind, as were memories of other Americans whose obscene deaths were also recorded there. Beyond the physical pain was hidden his unrelenting guilt for having been kept alive when so many of his fellow prisoners had not. With prodding from Dr. Schwimmer, Gerry unfolded his story, day by day. Stripped of the insulation of mortal fear, Gerry was experiencing pain that was more acute than ever before. The discussions continued without regard to Gerry's discomfort and somehow never seemed to focus on the more immediate problems that impeded his adjustment.

At the beginning of each session, he would begin a litany of issues: "My television set has no knobs on it. How do I change the station? I don't know how to set the clock on my stove. The eggs blew up in that microwave thing. I'd like to call my daughter, but I'm not sure how to work the phone. I can't get the lid off my medicine. My kitchen faucet only has one handle. The water's always hot. "What's a debit card? What's a pin number? What's e-mail? I hear people talking, but I don't understand the words."

"We'll cross those bridges when we get there, Gerry. Right now, it's important that we get those memories out in the open where we can rationalize them and put them behind us. OK? Now, you were telling me that you had just been moved to another camp. Do you know where?"

The interview continued for an hour, and while Dr. Schwimmer got answers to most of his questions, Gerry's questions were never addressed.

———

Gerry hung up the phone. He had just talked to a recording. It was the same whether he called his daughter or his ex-wife; he couldn't tell if his messages got through. It seemed that all his problems were manifested in that stupid phone. No one was ever on the other end. No one ever called back. Why even have a phone in the first place?

Gerry's eventual contact with his daughter was less than satisfactory. "Hello, Danielle? It sure is nice to talk to a real person. Can I come by this weekend? I'd like to see you and my grandkids. Maybe I could have lunch with you guys, my treat."

"Gee Gerry, that's nice of you, but . . . well, we're kinda busy this weekend. You know the kids are into a lot of things and we have to drag them all over the place."

"Sure. How about next weekend?"

"Pretty much the same thing. Maybe we can get together around the holidays . . . no we're going to Dan's grandmother's. Well, maybe you can come along."

"Sure, thanks."

The apartment was cold, as it had been for the past week. Gerry did what he had done for the past three nights, stand in front of the small gray box on the wall and wonder what he was supposed to do to make the room warmer. He read the words on the box several times. "Honeywell Programmable Thermostat." *What does that mean?* The little colored squares on the box didn't seem to do anything but beep when he touched them and the room stayed at 58 degrees.

"Make it warmer," he shouted at the thermostat. *With all this technology, maybe you can just reason with it,* he thought. The room stayed at 58 degrees. He called his ex-wife: *Maybe she can tell me how to work this thing.*

"You've reached the home of Frank and Julie Johnson. Please leave a message."

He called his daughter.

"Gee, Gerry; I just let Dan do all that. I'm a real dunce when it comes to that computer stuff. Look I've got to go. I'm late picking up Patsy."

"Wait!" Gerry pleaded. "Wait a minute, please. I know this isn't easy for you, having me show up after all those years . . . to find out that the father you never knew is alive. Lord knows, it must have turned your life upside down. Honey, you never knew me, but I knew you even before you were born. Your mom would send me letters telling me how you were growing inside her. I knew about your first kick and how your mom could actually see the imprint of your little foot from inside her belly.

"When we crashed in Nam, and I woke up in the POW camp, I thought I had lost everything. But just thinking about your mom and wondering about the little baby she was carrying, kept me from losing it. Without that, I never would have made it. I just want to get to know my baby . . . I just . . ." Gerry began to sob.

"Gerry, don't . . ."

"Look, please don't call me Gerry, like I'm some guy who paints your house or something. I'm your father, for God's sake; can't you call me dad?"

"I'm sorry, Gerry, I can't do that, Danielle replied without a moment's consideration. Frank has always been my dad. He adopted me after he and mom got married. He's the only dad I've ever known. It just wouldn't be fair to Frank. Look, call mom, she might know how to work that thermostat."

He called his ex-wife again.

"Sorry, Julie's out shopping," her husband told him. "But I really don't think she wants you calling here all the time. We've got our lives; you've got to get along with yours. I mean, she can't be at your beck and call every time you have a problem."

"But, I've only talked with her once."

"No offense, but I'd prefer that you not call her anymore."

Gerry walked out onto the balcony of his fourth floor apartment. The temperature was considerably colder than in his apartment, but he could only feel the frigid waves of loneliness that swept over him. In Vietnam, the physical pain and fear had numbed him from the pain of loneliness and there he could be warmed by thoughts of his wife. Now the chill he felt emanated not from the nighttime air, but from the single truth that no one cared . . . no one but Dr. Schwimmer. Gerry was in new territory and he was having trouble navigating through it. His compass had failed him and he felt more profoundly lost than ever in his life.

Looking down at the street, an unusual calm swept over him, as if a great decision had been made, an unbearable burden lifted. Gerry raised one leg over the railing, then the other. He leaned out over the street, hands behind him grasping the rail, heals perched on the lip of the ledge. He could just let go and disappear from this place where he didn't belong. Wasn't there once someplace where he did belong? There may have been. *Yes,* he thought, *there was.* Suddenly, standing on the edge of oblivion, he was overwhelmed with a new idea and a desire to see how it all would play out. He might still survive, and he was sure Dr. Schwimmer could help him do it.

The doctor's office was quiet, and Gerry feared that Schwimmer was not in. The only sound, a voice filtering through Schwimmer's office door, verified that the doctor was indeed there, talking on the phone.

"Look, all I need are a few more sessions with this guy and I'll have enough to complete the book. Trust me; this will be a best seller. Thirty-eight years a prisoner in Vietnam; he's lived two totally different lives. And he told me some stories about how our soldiers were treated in Vietnam that would turn your hair white. Doctor-patient privilege? No problem. I can get him to sign the proper releases. I could get him to sign anything. He trusts me. Believe me; this story will be worth millions."

Schwimmer turned around to see Gerry standing in the doorway. "Uh, Gerry, how long . . ."

"Dr. Schwimmer, I just came by to tell you I won't be coming back any more," Gerry said calmly. "Oh, and I'm not signing anything. And if you print one word of what I've told you in our confidential sessions, I'll sue you.

———

John Higgins looked up at the determined face. "You sure you want to do this, Gerry?"

"I'm sure."

"Do you have the envelopes?"

Gerry passed two envelopes across the desk to Higgins. "A letter for my daughter, and for Lee Xuan . . . my 38 years of military back pay."

"He'll probably need it since Congress voted down the trade bill. I'll see that the check gets into his account in Zurich," Higgins said, shaking his head. "Can't figure you out Gerry. You spent 38 years trying to get out of Vietnam, now you want to bribe somebody to get you back in."

"John, I busted my ass trying to escape from those damn POW camps, but after ten years, I stopped trying. I got tired of the beatings and being thrown into the cage without food or water every time I got caught. They called it "retraining". After a while I stopped believing there ever was anything to escape to. Maybe it was the retraining or maybe I just lost hope. One day they left the gate open and I just walked away. I found myself out in the middle of a rice paddy, so I became a rice farmer and I started a life again.

I eventually married a Vietnamese woman and we have two nice kids. We were pretty content until the troops came along and tossed me on that truck. When I saw you, an American, I started to think about my old life. I thought it could be the same, but it couldn't. A few days ago, after all that time just trying to survive, I was actually going to kill myself. That shocked me. I realized then that the country hadn't changed much, I had. It's a tough life in Vietnam, but like it or not, that's more my country than this is. I understand it and I have a family there who loves me. I didn't know until now how much I love them, and I'd pay any price to get back to them. I thought Dr. Schwimmer could help me do that, but he just wanted to sell a book. What about you, John, did you get your promotion?"

"Nah; with the President out, I'm just looking for a job. You might be the only son of a bitch in this whole mess who's getting what he wanted . . . and I wish you luck." Higgins forced a smile and took the envelopes.

Few people remembered the tiny airstrip in Vietnam. The CIA had built it in 1963 to accommodate B-24s that the government had planned to use for reconnaissance. Only one was ever used for that purpose, and even that was never acknowledged by the agency. Although the airstrip had fallen into serious disrepair, on this day it was more than adequate for the ancient DC-3 and its special cargo. The dilapidated truck pulled alongside the plane before it could come to a full stop. The plane's only passenger emerged and, as if he had rehearsed the move, hopped onto the truck bed. The driver popped the clutch and the vehicle headed off toward the bush where, several kilometers in, a family lovingly awaited the return of their missing father.

Elmer Perkins has left the room

After twenty-four years, Cynthia Perkins knew her marriage to Elmer was over. There was just one thing left to do; she had to tell him. She stared down at the small table that separated them, her hands at her sides to keep him from tenderly caressing them as he always did whenever she was upset. If he did that today, she would not be able to tell him. She raised her head slowly, shifting her gaze up from the tiny drops of sweat on her ice tea glass until her eyes met his . . . and she knew he knew.

"Don't cry," she said. "It'll only make this harder."

Her appeal went unheeded as a tear tentatively overflowed onto Elmer's cheek.

"What did I do wrong?" he barely choked.

"You couldn't help what went wrong," she said. "You're a sweet guy, Elmer, but I need more than you can give me." Cynthia leaned forward, cautiously placing her hands on the tabletop. "I've been married to you since I was nineteen. Now I'm almost forty-four and I've never been anywhere but here."

"Baby, I didn't think the age difference meant anything to you." Elmer let an ironic chuckle slip softly past his lips. "I guess 23 years is a pretty big difference, ain't it."

"It's not the age thing. It's this place . . ."

"I love you," the man pleaded. "Don't that count? I mean we had a kid and all. I was a good daddy, wasn't I?"

"You were a great daddy. Jessie worships the ground you walk on. But it was always you and him. It was never . . . us. It was always you and Jessie going out hunting and fishing. I was never included. I was always stuck here in this crummy little town."

"But baby, don't you remember the fun we'd have when Jessie and me'd git home and you'd cook us up the fish we caught? Then I'd git out the ol' guitar and you and Jessie would sing."

"Well, now Jessie's stationed in Germany, and without Jessie around . . ." Cynthia struggled for the right words that could spare the poor man's feelings, but failed. "Well, Elmer, let's face it, you're pretty boring."

Elmer stared at his ice tea glass, slowly rotating it on the small wet spot that had condensed on the table. "Ain't my fault I can't sing," he said finally, in a quivering baritone voice.

"It's not the singing, sweetie," she countered, trying to soften her last statement. "You're gone most of the time with your friends. I never get to go anywhere."

"It's only one friend and he don't come that often."

"Ok, one. What's his name? Wayne . . . from up around Memphis, ain't he? Sally said she and Rudy saw you and him at the Beer n' Steer just last week. You never even told me he was in town.

"Uh, well . . . he owed me some money and he was only here long enough to give it to me."

"And that's another thing. You're always loanin' out money. Everybody in town owes you. Sally told me that sometimes you give money to folks and don't even ask for it back. Where you gettin' all that money, Elmer? That little hardware store of ours don't make that much, does it? And we live pretty good too. Where's all that money coming from?"

Elmer shrugged his head down between his shoulders. "Well darling,' I did pretty good at my old job. I got some investments." "That's news to me. You never talk to me about money. You're always goin' off to those hardware conventions, but you never invite me to go along. How do I know you're goin' to a convention at all? You could be meetin' another woman for all I know."

"Baby, that ain't true; I don't want nobody but you."

I'm sorry, Elmer. I been on the outside lookin' in for too long. I gotta get a turn. I'm leavin'; I want a divorce."

Elmer leaned forward and reached for Cynthia's hand. She could not allow that. "No," she said, pulling her hands away, "I'm leavin' and I ain't lookin' back."

"Baby, I . . . I . . ."

Without warning Elmer's pitiful expression twisted into an aspect of agony as the color suddenly drained from his face. Cynthia froze with the realization that something was desperately wrong. Elmer was trying to hand her something—a business card—but Cynthia, paralyzed by the pain she saw in his sad blue eyes, couldn't reach for it.

"Call Wayne," Elmer rasped urgently, flipping the card across the table. "Darlin' . . . I love you," he gasped, ". . . and I always will."

His lifeless body fell forward across the table. The shattering of the ice tea glasses caused Cynthia to bolt upright, her arms still dangling at her sides, her eyes wide in disbelief.

———

The funeral was delayed for a week until Jessie returned from Germany. Wayne arrived the morning after Elmer's heart attack to help with the funeral arrangements.

"He was a good man," Wayne said, once all the neighbors had left the house.

"I suppose he was," Cynthia replied. "We were married almost 25 years, but I never really knew him. The night he died, I told him

I was leaving," Cynthia sobbed, burying her face in her hands to conceal her tears. "I think I killed him, Wayne."

"No," Wayne said, reaching across the kitchen table and gently touching Cynthia's hand. "You didn't kill him. His heart was damaged years ago. If anything, it was loving you that kept him alive this long." Wayne turned toward Jessie who was morosely unpacking a large wooden crate that had just arrived from Memphis. "Those are some of your daddy's things. They might help you understand the situation better."

"What situation," Jessie said sullenly, picking up something that looked like a trophy.

"Well, before he and your momma met, your daddy and I used to travel around a lot. You see, he was a pretty important man . . . important enough that a lot of people wanted to keep him healthy. That was my job. I was his doctor, long before I was his friend. As his doctor, I did a pretty good job, but as a friend, I'm afraid I let him down." Wayne folded his hands in front of him and looked down at his thumbs. He was silent for a while. Cynthia could see water glistening in his eyes when he finally raised his head to resume.

"His schedule kept him on the road constantly. I watched it take its toll, day after day, month after month. He wasn't eating right . . . drank too much. He got way out of shape." Wayne took a deep breath.

"When his mother died, he went to pieces and started drinking pretty hard. His schedule got worse and he withdrew more and more. One night in Memphis, he begged me for something to help him get some sleep. I knew that in his state of mind it was risky, but as a friend, I couldn't deny him, so I gave him something. I never imagined he would take the whole bottle. We found him just in time to save his life, but not soon enough to avoid the heart damage."

"The press reported that he had died. We just let 'em keep thinking it, because with his damaged heart he couldn't work again anyway. The stress of his illness had changed his appearance so much that even his best friends didn't recognize him. So I paid the coroner to forge a death certificate, and I brought him here to build a new life. He decided on the name Elmer Perkins, because it matched the initials on the cufflinks his mother had given him."

"That was twenty five years ago, Cynthia. About a year before you and your folks moved to town. You two met and the rest is history. Those trips to hardware conventions? Well he lied a little. They were actually trips to the Mayo Clinic for his heart problems. About the money? I sold some of his stuff that wasn't inventoried in his estate. The interest provided a good income."

Jessie was intently studying the trophy that he had dug out of the crate. Slowly, a smile born of newly gained knowledge began to spread across his face.

"Was this really my Dad's?"

Wayne smiled at the young man. "Yep, that's the real one; there's a copy back in Memphis."

Jessie handed the object to his mother. "Momma, you might want to look at this," he said.

Cynthia held the heavy object out to where she could read the inscription engraved below the golden gramophone.

15th *Annual Grammy Awards*
Best Gospel Album for 1972
"He Touched Me"
Elvis Presley

Cynthia felt the air in the room stir as if someone had suddenly left.

Boy on a Bus

The industrial lights that hung in rows from the metal beams of the discarded warehouse dimmed as the coffin-sized machine reappeared upon the wood-framed stage at the center of the sprawling building. From out of a glassed-in corner office came two people, one running toward the machine, the other much older one, calmly walking.

Paul Baird, assistant to Professor Howard Kranz,, was only twenty-three, but already held degrees in physics, cosmology and electrical engineering, almost as many as Kranz, who also was a doctor of chemistry and held the Niels Bohr Chair for Theoretical Physics that had recently been established at the university. Kranz and Baird each had immeasurable I.Q.s and it had been said that if they stood outside at the same time, the sun would dim out of respect. As intimidating as that brain trust should have been, it was not enough to secure funding for the project that had been assembled in the dilapidated warehouse. Everything involved with the project, including the warehouse, had been purchased with Kranz's personal fortune gained from the licensing of his numerous patents. No one but Kranz and Baird had any knowledge of the project, and that's the way they wanted to keep it until they were ready to announce it following the full-scale test. If the specimen had survived today's test, that launch would be tomorrow.

"She appears to be in good shape," Baird said as he removed the restraints from Doris, the Chimpanzee that had just returned from twelve hours in the past. The two scientists already knew that their attempt to send the chimp back had worked, since twelve hours earlier they were waiting for her when she arrived at this exact place. The question that then remained was could they reverse the process and return her alive to the present. That question was answered by the chattering chimp herself as she whirled and rolled across the concrete floor of the ancient warehouse.

Swept up in emotion paralleling that of a child finding an E-ticket at Disney World, the young assistant could not suppress the tears that now flowed down his grinning cheeks.

"You did it, professor," Baird said breathlessly. "You have done what scientists and philosophers have dreamed about for millennia. You proved Einstein to be correct and Cox to be wrong."

Indeed, time travel had been hinted at in numerous scientific papers and ancient texts including Hindu mythology, the Bible, Talmud and others. Einstein believed his Theory of General Relativity indicated that time travel could be achieved. Other notable scientists such as British particle physicist Brian Cox believed that time travel might be possible, but only in one direction. Kranz and Baird had just proven that time was a two-way street, and that would change the world forever.

"Looks like we're on for full-scale tomorrow," Baird said.

"Right," Kranz replied stoically. "We've done it with a chimp. Tomorrow will see if a human can handle the trip. I already have entered the data for my visit and automatic return."

Kranz saw Baird shaking his head and pinching the bridge of his nose as if in deep thought. It was an indication that Paul was trying to puzzle through something that even his huge intellect couldn't fathom.

"You have a question?" Kranz asked.

"Well yes, two actually. First, why shouldn't I be the one to take the risk tomorrow? After all, I'm younger and more fit, and . . . well, if something should go wrong, I wouldn't be missed as much as you would be." Then recalling that Kranz had no living family, he added, ". . . you know, by the scientific community. And second, why have you chosen December 12th, 1955? I looked it up and nothing of much importance occurred around that time."

"To answer your first question," Kranz said, "Don't sell yourself short. I've lived a long, productive life. My time is fading; yours is just beginning. You're brilliant and have so much more to give. You'd be a much greater loss to science than I. As to your second question and, with all due respect for your excellent capabilities, there is one facet of this experiment that only I am qualified to accomplish." Kranz shrugged, "Besides, 1955 was a damned good year. Why not?"

Baird, with his head cocked to the side, looked as if he were trying to comprehend some esoteric scientific theory. Kranz went back into the glassed-in office and closed the door behind him.

———

For little Howie Kranz, 1955 was indeed a pretty good year and December 12th would turn out to be the most important day in Howie's life. It was a Monday and still cold enough to make the snow that had fallen over the weekend crunch under his feet. Everyone knew Howie was smart, but his actual intelligence would not be determined until today when he would be relieved of the mind-numbing exercises of third grade to take a battery of tests that would make that exact determination. The boredom of the classroom was one thing; dealing with his classmates was a different matter entirely. They thought he was some kind of a nerd, a dork, or worse, a wimp, because he didn't play their schoolyard games or join in their mundane conversations. He mostly stayed by himself and daydreamed. He didn't mind school, waste of time that he thought it was, but before he could get to school, he had to ride the city bus that stopped a block from his house, and then he had to survive the abuse conferred on him by the four or five other third graders whose homes were on the bus route. Howie always sat alone, with his books and sack-lunch in the empty seat next to him. The kids called him egghead and sometimes slapped him on the head as they did. But in time they would go to the back of the bus and he was glad for the solitude and his daydreams.

This morning was no different. The kids slapped him, shot him with spitballs and called him egghead. It was all in a day's ride to school. It would be the same on the ride home.

He had received the egghead appellation during a classroom exercise about each child's favorite subject. Howie chose Physics and tried unsuccessfully to explain the Heisenberg Uncertainty Principle to his classmates. His perplexed teacher said, "That's nice, Howie," and told him to sit down.

Today, instead of attending class where he would have to suffer through Mrs. Johansson's instruction on basic reading, writing and arithmetic, Howie would be taken to a special room where he would be tested, along with two other children to determine their eligibility for the advanced school. He knew he would do well, but wondered if he should hold back a little so as not to intimidate the testing people. Regardless, he was pretty sure he would be celebrating his success on the bus ride home, and perhaps his nightmare of being different would end.

With the exception of Howie, everyone was amazed at how well he had done on the tests. Howie's I.Q was off the chart, as was his psychological profile; he fell short only in social interactions, but that could be rectified. The Principal called his mother and by the end of the day, he was enrolled in a special school for gifted children that had an opening for the January semester. None of this was communicated to Howie, who got on the bus at the end of the school day thinking nothing had changed.

Howie took his usual seat and was about to place his books on the seat next to him when an old man walked up from the back of the bus and sat. Howie had never seen a bum before, but he thought this man might qualify. His clothes looked well-worn and the ill-fitting overcoat emitted a peculiar odor. Young Howie hoped he wouldn't have to talk to the guy, but it appeared that the old man wanted to carry on a conversation with him. The loquacious old tramp asked if Howie was coming from school, what he'd been studying and all kinds of questions that the eight-year old answered curtly. Then Howie launched into his interpretation of the "Planck Constant", thinking the old guy would just shut up and go away. Instead he just smiled, shrugged and said "You're pretty smart, aren't you.

Howie looked out the window and saw that the bus had just gone passed his normal stop. "Aw heck, I missed my stop." Now he would have to trudge an additional two blocks on the snow clogged sidewalks to get home.

At the next stop, Howie was standing on the step, braced for the blast of cold air as the bus door opened. As he stepped down from the bus he thought he heard the old man yell something at him. Ignoring it, he began the three-block trek through the deep snow. The streets, which were plowed and salted as the snow fell, were passable, but the snow that had thawed from the morning sun, had refrozen into dangerous patches as clouds had gathered again and the temperature dropped in the afternoon.

Crossing the icy street, Howie had just reached the spot where the sidewalk should have been when he heard the screeching crash, the sound of two cars slamming together. He turned to see one of the cars skidding toward him. With the snow weighing down his feet he was literally frozen, as the automobile careened toward him, and instead of moving in one direction or another, he fell backward. As he did, he was hit from another direction, swooped up and tossed out of the path of the vehicle.

Howie landed in a snowbank as the car passed just inches from him. He struggled to his feet in time to see the car slide sideways into a tree. Then he saw the old man from the bus lying face up in red colored snow. The old brown coat had been ripped from his body and was now attached to the bumper of the car. Howie trudged over to the man's side. He had never seen a person die before, but he was sure the old man was dying. Then the man raised his hand slightly.

"Are you all right?" the man said, his words barely audible.

Howie tilted his head slightly, then nodded. Death was a very strange thing. Howie did not know the man—had never seen him before today—yet he felt such a deep sadness, the same feeling of loss he had when his father died two years ago. Not knowing what to do, the eight year-old just stood there and watched as life drained from the old man. Their eyes stayed in contact. Then the old man smiled and took one last breath.

The few people who had come out of their homes to determine the cause of the horrendous sound were tending to the victims in the two cars; they hadn't even seen the man lying in the snow. It was ten minutes before they noticed the little boy who was still staring wonderingly at the man who had died to save his life. As the people led Howie away from the scene, he craned his head around to, one last time, view the man to whom he knew he owed an unpayable debt.

The headline in the next day's Gazette was "Boy Saved by Nameless Vagrant."

————

For Professor Howard Kranz the memory was as fresh as it was on that day sixty years ago. Believing that he was responsible for the old man's death, he bore an unrelenting burden of guilt, and every day since that time, he prayed that he could somehow repay his debt.

"I have something for you Doctor Kranz," Paul said as he entered the small office. "You're going to need some money."

Kranz looked up from his desk, his mind still engrossed in the memory of that distant day. "I have money; I got five hundred from the ATM this morning."

"No, you need money that won't look counterfeit to the people in 1955. Money has changed, so I went to my grandmother and asked if she had any old money. She did. I told her that I knew a guy who would give her ten times face value for it and convinced her to sell it. I got about $50."

"Just fifty?"

"That will go a long way in 1955. It ought to last you the few hours you're going to be there."

"Yes, I suppose it will."

"I also got some of my granddad's old clothes. She kept them in her cedar chest after granddad died. They look kind of fifty-ish and they're in pretty good shape I guess."

"Thanks, Paul. I've been so focused on the calculations that I had not even thought of those details."

"No problem. That's why I get the big bucks," Paul replied.

Kranz donned the clothes, and stuffed the money into one of the deep pockets of the heavy coat. Then giving a slight nod to his assistant, he entered the vehicle. Following a five second countdown, the professor flicked a toggle switch on the sparse console. Paul watched as the vehicle faded, then disappeared completely. He felt confident it would emerge in the same spot, only sixty years earlier. The warehouse was an ideal venue for the experiment, as Paul's research had shown that it had been emptied, locked and unused for more than sixty-five years.

———

Professor Howard Kranz stepped onto the bus at the stop where the route originated and walked to the back so he could see all the passengers who got on. He had no idea where the old man had gotten on, but wanted to talk with him and perhaps give him some of the money Paul had gotten from his grandmother. After having paid only fifteen cents for bus fare, it was obvious that the "old" money would indeed go a long way in 1955, especially for the old vagrant who would soon save young Howie's life. But perhaps it didn't have to be that way at all. If Kranz could distract Howie long enough to get past the accident, both the boy and the vagrant would survive and Kranz would have repaid his debt; better still, there would be no debt to repay.

Regardless, he wanted to have some time to talk with the old man; to find out just what kind of person would so selflessly give his own life to save that of another. The old man had been his hero for all those years and Kranz never knew even as much as his name.

Several young boys had gotten on at the stop nearest the school. Then he saw him; an old man in a brown overcoat was walking toward him. This had to be the man who would save little Howie's life . . . his life. The old man plopped down next to him in the long bench seat that straddled the rear of the bus. He exuded a peculiar odor—sweet—*probably Gin*, Kranz thought. Kranz felt the money in the pocket of his overcoat and crumpling all the bills into a ball, transferred them stealthily into the old man's coat pocket. *There, that ought to take care of you for a while, old timer*, Kranz thought.

The boys who had entered earlier were typically rowdy, changing seats and talking loudly. He noticed the boys' attention suddenly shift to a child, sitting alone five rows ahead. They were taunting him and calling him egghead. The impulse to go up and protect his young self from the derision of the other boys was overwhelming, and he still had to somehow distract the boy to keep the tragedy from happening.

146

"Do you mind if I sit here?" Kranz asked, pointing to the empty seat next to Howie. "Those kids are so noisy, I can hardly think."

"No," the boy answered, "as long as you don't talk. "I'm thinking about some stuff myself."

"Do you mind if I ask what you're thinking about?" Kranz asked.

"Some tests I took today . . . y'know, to see if I'm smart enough to skip a few grades. I'm thinking about that."

"Are you smart enough?" Kranz asked.

"I think so. I've been studying stuff like Physics and astronomy since I was little."

"Since you were little," Kranz repeated, trying to conceal a smile. "So what do you know about those things?"

"Well, I know about the Theory of Relativity, which is pretty interesting, but what's really great is Quantum Theory, you know, how really small things work. I've just now started to think about the Heisenberg Uncertainly Principle and . . ." the little boy paused. "Do you know about the Planck Constant?"

"Kranz smiled and shrugged his shoulders."

Then the boy launched into his explanation of how the Plank Constant helps define the relationship between particles and waves.

The bus stopped briefly, then started up. The boy turned toward the window just in time to watch as his bus stop went past.

"Aw heck," he said, "I missed my stop." He jumped up pulled the exit cord and ran to the center door.

Ah, he missed his stop, Kranz thought. That means the disaster has been averted, the boy is safe and the old man didn't die after all. Satisfied that he had saved the lives of the old man and the boy, Kranz basked in the warm feeling that his debt had finally been paid. Kranz watched the boy as he stepped from the bus and began trudging across the street toward the sidewalk on the opposite side. Then he saw two cars skidding toward one another as the recollection of another time flashed painfully in his mind.

147

"No," he shouted, as he remembered that the tragedy had not been *prevented* by the boy missing his stop, but was *caused* by it.

He expected to see the old man from the back of the bus dash out to rescue the boy as he had seen it in his mind for the past sixty years, but today that wasn't happening.

He looked around the bus. The boys in the back were still rowdy. He saw little Howie in the middle of the street, he saw the two cars sliding toward an inevitable collision, and he saw the old man, who he had thought was his hero, in a drunken sleep, clutching a half empty bottle of Gin, still in the back of the bus. Suddenly what he had to do became crystal clear to Professor Kranz; it was what he now realized he had done before, what he could never escape doing. He rushed toward the bus door.

"Please sit down," the bus driver shouted as Kranz reached the center exit and had forced the doors open.

Stumbling off the bus, he could see the cars colliding, one of them beginning a long skid from one side of the street to the other.

"Howie, wait," Kranz screamed as the boy slogged through the street.

The boy had nearly reached the other side of the intersection when Kranz lunged for him just in time to scoop him up and throw him clear. Kranz's overcoat caught on the car's bumper, dragging him under the vehicle and crushing his chest. When the fabric of the old brown coat finally ripped, Kranz was rolled into a snowbank, invisible to everyone accept the little boy who was struggling to pull himself up only a few feet away.

Barely conscious, Kranz now looked up into the eyes of the little boy. "Are you all right?" he gasped.

The boy nodded, tilting his head to the side as if trying to understand what had happened. Kranz maintained eye contact with the boy for what seemed an eternity. There was no pain, no cold; in fact he felt nothing at all, other than the satisfaction that he had completed his mission. He had saved the boy and absolved the burden of debt that he thought he had to an unknown man who once had saved his life. He could only smile. Then slowly, the boy began to fade from his vision.

Paul Baird was relieved when the coffin-sized craft reappeared on the wooden stage, but was struck with sadness to find that it was empty. He could never know why professor Kranz had not returned, or how events of that day had played out. He would never know that the small craft was more than a machine for traveling through time; indeed, it was an inexorable conveyance, one that would relentlessly and eternally transport Professor Howard Kranz to his destiny.

The Devil in the Details

Lorenzo Philbin's pending divorce was just beginning to settle into his psyche. Although he would be the first to admit that he wasn't the best of husbands—not even a good husband—he could not bear the fact that Loreen was leaving him. He was over the anger that he had felt when she "pulled up stakes and left." He was currently going through what his drinking buddy, Clem Daugherty, called the mourning stage. Clem swore that as soon as the divorce was final Lorenzo would begin the recovery stage, which Clem said was the most fun. Unfortunately, since Lorenzo hadn't signed the divorce papers he remained stuck in the mourning stage, dubbed by Clem as the miseries. The fact was, he was both pissed off and holding out hope that Loreen would come back. If she did come back, Lorenzo didn't know if he would hug her or beat the crap out of her. He had done both during their volatile two-year marriage. He was still trying to figure out whose fault it was and he hadn't gotten around to pointing the finger at himself. He probably never would; Lorenzo Philbin just wasn't that kind of guy.

Money had always been a problem. Lorenzo couldn't hold a steady job and when Loreen talked him into loaning her worthless brother the five grand for that get-rich-quick scheme, well, they didn't have enough money to hold their tenuous marriage together. The five grand was Lorenzo's biggest payday at the track, and he planned to parlay that into a million. He and Loreen could have been living large, but now it was all pissed away on who knows what. All he could afford now was the lousy Mega-Pik lottery ticket that he bought with his last two bucks. The fault was all that of his brother-in-law, Paulie Ray Ritter. "I'd like to kill that son of a bitch," Lorenzo would say whenever the subject came up; and it came up often after he and Clem had a few beers.

He sat in the tattered overstuffed chair and stared at the grey paint-chipped apartment door as if waiting for someone to walk through at any minute.

"Maybe if I concentrate hard enough, she'll come back," he mumbled, and narrowed his gaze at the door. "Come on Loreen, baby, walk through that door." Then, taking the last sip from his beer can, "Come on baby, knock."

Knock, knock.

"Well I'll be damned, it worked," he said as he leaped from his chair, clearing the six feet to the door and flinging it open in one less-than-fluid motion. "Lor . . ." he cut his greeting short, his sudden elation turning just as suddenly to aggravation. "Who the hell are you?"

"Excuse me," the tall distinguished man said. "Mr. Philbin, my name is Bradley, and I'm here to grant you your request. How would you want it done?"

"What're you talking about, grant me my request? What request?"

"Why, you just asked for your wife to walk through that door, but before I can do that for you, I need some specifics; you know, details."

"What are you, some kind of genie, or something? You're gonna grant me three wishes?

"If that's what you want, I suppose you could make it a . . . three-part request. That might be even more exciting. Sure, three wishes it is. Now where do you want to start?"

"OK, fruitcake, get outa here. If Clem sent you, tell him it ain't funny and I'll be talking to him about this next time I see him." Lorenzo balled up his fist and placed it under the man's nose, ". . . if you know what I mean."

"I'm afraid I don't know what you mean, and I don't know this Clem fellow. Look Lorenzo, I'm just here to be of help," the man said, pushing himself into the apartment. I assure you, I have the power to grant your request . . . uh . . . wishes, but I need you to tell me exactly how you want it done."

"So, you're like an angel. Is that it?"

"Well, I suppose you could say I'm not entirely of this world, but I wouldn't exactly say that I'm an angel either."

"You're not that . . . that other guy, are you?"

"Satan? Oh, mercy, no. He would probably ask you to pay for the service with something like your immortal soul or your first born perhaps. My services are entirely free. I do it because I get a lot of pleasure from it. It's a wonderful hobby."

"So, let me get this straight, Bradley. By the way, is that your first name or your last?"

"It could be either, and you can call me Brad, if you like."

"So, let me get this straight, Brad. You're just gonna grant me some wishes, because you get a kick outta granting wishes. This ain't gonna cost me nothing?"

"That's correct. All you need do is lay out the scenario for me and I will make it happen exactly as you want it to happen, right down to the final detail."

"And I won't go to hell . . . like when I die or anything?"

"No. I couldn't get you into hell even if you asked me to. That's not my purview."

There was something about Bradley's demeanor that made Lorenzo want to believe that this just wasn't some sick joke that Clem thought up after consuming a six pack or two. If Brad could do what he said he could do, then his problems would be solved. *If he was just a nutcase, so what?* Lorenzo reasoned. *I have no skin in the game.*

"OK, OK," Lorenzo said, trying to contain his rising excitement. "All you need for me to do is tell you exactly how you want this thing to go down, right?"

"That's right," Bradley replied. "Give me the details and I'll make sure it'll 'go down' just that way." Bradley eased over toward the threadbare couch. "Perhaps we could sit down while you think about it."

Lorenzo plunked back into the overstuffed chair and Bradley sat delicately on the edge of the couch next to the door.

"There's only one thing," Bradley said, raising his index finger, "Everything must happen in a relatively logical fashion. That is, I can't just snap my fingers and make things happen . . . well, I could, but that wouldn't be any fun, so I won't. I suggest you develop a scenario—like a play—that would at least appear not to break any universal laws of physics."

"You mean, it's gotta seem natural."

"That's exactly what I mean. Oh, and since this is a three-part request, all the parts must be related and sequential."

"OK. Let me think."

If Lorenzo continued to have doubts about Bradley's sincerity, it wasn't evident in his deliberation; he stared at the yellow legal pad that Bradley had handed him for more than an hour, and then, as if he had come to some startling conclusion, he started writing. He saw no need to provide a complete script, just the desired outcomes, so when he was finished he had filled less than half a page.

"OK, I got it," Lorenzo said, ripping off a sheet of yellow paper and handing it to the man sitting across from him. Bradley hadn't moved at all during the past few hours. He was still sitting stiffly on the old couch. If Lorenzo had not been so focused on his writing, he might have noticed that his new benefactor hadn't even blinked.

Bradley turned the page front to back to make sure he was seeing all of it, scanning the scribbled words as he did. "Is this everything?" he asked. "You have been a little sketchy on the details, I must say."

"Yep. It's pretty clear cut." Lorenzo replied. "If you can pull that off, I'd say you're pretty damn good. I'll leave the details to you."

"Well since you're being so accommodating," Bradley said, "I guess I could throw in an extra wish, if you'd like; sort of a bonus for allowing me to have some latitude."

"Sure, I might have another wish," Lorenzo said, grabbing the paper back and scrawling something on it. "Here, fit this one in there."

"Do you want these in any particular order?"

"Nah; just make it all happen quick. I'm dying here."

"Very well," Bradley said, adding as he handed the yellow note paper back to Lorenzo, "You can keep this if you like. I have it memorized."

Lorenzo stared at the peeling paint on the door as it closed behind his visitor; an uneasy feeling, like he had just been had, settled over him as he tossed the yellow paper into the shoebox where he kept his unpaid bills. He retrieved a fresh brew from the smelly refrigerator and muttered, "Clem, you son of a bitch, if this is some stupid prank, I'll get you back for trying to make a fool outta me."

The filthy overstuffed chair that he had scavenged from the downstairs dumpster was a reminder to Lorenzo of just how far his fortunes had declined since he made the loan to his brother-in-law and hatred welled up in him like a virulent foam. Staring at the ripped and stained chair he wondered how much vermin might have taken up residence there. He didn't even want to touch it, but curbing his disgust; he plopped down in the chair and switched on the small-screen TV in hopes of getting the score on the Cardinals–Red Sox game that he missed because of his recent visitor.

The yellow ping pong balls rolled out one at time. "Fifteen," the announcer said. "Twenty-four . . . thirty seven . . . thirty nine . . . and forty six; and the Mega-ball is nine."

These weren't the sports scores, but the Mega-Pik lottery numbers for the $75 million dollar prize. Lorenzo knew those numbers; he had been playing them consistently for the past five years. Those were his numbers, and he knew they matched the ones on the lottery ticket lying on the table just three feet from him.

Lorenzo's immediate impulse was to get to the lottery ticket to double check the numbers, but the unfathomable concept of winning 75 million bucks froze his body. It seemed that all of Lorenzo's muscles wanted to flex at the same time inducing a momentary paralysis that locked him into the chair. His heart felt as if it would escape his chest as it pumped blood to his brain in such volumes that he nearly passed out. With the exception of a few ecstatic evenings with Loreen, it was a feeling he had seldom experienced in his otherwise miserable life.

"There they are," the announcer said. "If those are your numbers, you are the big winner of the Mega-Pik lottery and seventy-five million dollars."

"Holy crap," Lorenzo shouted as he checked the numbers on his ticket for the fourth time. "I'm the winner!"

Lorenzo's elation waned somewhat when he discovered that there were three other people with the same numbers, and he had to share the prize with them. Of course the IRS took their initial 20 percent, and warned him that there would be additional taxes owing on April 15th. But that left him with a cool $15 million. His fortune had certainly changed. Having been generally ignored most of his life,

Lorenzo now was being followed around by reporters trying to get warm fuzzy stories about the underdog who suddenly became rich. "What are you going to do with the all that money?" one of them asked.

"Spend it," Lorenzo answered.

"Do you have any charitable organizations that might benefit?"

"Hell no! No 'charity' never did nothin' for me." Lorenzo spat the word 'charity' as if he had just bit into a wormy apple.

A week after collecting his winnings, he moved into a five-million-dollar home in the suburbs. Two days later Loreen showed up, begging for forgiveness, saying that she had been wrong and no longer wanted a divorce. She had gained a little weight and her platinum blond hair was now auburn; not auburn red, but Auburn University burnt orange. Nevertheless, Lorenzo was glad to have one of his possessions back and he always thought of Loreen as a possession. It mattered not that Loreen's penitence was simply a matter of the money, and not any guilt on her part. Lorenzo was content that he now had her totally under his thumb. That was nice.

Paulie was another matter. Loreen's brother still owed Lorenzo five grand. "If that S.O.B. ever shows up here without my money, he'll eat a bullet," Lorenzo would say every time Paulie's name came up. Then one day, Paulie showed up.

———

A guard at the state prison wheeled the ancient looking man into the small sparsely decorated room where another, much younger man was waiting.

"Hello, Lorenzo," the younger man said. "It's been awhile."

"Do I know you?" Lorenzo asked, fumbling for his bifocals hidden somewhere in the wheelchair saddlebag.

"Yes, you do. I'm Bradley. We met . . . oh, nearly 60 years ago."

"Bradley . . . that your first or last name?"

"It could be either, but you can call me Brad."

"Yeah, I remember you. The prank Clem played on me. You were in on it. I almost fell for it, but then I ended up here. Three wishes . . . Hah!" Lorenzo spat.

"Actually four, and it wasn't a prank," the man said sitting perfectly straight in the steel chair. You got your wishes exactly as you wrote them down.

"First you said you wanted to win the lottery . . . and you did. And you wanted Loreen to come back, and she did . . ."

"But I still owe the IRS two million dollars, and Loreen's dead," Lorenzo protested.

"Well that's because you shot her when she stepped in front of you to keep you from killing Paulie, into whom you then pumped eleven nine millimeter hollow point rounds in a marvelous fit of rage. I must say, you were magnificent. That was your bonus wish. You wrote very large across the page, 'I want Paulie dead'. Your wish was so clear that the prosecutor used that piece of note paper they found in your shoebox to get you sentenced to life without parole on two counts of premeditated murder with prejudice."

Lorenzo tried to get up, but fell back into his chair. "Why did you do that to me? Why couldn't you just grant the wishes like I wrote them?"

"Oh, we did; all your requests were granted just as you wrote them, but since you provided so few details, we had to supply them. Everything happened in a logical order and very naturally. Think about it, Lorenzo. All your life you have hated. You have flouted the law, your morals are abysmal and you think only of yourself. Bravo! You're my kind of guy. I just applied those elements of your character—or lack of character—to create the details. Everything that happened in regard to your requests, or wishes, happened naturally based upon your past behavior. That's all I had to go on, really, and you did leave the details up to me. Remember?" Brad grinned sheepishly as if he was sorry for

Lorenzo's plight. "Had you taken the time to supply the details, the outcome may have been different."

Then taking on a firmer demeanor, Bradley asked, "How old are you now, Lorenzo—ninety?"

The old man nodded affirmatively. "Yeah, I'll be dead soon . . . with any luck."

"Can't walk," Bradley pressed. "Probably in a lot of pain . . . arthritis. Can't taste your food. Haven't had a woman in—what— sixty years?" If Lorenzo had not been gazing at the floor he might have noticed the gleam in Bradley's eyes and a slight smile.

"Yeah, that and stuck in this place for the rest of my life," Lorenzo answered. "Why are you here . . . to rub it in?" Lorenzo asked.

"Oh no, quite the contrary. I'm here to assure you that while I have already granted three of your wishes, I haven't forgotten that you had four altogether, and that wish will be granted as well?"

Lorenzo's mind struggled to recall that bizarre encounter some sixty years earlier. "I . . . I don't remember," he said.

"Oh well, Lorenzo, I remember like it was yesterday, and I'm here to grant your request exactly as you wrote it. To use your words, 'it's clear cut.' You wrote very unambiguously, 'I want to live forever.'"

A look of stark realization crossed Lorenzo's features. His pale countenance turned ashen, his eyes widened as his own words flowed over him like hot lava, and Lorenzo Philbin cried for the first time in his miserable life.

IV

"When I despair, I remember that all through history the way of truth and love has always won. There have been tyrants and murderers, and for a time, they can seem invincible, but in the end, they always fall. Think of it----always."
— Mahatma Gandhi

Death and Resurrection

The coffee is the same as the stuff Liz used to make, but drinking it without her pretty face smiling at me from across the table forces me to really taste it. Somehow our morning conversations were always able to disguise the fact that this isn't coffee at all, but a chemical concoction of artificial flavors, coloring and polluted water.

I miss her most in the mornings; it was the only time she and I could really be together, the only time when we could talk, and the only time we could make love. I try to drink my chemical coffee more quickly now in order to get out of the apartment before the guilt sets in. After all, I'm responsible for her death. I was the initiator who didn't heed her warning to use the government-supplied condom. I was the one who didn't check the validity of our pregnancy permit that had expired a week earlier, but who could have imagined the consequences would be so devastating.

It seemed innocent enough. I was on my way out to my morning shift and she had just returned from her evening shift. As usual we spent our allotted ninety minutes of conjugal time, making small talk and sharing the warmth that emanated from the two burner hot plate in our living space. It was such a pleasure just to look at her.

160

She never changed, yet each morning her beauty was surprising to me, as if I was seeing her for the first time. Her sweet expression told me that she felt the same for me. I ached to touch her, but not touching her somehow increased the pleasure of just looking at her. Without saying a word, she leaned forward to touch my hand, the action allowing her lose-fitting gown to fall forward, exposing her lovely breasts to my admiring glance. We made love and I was not able to stop even long enough to protect her from what was to be.

Liz was overjoyed when she announced to me that she was pregnant, a joy that diminished with each day as her condition began to reveal itself. We both knew that the authorities would not allow a non-permitted pregnancy.

In her sixth month, she was taken off the line during her evening shift, a metal utensil was inserted and the unborn child was rudely ripped from her body. Her coworkers were kind enough to bring her home to me when it became obvious that she couldn't carry on with her duties on the line. She bled to death in my arms that night. I held her until the truck came to take me to the morning shift. I think she was buried, but exactly where, I'm not certain. I assumed that she was in the mass grave near the burned out church on the south side of the city, so I go there every morning, before my shift, to be near her. I used to bring her flowers if I could find some to pick, but that has become nearly impossible now. Nothing grows anymore.

I must hurry now to get to her grave before my shift starts. The pale disc of the sun has nearly overcome the black smoky clouds that have shrouded the world since the "Great Change" some fifteen years ago. The fire-storms that destroyed New York, Boston and Washington are distant memories, with only the constant smoke and cold as reminders. I remember the way the sky looked when I was a child, an infinite hue of colors from purple to bright white. I miss the colors, but have almost gotten accustomed to the varying shades of gray.

There is a man standing near the old church. That's unusual; few come here since the practice of religion was criminalized.

"Hello," the man said. "Do you have someone here?"

"Yes, I replied, "I think . . . my wife. You?"

"Yes; my father."

We stood in silence looking at a large mound of dirt that may have been a grave. There were large birds picking at the dirt looking for something to eat. The man threw a rock to scare them away. We watched them fly up to avoid the threatening projectile, then return to begin picking again.

"Did the CIA kill her?" the man asked.

"No, she was pregnant. Our permit had expired." I was ashamed of my tears, and I turned away so the man couldn't see. "It was my fault."

"I see. My father was killed by the CIA shortly after Kasam consolidated his power," the man said. "Dad was a scientist. He knew nothing of politics and supported Kasam when he ran for president . . . back when we still had elections. Then when it became apparent that Kasam wasn't the man he claimed to be, Dad started to pay more attention and began speaking out against his senseless executive orders, warrantless searches, and arrests.

"After several of our neighbors were arrested for conspiracy, Dad became increasingly vocal about the regime's abuses. Since his research was a valuable asset for government, they gave him several warnings, which he didn't heed. After a while, he refused to work or do any research that might support Kasam's agenda. That's when they did it. One evening they just came to our house and shot him while we were watching television. Do you remember television?"

"Yes."

"I remember his blood splattered on the TV screen. They dragged his body out and threw it on a truck with some other bodies. My mother begged them to let us bury him, but they pushed

162

her away and drove off. We followed them in our car—back when people could still own a car—and watched them toss the bodies into a trench right about here." The man pointed to an elongated scar in the earth. "Then a backhoe came in and covered it up. My mother said a prayer. Then she cried every day until she died a few years later. She's here too, somewhere."

The man fell silent and the two of us stared at the mound. The dark clouds seemed to be getting thicker and appeared almost to stick to the branches of the craggy, black, leafless trees that still stood near the church.

"Do you pray when you come here?" The man asked.

"No, I haven't prayed in a long time."

"I do."

"Why?"

"It gives me something . . . something to believe in, beyond this."

"You know, if I were CIA, I could shoot you for practicing religion," I said.

"I know, but you're not CIA. I can tell."

"No, I'm not CIA."

We parted company without saying another word. He went toward the country and I back to the city where the "line" awaited me.

I saw him again about a week later. I had gotten to the mass grave earlier and he approached from the other side after I had been there for about ten minutes.

"It's comforting to be here, in a strange sort of way," he said. "Do you come here every day?"

"Yes, when I don't have to work a double shift."

"I try to come here often, but sometimes I lose track of the time and can't get here before dark. I work kind of unusual hours."

"Oh? What do you do?"

"I'm a physicist."

"Like your father?"

"Yes. My normal job is at the Science Ministry Labs, but in the evenings I work at home on some work that my father left unfinished. It probably wouldn't interest you," he said. Then he changed the subject abruptly. "I never got your name. I'm William Blake . . . Bill Blake."

"I'm Norman Atkins," I responded. Everyone calls me Norman but you can call me Norm. That's what Liz always called me."

There was silence and both of us, hands in our coat pockets, simultaneously shrugged our shoulders up around our ears to ward off a sudden wind gust that accentuated the bitter cold of the September day.

"What are your thoughts about Kasam?" He asked.

"I don't know. I'm not a political person. I don't know anything about the man."

"No one knows anything about him. All I know is that he murdered my father, and I hate him for it."

"Aren't you afraid I might tell the authorities that you said that? It would mean a few more watt-hours of electricity for me if I did, you know."

"You won't tell anyone. They killed your wife. What's electricity to you?"

"I was responsible for what happened to Liz," I protested.

"No Kasam's policies killed your wife. Your only guilt should be in blaming yourself, not in making love to Liz."

I turned away again and cried shamelessly, for I knew Bill was right. I felt Bill's gloved hand on my shoulder and my sudden emotion was calmed by his comforting voice.

"There may be a way to hurt Kasam. Would you like to do that?"

"Yes," I said, turning to look into his dark, deep-set eyes. "I hate him . . . I want to hurt him." A flash of raw emotion boiled up into my throat until I could hardly speak "I want to hurt him bad."

"Good," he said, his voice soft and soothing, "then come with me. You won't be working on the line ever again, and no one will know where you went."

We walked away from the city toward a tree line in the distance. It took us an hour before we reached the dense woods where an automobile was hidden.

"You have a car?" I said, as we approached a rusty vehicle that was tucked in behind a stand of withered saplings.

"Yes," Bill replied, pulling some of the camouflaging branches off the top of the car. "Highly illegal, as you know, so this is as close to the city as I can drive it. There are several abandon gas stations around with enough residual fuel in their tanks to last several lifetimes, and spare parts are abundant."

We drove cross country for another hour, staying within the shelter of the woods. Soon we came upon an old farmhouse that looked as if it had been abandoned for decades. Bill explained that it had in fact been sitting idle since well before the turn of the century and that, while he worked and maintained an apartment in the city as a front, he actually lived here where he could continue his father's work. The interior of the old house was in much better shape than the exterior.

"Electricity?" I inquired, amazed that the electric lights worked, providing more brightness than I had seen since before Kasam's takeover.

"Of course. It comes from car storage batteries charged by an old welding generator out in the barn."

Bill showed me all around the two story farm house. It had a well-stocked kitchen with running water, which he explained came from the original deep-rock well that had been drilled more than 100 years earlier. In what appeared to be the parlor, Bill instructed me to have a seat on one of the overstuffed chairs that populated the room.

Bill stepped over to a long sideboard cabinet. "Would you care for a drink; perhaps some brandy? I make it myself from whatever still grows in the woods. It's pretty good, even if I do say so myself."

"I haven't had anything to drink since Kasam shut down the distilleries," I replied, "but tonight, I think I could use one."

Bill raised his glass as if to propose a toast, but he said nothing. I was surprised by the warm, pleasant flavor and the delicate aroma of the brandy. We sat and savored the sweet drink in silence for a while, then I asked the question that had been on my mind ever since we started our trek from the church.

"Why did you bring me here?"

"That will require some explanation from me and a great deal of trust from you."

"You said I could hurt Kasam."

"Yes and I'll get to that, but first, what do you know about Kasam?"

"Well, I know that he seemed OK when he was first elected, but then in his second term, he started grabbing power, issuing executive orders, ignoring laws he didn't like and issuing ones that fit his agenda. He ignored congress and used recess appointments to stack the Supreme Court. It all went down hill fast after that. When Kasam tried to stop the riots that ensued, the protestors burned down the cities and the smoke has fouled the environment."

"That's what you're supposed to believe. Kasam ginned up the riots and his thugs set those fires so he could declare martial law and grab more power. Kasam is a megalomaniac and was able to gain control by pitting lower class against upper class, poor against rich and inciting terror against his own countrymen; he maintains control by the same means. Now he is waging war all across the globe to grab more power, and he doesn't care if he kills everyone on Earth in the process. But that's not the worst of it. This artificial winter that we have been in for the past several years has catastrophically interrupted the food chain. The most recent estimates are that it will take at least a hundred years to heal the environment and we don't have that long. Starvation will kill everyone in much less time than that.

"If the situation is so futile, why am I here?" I asked.

"Come with me. I've been saving the best for last," he said as we descended the stairs to the basement. "This is my lab."

It was magnificent. The lights were bright enough to hurt my unaccustomed eyes. I had never been inside a laboratory before. Large, black racks of electronic equipment loomed against the walls of the room. They all seemed to be focused on a large ball shaped object in the center of the room. It appeared to be made out of glass. It was perched upon a black pedestal like a fortune teller's crystal ball, only it stood nearly eight feet high. Thick cables stretched out from below the pedestal, giving the apparatus the appearance of a huge jellyfish.

"What is it?" I asked.

It's a device based on a theory that my father developed. I don't think even he believed it could be built, but I built it.

"What does it do?"

"Here's where the trust comes in," he said. "My father was a great scientist. When he was murdered, he had already finished a large portion of his work, and although I was only a teenager, he had allowed me to work closely with him. Following Dad's murder, I vowed to complete his work and use it against Kasam. With your help, I will do just that. You see, what you're looking at is the practical application of my father's theory. I guess you would call it a . . . a time machine."

His words stunned me to the point of near speechlessness. He was either totally insane or a genius who had done something that most had thought impossible.

"I know it sounds impossible," he continued. "But if it works, it will allow us to go to one point in the past and eliminate Kasam at a time before he could formulate his evil plan—at his most vulnerable point—when he's a child."

"Kill a child?"

"It sounds cruel, but in fact it would be saving the lives of millions if not billions of children that he will kill as an adult."

"Have . . . have you tested it yet?"

"No. I have only enough fuel for one time. That's the reason I continued to work at the ministry of science, to get the fuel. I had to sneak it out of the lab in such small quantities that it took four years to get enough. Enriched Uranium is very difficult to steal, so we have just one shot at this. It will be your job to go back, locate Kasam the child, and kill him."

"Me?"

You will have to do it. You see, if you fail, I may still have time left to steal enough fuel for one last attempt. I chose you, not because of your intelligence or abilities, but because you have nothing here to live for anyway. And if you succeed, you will change the world to one that still has your beloved Liz in it."

"Do I need to learn how to operate that thing?

"No, I will do whatever needs to be done from here. Once I energize the system, it becomes automatic."

Bill stared at the floor for a long moment. I knew he was trying to put this strange concept into terms I could understand. "Think of time existing as a piece of very elastic fabric. It takes a great deal of energy to stretch the fabric, but once enough energy is applied, time can be contorted so that it can exist anywhere within the boundaries of the fabric. And as long as the energy holds out, the . . . uh . . . 'time traveler' can stay at that point in time. When the energy is removed, the elastic fabric snaps back just like the waistband on your underwear and the traveler returns automatically to his starting point in time plus the amount of time that elapsed during his travels."

"How much time will I have to do the job?"

"I was able to sneak out enough fuel for about one month, give or take a few days. If you haven't completed your task in that time, you will return to a world that will be pretty much the same as you left it. Of course, if I've missed something or if the theory is fallacious, you may not go anywhere, you may be sent to some place or some time that I didn't anticipate . . . or you could . . . die.

"What if I refuse?"

"Well, you will return to your miserable life, and I will try to find someone else to do it."

"I don't know. It's frightening," I said.

Bill turned his back on me to adjust a piece of equipment. "As frightening as what happened to Liz?"

"No," I said. "It couldn't be."

I had received too much information too fast and my mind was still trying to assimilate it. I could think of only one thing, Liz's death must be avenged.

"When do we do it?" I finally blurted out, not yet fully understanding the what or the how of the "it" to which I referred.

He turned back, and for the first time, I saw Bill smile. His expression was warm and comforting, and I glimpsed deep compassion in his dark, tired eyes.

"Not today," he said. "I'll cook us a nice dinner and we'll get some rest. I'll lay out the time-table tomorrow."

Bill and I returned to the first floor, he to the kitchen and I to the parlor where I attempted to read fifteen year old issues of the Journal Science that were stacked in a built-in bookshelf. An hour into my attempts at higher learning, Bill summoned me to the dining room for dinner. It was a delightful stew with real meat and vegetables that Bill told me he had vacuum sealed and frozen five years earlier when such perishables were still available on the black market. This was accompanied by a red wine that Bill told me his father had put back more than twenty years ago, and that Bill had been saving for just this occasion. It was one of the few mementos that he had from his parents. The other was a glass vacuum sealed humidor filled with cigars.

"Pre-revolution," Bill announced, as we sipped our after dinner brandy. "I mean pre-Cuban revolution; these cigars are more than sixty years old. My grandfather bought them 'green' in Cuba just before the embargo."

I had not heard of an embargo or any revolution in Cuba, and I didn't know what a "green" cigar was, except that it was wonderful. We retired shortly after that and I enjoyed the most restful sleep I had had in many years.

———

The next few weeks went by quickly as they were filled with training for the task ahead. I became proficient with the nine millimeter pistol that Bill's father had purchased when gun ownership was still allowed. I studied the history of the time to which I was to return, 1980 when Kasam was ten years old. Bill felt that would be the best age, because he would not be under the protection of his parents at all times, and would have been too young to infect others with the venom of his evil mind. Of most importance, I studied everything that was known about Kasam and his family. There was not much available on his childhood, because most of it had been expunged after the Great Change so that it wouldn't conflict with the brilliant life story that his public relations hacks had cooked up.

Bill's father had saved some newspapers and magazines from before the Great Change, which carried stories about Kasam, the young Senator who many thought could be a contender for the presidency. Some of the articles contained clippings from newspaper stories that marked milestones in the Senator's life.

I discovered from the yellowing newspapers that Kasam had grown up in Bloomfield, Indiana and lived there until he was nineteen years old. A few of the stories contained information about his childhood along with photos of him and his parents. One such article had a picture of Kasam at age eight, having just won the Warren County spelling bee. The picture also included his mother whom the caption claimed had matched her son's prodigious spelling feat some twenty-six years earlier. The caption read:

> **Like mother, like son** -- Eight year old David Kasam of Madison elementary school is congratulated by his mother after winning the Warren County Spelling Bee. Mrs. Kasam, the former Molly Werner, won the competition for the same school in 1952.

I studied the picture carefully in order to memorize the face of the child I would have to kill. The photo of the squat, round-faced child standing next to the pretty, statuesque blond woman made it obvious that the child must have gotten his looks from Mr. Kasam. Other clippings included the wedding announcement of little David Kasam's parents in 1968.

Werner-Kasam

> The First Baptist Church was the site of nuptials between Miss Molly Werner of Bloomfield and Mr. Armand Kasam of Paramus, New Jersey. The bride wore a full length gown of embroidered Swiss organdy with bell sleeves and a scoop neck bodice of silk brocade, encrusted with beads and sequins. She carried a nosegay of orange blossoms, heather and forget-me-nots. The Bride's attendants wore floor-length dresses of pink satin and organdy. The groom and groomsmen were attired in black tuxedos.
>
> Mr. Kasam is a materials engineer at the Chrysler Corporation's design division in Indianapolis. The Bride recently graduated from Indiana University.
>
> The couple will honeymoon at Lake Geneva, Wisconsin, and make their home in Bloomfield.

I stared at the photo of the radiant bride and wondered how such a woman could have produced the likes of David Kasam.

"Will you be ready tomorrow," Bill asked as he entered the parlor where I had been studying.

"I'm ready now," I replied.

"Tomorrow will be soon enough. Norman . . ." Bill said, uncharacteristically using the formal version of my name. ". . . there's something I haven't told you about this, uh . . . journey. And if you change your mind after I tell you, I'll understand."

I couldn't imagine what Bill could tell me at that point that could affect my decision to go.

"What is it," I asked.

"I told you that when the energy was dissipated you would automatically snap back like an elastic band. I believe that may be true only under specific circumstances."

"Like what circumstances."

"Like only if you fail to kill Kasam. If you do kill him, it will alter the future, Kasam's regime will never have existed and the need to even build the machine would be eliminated. My father will be here as will Liz; however, you won't. The machine that would snap you back will not be here. You will have altered time permanently."

"Where will I be?"

"You will remain in the past. Mind you, it could be a pretty good life. With Kasam out of the way, you will never have to live under his tyranny no matter how long you live . . . and neither will any of us. Obviously, if you fail, nothing will have changed, and in a month when the fuel runs out, you will snap back to the same miserable life you have now. No matter what happens, you probably will never see Liz again. I'm sorry."

My mind revolted at the thought. "Why are you just telling me this now?" I asked, trying in vain to control my quivering voice.

"I wasn't going to tell you at all," Bill answered. "But over the past few weeks, I've come to see you as a friend. I had not anticipated that happening. As a friend, I had to tell you, so you could have all the information you needed to make a decision you could be content with."

"If I'm successful, you will lose a friend. Won't that bother you?"

"No. I won't miss you, because I will never have known you. I know this is a lot to ask. Why don't you just think about it and give me your answer in the morning."

"I don't have to think about it," I said. Nothing has changed; I'll do it. At least Liz will get a fair chance at a normal life. Even if I don't come back, I can take some comfort in that."

"Well, then maybe we should have one brandy after all," Bill said, his tone still subdued.

I spent the night thinking about how I would do the job. The first thing I had to do after arriving at 1980 was cash in some old savings bonds that were part of Bill's inheritance after his mother died. Kasam's economic policies made the bonds worthless in the present, but since they were purchased in the early nineteen-sixties by Bill's grandfather, they would net me enough operating cash to sustain me for at least a month.

The second thing I needed to do was travel to Bloomfield, Indiana and get a room. The next thing would be to find David Kasam—the last thing, to kill him.

The large ball shimmered as I approached it. Although it looked like crystal, it was in fact, a plasma container that acted as a hallway, as Bill had described it to me, to anywhere in time. I understood little more than that, other than my overwhelming confidence in Bill's ability to get me there and back.

"I have set the controls as precisely as I can," Bill told me. "So you should 'land' sometime in 1980. But everything we do from now on is plowing new ground, so be prepared to make adjustments in case you miss by more than a few days. Just remember that if you don't kill Kasam, no matter where you are in about a month when the fuel has dissipated, you will snap back to this very room"

That was the first time I had heard even a shadow of a doubt in Bill's voice. I stepped toward the shimmering ball in the center of the lab, my suitcase in hand like a man about to board a bus. The glassy walls of the ball stretched inward, resisting me at first, then engulfing me. I found myself inside the ball and looking out at Bill who was sitting at a computer keyboard. I watched with detached interest as his hand moved deftly across the keys. In an instant, he disappeared along with the computer and all else in the room. Even the glassy ball that had surrounded me was gone. I was in the same house, but it was not a lab, but a basement with an oil furnace near the wall where the racks of electronic equipment had stood. The only light came through two window slits high on opposing walls. I found my way to the stairs and ascended to the parlor. It left no doubt that the house had been abandoned for decades. The light streaming through the broken parlor windows was blinding. The rays of sun were like spotlights that highlighted millions of minute dust particles awakened by my presence.

Outside, the sky was that of my childhood, blue and white with a sun too bright to look at. The air was light with not a hint of smoke, and a sweet fragrance had attached itself to the warm morning breeze. I was immediately aware that I was overdressed for the weather and removed my flannel shirt. The tee shirt underneath was more than enough for the mild September temperature. Even with that I would soon begin to sweat as I made the long walk toward the city.

Within a half hour I could see the skyline. It was nothing like what remained of the city in my time. The buildings glistened and the clear air allowed me to discern details even though I was still many miles away. *This is the way it will be again, when I finish my job here*, I thought.

A chain link fence that appeared to stretch for miles stopped me from moving ahead further. On the other side of the fence, hundreds of automobiles and trucks sped both toward and away from the city. Locating a tear in the fence, I pushed my body through and began walking on the berm of the road.

"Hey buddy," a motorist called as he pulled up behind me. "You got car trouble or somethin'."

"Uh yeah," I replied. "A couple of miles back."

"Well, get in, I'll take you in to a service station. You can call a wrecker."

"Yeah, thanks."

The service station was only a few blocks from the Greyhound terminal. There was a bank in the same block where I was able to cash in the bonds. Bill's father's driver's license with my photo came in handy. I then walked to the bus station and bought a ticket to Bloomfield. The only change in buses would be in Indianapolis.

The man at the ticket counter pulled a blue ticket out of its cubby hole and after writing something on it, pressed a large time/date stamp down on it. "That'll be forty-nine, ninety-nine," he said as he slid the ticket under the grill that separated us.

I walked away from the counter, absentmindedly scanning the ticket in my hand. *This will be the ticket to freedom for the entire world*, I thought. Then something on the ticket froze the blood in my veins. "This can't be right," I said aloud as I forced my way in front of a man who was asking for a schedule.

"Is this date correct?" I asked the man at the ticket window.

He turned the ticket around to check it. "Uh, yeah, September 23rd. You did want the ticket for today, didn't you?"

"No I mean the year," I said, poking my finger at the date.

"Sure, 1966. That's right."

The calendar behind the man verified his statement; September 23, 1966, was printed on it in large black letters. I had missed my time destination not by a few days, but by fourteen years. It would be four years before Kasam would even be born, and I would only be here for one month. I wondered if Bill had been wrong about that too.

I had twelve hours before we reached Indianapolis to figure out just what, if anything I could do to save the situation. It was hard to concentrate with all the colorful scenery whizzing past the bus window, so I let my mind fill with thoughts of Liz and the wonderful life I will soon give her. It was late by the time we reached Indianapolis, and I wondered if I should even continue on to Bloomfield. There was a thirty minute layover before the bus would board again. It was time I could use to walk around just to read the colorful signs and read brochures for museums and places of interest and get acclimated to this part of Indiana.

The answer to my dilemma struck me like a bullet between the eyes. The brochure said Indiana University at Bloomington, Indiana, the home of Hoosier basketball. I had seen the name of that University before, in one of the folders I had studied in Bill's parlor. The 1968 newspaper article said The Bride recently graduated from Indiana University. That meant she probably was a student in 1966. I hurried to the ticket counter. "I made a mistake," I told the ticket seller. "I must have said Bloomfield, but I meant Bloomington. Can you change it for me?"

"Sure, you'll even get a couple of bucks back."

—

The Volkswagen minivan wobbled to a stop at the curb in front of the little white frame house on Elm Street. The apartments in the row of old homes must have been one of the choice places on campus to live. Just a short walk from the music hall and library, the location also gave easy access to the small town of Bloomington.

An attractive blond coed got out of the passenger side of the car. She stood by the door and talked with the driver for a moment. Then she pushed the door shut and waved as the car drove off. Her blond hair and striking figure made Molly Werner easy to spot. As I watched in my rearview mirror from about a half block up the

176

street, I watched another car door open. The red Corvette Stingray had been sitting across the street from the little house when I arrived. The man ran from the car toward the house, cutting off the young blond girl before she could get inside.

It was a particularly vicious attack. He clamped his hand across Molly's mouth and dragged her off the porch stoop and behind a clump of Spirea bushes that delineated the front and side yards. I felt like a voyeur, sitting in my rented car, as the scene unfolded. The man became rougher as the girl struggled to free herself. He was a towering hulk and she was no match for him. He shoved her to the ground and the couple disappeared behind the foliage. I could only imagine what must have happened then. Less than five minutes later the man emerged from the bushes, walked calmly to his car and drove away. When the car was a safe distance ahead, I started my rented car and followed the Corvette for several blocks until it turned down an alley that ran behind several fraternity houses. I didn't need to go farther; I had gotten the tag number. I wasn't sure how, but I felt that information would be helpful later on.

Perhaps the attacker had done my job for me, I thought. But no, as unpleasant as this event had been for the young lady, history would show that the girl had survived to become Mrs. Kasam and the mother of the beast who would control most of the world.

I took a room at an old hotel in town and purchased some clothes at the Salvation Army store that made me indistinguishable from the rest of the residents. If I was successful, I would be stuck in this time for the rest of my life. I would not have the option of escaping to the future to avoid detection, so I would have to do my job without leaving any trace that I was ever in the vicinity. My fingerprints could not have been on file anywhere in this time, and I wore a pair of leather driving gloves most of the time, so they never would be.

Molly's rape made the headline on the front page of the Bloomington Times morning edition. The accompanying story said that this had been the third in a series of similar attacks on campus. Police assumed they were all connected. After breakfast, I used the pay phone several blocks from the hotel to call the patient information desk of the student infirmary for an update on Molly Werner's condition.

"She probably will be released in three days," the voice on the other end told me. That meant I could get to her easily in her own apartment, and do the job with the nine millimeter pistol that was registered sometime in the future. If it was ever found, it too would be untraceable. For the next three days, I watched the house at different times to get an idea of the traffic patterns—who came and went from the house, at what times and how much auto traffic there was on the street. At times, I parked down the street from the house and watched in the side view mirror; at other times I acted like a pedestrian, walking on the sidewalk past the house to get a better lay of the land.

———

Molly Werner still wore the bruises on her face, but even they could not hide the girl's beauty. I felt a surprising anger welling inside me toward the evil man who had done this. He would have done well in Kasam's world. I was revolted by his heinous act. Yet, I soon would do something to her that would be far worse. It would not be today, however.

For more than a week, she was in the constant company of friends and relatives, leaving me no good opportunities to do the job. I had a little more than one week left before I would be flung back into my present . . . if I wasn't successful. I used the time to learn the layout of the house. The traffic of well-wishers in and out of the house made my appearance on the front doorstep seem normal. There were four metal mail boxes in a line to the right of the door.

The name on the box marked Apt. 3 was that of Molly Werner. The glass sidelights flanking the massive front door gave me a good view of a long hall on the left, and on the right an open stairway leading to a second floor. A large dining room was to the right of the stairway and it appeared that all the apartments were on the left side of the hall. I tried the door and it swung open. In front of the last door on the hall were two large floral arrangements that I had seen being delivered earlier.

Below the stairway opposite the row of apartment doors was another door, which I guessed was the basement stairway. The door was locked.

Just then the door of apartment number three opened and I was face to face with Molly Werner. She was still in her robe as though she had just gotten out of bed, although it was past noon. Even without her makeup, she was beautiful. Her skin seemed flawless and almost translucent, a quality that revealed a pink flush in her face brought on by the surprise of seeing me in the hallway. Recovering from my own surprise, I managed a wave that resembled a feeble salute. "Just delivering another batch of flowers, ma'am. Hope you enjoy 'em."

"Thank you," she said in a softly sweet voice, as she slid the two large planters into her apartment.

Hoping my visit hadn't raised her suspicion, I quickly left the house and walked down the street to my car. A slow drive down the alley that serviced the garages behind the old homes revealed a basement window in the rear of the apartment house. One of the panes of glass was broken. I had found my way in.

———

The headline on page 3b of the Bloomington Times read:

Rapist still at large
Victims live in fear

Two of the four women who had fallen prey to the campus rapist were interviewed; their names were withheld. I wondered how the reporter got their names in the first place. They both said they didn't know their rapist, but that he had threatened to come back and kill them if they talked to the police.

The thought that the rapist would be blamed for my act of murder was of little consolation; I couldn't get past the fact that killing another human being was wrong regardless of the circumstances. Would killing Molly make me just as evil as Kasam? Can one evil act offset another? In this case killing this woman wouldn't just offset Kasam's evil, it would obliterate it so completely that not even a memory of it would survive. By killing Molly, Kasam will never have existed to rain his horror on the world. Aren't some wars fought for just causes, and isn't this a war? Am I not a soldier in a war against tyranny? I had been there; I saw the blood, the stacked bodies, the polluted atmosphere and the dying Earth that was the hallmark of Kasam's tyranny. No, killing this woman would not be evil. It would be the best thing I could ever do, and I would have to live with it. The mass grave was real, or will be if I don't do my duty.

My month was nearly up and I determined that this would have to be the night when I would kill a human being for the first time. I had checked out of the hotel earlier in the day and now was driving slowly past the small white house on Elm Street.

It was past midnight. All the lights in the little house had been off for nearly an hour, and Molly had no doubt gone to bed. Parking the rented car two blocks up from the house, I reached over and opened the glove box. The gun was already loaded. I pushed it into my jacket pocket and slid out of the car. I would not use the gun unless I had to, and as I pulled the black leather driving gloves tighter on my hands I realized that they would be my weapons.

As I had guessed, the basement window allowed easy access into the house. The dim reflection of the overhead light in the alley was adequate for me find the stairs to the first floor, and after carefully ascending, I reached the landing and the door that opened to the first floor. It was locked. Gripping the old door knob with both hands I gradually increased the pressure until, with a dull snap, the knob turned and I was standing in the dark hallway.

I approached the door of apartment three, grasped the old door knob and gave a quick twist. Another snap and the handle turned. I ran my hand up the edge of the slightly opened door, feeling for a chain lock. There was none. Despite the recent events on campus, the fear and paranoia that pervaded my time apparently had yet to arrive in this insulated place at this insulated time.

I felt my way along a wall, encountering only a few small obstacles as I went. My hand felt a door frame blocked only by a curtain of some sort. A figure lay on the bed in the small room. As I approached the bed, lights from a passing car outside briefly illuminated the room enough to confirm that it was indeed Molly Werner. She was asleep, and I hoped I could complete the job without her waking. My hands encircled her throat and I positioned my thumbs over her larynx and with all the strength I could muster, began to throttle her.

Even the darkness of the room could not conceal the panic on her face. Her struggling was ineffective against my determined grip, and I was grateful when her body finally went limp. She died quickly, but I continued squeezing for several minutes until my fingers became numb. Then, I gently placed her head down on the pillow and closed her eyes. She appeared to be sleeping again. I stood, staring down at her body, trying to fathom the reality of the atrocity I had just committed. My body shook with a horrible anguish of knowing that I had snuffed out a beautiful life, an act that could not be undone. Only the thought that I had just saved the lives of millions in the future that Molly would never see kept me from screaming. My legs were rubbery, collapsing under my weight until I was forced to sit on the edge of the bed to keep from falling. Unwanted tears came generously, wetting my face, now buried in my trembling hands . . . tears for the poor girl and tears for my own soul. My act had killed them both, and no power on earth could resurrect them. I instinctively pulled the comforter up to cover Molly's shoulders, and saw that even in death she was beautiful. I left the way I had come.

My instincts were telling me to run from the house, to keep on running and get as far from this place as possible. But it was clear that the only place far enough away was in a different time that didn't even exist yet, and having succeeded in this murder, I had closed the door to any possible return to that time. By the time I reached the car my body was shaking and it was everything I could do to control my hand as I put the key in the ignition. Revulsion swept through me like a cold dark wave that curdled the contents of my stomach and caused my brain to pound, and sweat to dampen my heavy wool shirt. With my eyes tightly closed as if to keep my brain from exploding, I could still see Molly's face; her expression, a silent scream that pointed an accusatory finger straight into what was left of my soul. No amount of rationalization could excuse what I had done. The air inside the car became stifling and the contents of my stomach were in my throat. Throwing open the car door, I exited just in time to be sick. I remained doubled over for what seemed an eternity. Finally, I returned to the car and drove off slowly toward the bus station where I had picked up the rental car. There, I would turn in the car and purchase a ticket to take me as far away as possible.

The bus wasn't scheduled to depart for another hour, so I purchased a humor magazine called *Mad* in the hope that it would divert my thoughts from my heinous crime. It didn't. Instead, I pretended to read while peering over the top of the page to watch the travelers as they traversed the bus station.

Two men in heavy overcoats walked hurriedly, passing right in front of me then over to the car rental desk. The rental clerk spoke briefly and nodded in my direction. As the two men came toward me, I subconsciously withdrew into my jacket and raised the magazine higher in an attempt to ignore them.

"Mr. Blake?" the taller man asked.

No one had ever actually called me by the name on my forged driver's license and I thought he may have been talking to someone else. I looked around, but there was no one else.

"Are you William Blake?"

"Uh, yes," I answered, feeling my heart stop for a moment.

"Did you just return a red Chevelle Rental car?"

"Uh, yes . . . I guess it was a . . . uh . . . Chevelle?"

The taller man flipped open a leather case containing a badge. "Mr. Blake, you'll have to come with us," he said as the two men grabbed my arms and lifted me out of the chair.

———

I sat in one of three straight back steel gray chairs in the small room. I was alone. The chairs and a steel table were the only furniture. The shorter of the two men had brought me a brown beverage in a can, the taste of which I remembered from when I was a kid, before such sweet drinks were banned. The activities of the evening had left me quite thirsty and the first can of the sweet drink went down quickly. The detective brought me another and told me he would be back in a few minutes. After what seemed to be a few hours, my bladder began asking for relief, but there was nowhere in the room to go.

"May I go to the rest room?" I ask the shorter detective when the two finally returned.

"Sure, in a few minutes," he said. "We just want to ask you a few questions first. OK?"

"OK, but hurry. I really have to go."

"I imagine you do," the taller said. "You nearly inhaled those two Cokes. Do anything last night to make you so thirsty?"

"No."

"Mister Blake, I'm Lieutenant Hathaway," the taller man said. "And this is Lieutenant Goldstein. We know your driver's license is a forgery and we can find no record of you in the State files. We'd like you to tell us your real name."

"William Blake."

"OK, Mr. Blake, if you insist. We'll go with that for now," Hathaway said. "Now Mr. Blake, can you tell us where you were last evening . . . say, between 9 p.m. and 2 a.m."

"I was driving around. I'm new in town and I wanted to see the university."

"So is that why you've been sitting in your car over on Elm Street for the past few weeks . . . Just looking at the university?"

"What?"

"Several of the neighbors saw you, Mr. Blake," Goldstein said. "You see they were scared and they reported your license number to the police. It seems that someone has been raping college girls; one of them right on that same street. Last night, someone killed one of them. We think it might have been you."

"No . . . no . . . I . . ."

"Of course, you were just driving around," Hathaway said. "No, Mr. Blake, one of the neighbors saw your car sitting down the street from the murdered girl's house. Then around 2 a.m. he saw you throwing up next to your car. You made a lot of noise. Why were you throwing up, Mr. Blake?"

"I was sick. I ate some bad food or something."

"I think you were sick all right. Sick because of what you did to that girl. It wasn't bad enough that you raped her, but you had to come back and murder her didn't you."

"No," I protested, "I'm not a murderer. You don't understand."

"Oh you're a murderer all right. You're just not very good at it. That's why you got sick. You raped her and then when you thought she might be able to identify you, you killed her. Isn't that right?"

"No, I didn't rape her. No, I didn't do it."

"What about the gun in your jacket, Blake?" Goldstein interjected. "Was that your backup in case strangling her wasn't enough?"

"No!" My bladder was bursting. "Please can I go to the bathroom?"

"Later! Blake, we've got witnesses who can confirm that you were in the vicinity of both the rape and the murder," Hathaway said. "We have two people who said a car that looked a lot like yours was parked in the neighborhood several times before and after the rape. Some of them saw the driver too . . . and I bet they'll be able to pick you out of a lineup."

"OK, OK, I was there. I saw the rape. It was a guy in a red Corvette. I followed him. I think he might belong to one of the fraternities on campus."

"I don't suppose you got the license number of that red Corvette?" Hathaway asked.

"Yes, I did," I answered as I reached into my pocket for the small slip of paper where I had written it. I handed it to Hathaway.

"What are you trying to pull, this is a gum wrapper," he shouted.

"Other side," I said.

Hathaway ran out of the room and handed the paper to a young man sitting at a desk in the office bay. He appeared to be giving him some instructions.

When Hathaway returned he said, "OK, were checking that out. I doubt it will turn up anything, because here's what I think

185

happened; I think you are our rapist. I think you raped Molly Werner, then when you thought she could I.D. you, you went back and killed her. The number on that gum wrapper could have been anything."

As Goldstein walked around the table toward me a feeling of disorientation struck me as if for a moment I was looking at everything through a fishbowl. It left as quickly as it had come, but it left me dizzy as if I had just awakened from a sound sleep and stood up too fast. Goldstein's expression held a glimmer of compassion almost sympathy as he approached me. "Look Blake, why don't you just come clean. You'll feel better. You probably didn't mean to kill her. It was an accident, right? You just wanted to scare her a little. You know so she wouldn't talk . . . and things just got a little out of hand. A jury might understand that. Come on Blake. We want to get some sleep and you . . . well, you want to go to the bathroom. Tell us the truth and we'll all get what we want."

"No," I answered weakly as the room seemed to shift before my eyes. This time the disorientation lasted longer than before.

Hathaway, standing on the opposite side of the table, placed his hands in the center and leaned across toward me, his expression glowering. "Blake you could get the chair for what you did and I hope I'm the one who straps you in. I spit on perverts like you. You coward; picking on defenseless women because you don't have the balls to do anything else. Do you know what you did to that girl, the one you murdered? First you beat her than you raped her. Then you know what you did? You beat her again. In fact you beat her so brutally that the coroner who examined her body said that if she had lived, she never would have been able to bear children. First you took that away from her, and then you came back later and killed her. She was only eighteen years old. A jury is going to see you for the piece of dirt you are, and they will rush to put you in the chair."

The room seemed to be spinning.

"What did you say? She couldn't have children?"

The room appeared to explode in front of my eyes and I felt as if I was being pulled out into space.

———

"Are you all right?" Bill asked as he led me away from the shimmering bubble. "What happened?"

"Maybe I ought to ask you," I said, my mind still trying to fathom what I had just heard from the interrogator who by now must have been dead for many years. "You said I might miss by a few months, but I went back fourteen years too far. Has anything changed?"

"Kasam is still in control, if that's what you mean. Anything you may have changed would have changed in this time too, so I wouldn't notice it. You might, however."

It was all I could do to ascend the stairs to the parlor where my legs refused to carry my weight farther, and I collapsed on the chaise.

I assumed it was morning when I awoke, not because of any additional light in the sky but because Bill had prepared breakfast. Outside, the angry black smoke clouds roiling through the atmosphere presented a stark contrast to the bright time and place from which I had just returned.

I stared at the food—it was more meager than I had remembered—but I couldn't eat. "I did a terrible thing," I said. "I killed a woman."

Bill looked up, his eyes locking on me for the first time since my return. His expression was filled with questions. "Tell me everything that happened," he said.

For the next two hours, I told him everything that had happened after he had sent me back.

"I thought she was Kasam's mother, but she couldn't have been," I said. "The woman I killed couldn't bear children, but I discovered that too late. She must have been his stepmother. What do we do now?" I asked, as I picked my fork into some sort of green vegetable.

"We wait. And when I have enough fuel for another try, we'll do it again. Tomorrow I'll drive you back to the tree line and you can walk the rest of the way . . . and Norman, thanks for giving it a good try."

—

They were waiting for me when I got back. A stocky man in a dark coat was sitting at the table in my room; two others were leaning against the back wall when I opened the door.

"CIA," was all the man said before one of the other men snapped handcuffs on my wrists. Saying nothing more, they shoved me out of the living space, down the stairs and into an unmarked vehicle.

The interrogation began with the anticipated questions about where I had been for the past month and some threats relating to punishment for missing work. But instead of being sent back to my living space with reduced rations, I was led to a cell in the basement of the old building where there were no lights and nothing to sit on save the damp concrete floor. After several hours, two men entered the cell and dragged me roughly into the glare of the hallway. One of the men twisted my arm painfully behind my back. I struggled momentarily and was struck behind my right ear with something that felt like a lead pipe, causing me to black out.

I awoke strapped into a hospital bed in a brightly lighted room. There was a tube taped to my left forearm. The tube led to a bottle of clear liquid hanging from a stand. The prospect of its contents sent a shudder of cold fear through my body. I noticed with relief that the tube was clamped off and the liquid had not yet been introduced into my blood stream. A small, balding man entered the room and stood at the foot of the bed.

"Do you know who I am," he asked.

"No."

"I'm David Kasam."

"What?" My mind was racing to catch up. There were too many new concepts in his statement; too much for me to grasp. "You're not Kasam," I said. "You can't be. Kasam's a big man. He's strong."

Kasam's lips slowly curled into a desiccated smile, as if he had just heard something simultaneously surprising and satisfying. "And I'm just a runt. Is that it? Amazing what a good PR campaign can do for one's image, isn't it. Yes, Norman, I am David Kasam and I'm in charge of everything, so I guess that does make me big . . . and strong. Now tell me about your little trip to the 1960s."

"What?"

"Now don't be coy, Norman. You know, how you used that 'time machine' to return to my childhood to kill me—only you went back too far. What did you do back there, Norman? Who did you kill?"

"How . . . how do you . . . how could you know?"

A gleeful chuckle wheezed passed the little man's lips. "Because Mr. Blake and I sent you there."

"But Bill is my friend. He . . ."

Kasam's smile broadened as he shifted his gaze to a dark corner of the room. My eyes followed suit and focused on the man emerging from the darkness.

"Sorry Norm, I work for him," Bill Blake said. Kasam and I have been planning this day for quite some time. I went to the 'graveyard' to find someone like you. Oh, don't feel like you're anything special. Just about anyone who visits that place regularly has reason to hate Kasam enough to want to see him dead. You just happened to be there at the right time."

I felt as if I had just stepped into a surreal landscape where everything was reversed. My mind could not process the information as fast as it was being presented. My brain began pounding with each heartbeat, faster and faster until my head felt as if something inside was trying to get out. I could not speak, only stare at this man who had created a nightmare for the world and now was unfolding another one for me, and he was getting a perverse pleasure from doing it.

"You see," Blake continued. "You were the first to test this device; our test pilot, as it were. We really didn't know if we'd be able to bring you back or even if you'd survive. We wanted you to perform certain tasks so we could gauge the effect a change in the past might have on our present, and we needed to give you an incentive to risk your life to do it. The unfortunate thing about it is that if you did change something, everything related to the thing you changed would also have changed, so anyone living in the present would have no memory of how things were before the change. We don't even know for sure what we really sent you into the past to do. All we know is we sent you there ostensibly to kill Kasam, and I purposely sent you back too far so you couldn't."

Kasam broke in, "After all, I'm not suicidal. You did survive. You did return, and from what you told Blake you made some edits in the past. Blake has told me about your killing the woman you thought was going to be my mother. That appears to be of little or no consequence to us today, but we can't know for sure until we have extracted everything that is in your head. You see only you know what the present was like before you left. You are going to provide us with the comparison."

My thoughts began to come clearer even in the face of Kasam's new revelation. "Why are you doing this?" I asked.

"I guess it won't hurt to tell you," Kasam answered. "You see, in order for me and my new order to come to power, I had to employ some extraordinary measures—perhaps 'drastic' would be more apropos. Well, these drastic measures pretty much put this planet in the crapper. The Earth is dying, the people are dying, and just a few of us are left to fight for the spoils. I got to tell you, Norman, the spoils really aren't worth fighting for."

Kasam turned to face the window and sighed. "You know, it really takes the fun out of being a despot."

"Do you expect me to feel sorry for you?" I asked.

"Oh no, Norman. You asked me why I'm doing this and I'm telling you. I plan to go back into the past. Perhaps start earlier and take advantage of knowledge that I can bring from the future. I plan to conquer the world without destroying it. Then, Norman . . . then the spoils will mean something."

"You're insane. I won't tell you anything."

"Oh sure you will. That little bottle attached to your arm makes the truth so easy to tell. All we have to do is turn it on and you'll tell us everything we need to know."

The fear that I had felt before attenuated, reverberating through my body as the young guard, responding to Kasam's nod, reached up and twisted the petcock that had stemmed the flow of the liquid.

"Now let's begin at the beginning," Kasam prompted.

———

I awoke in a room that looked like Bill's lab. Everything was the same except that instead of Bill standing next to the large shimmering sphere, it was Kasam.

"I know what I need to know," he said, his bent body forming a grotesque S-shape that forced him to cock his head sideways so he could look up into my face. If not for his malformed spine, he might have been tall. "Now I have the information to go back and take it all. I suppose I should thank you. Norman, when you look at me, what do you see?" Kasam asked.

"A deformed madman?" I answered, my fear somehow abated.

"Well, you are half right. My deformity is the result of a childhood disease . . . a disease for which a cure was found some twenty years too late for me. The vaccine that was finally developed is only effective if administered before the first symptoms become manifest. In fact, once the symptoms show up, the injection becomes deadly."

Kasam paused; his crooked smiled diminished to a frown. "Does the name Richard Gerard mean anything to you, Norman?"

"No, should it?"

"Not really . . . Dr. Richard Gerard is the brilliant physician who developed the vaccine for my disease. Gerard was a professor at Indiana University back in the sixties. The poor doctor had an unfortunate proclivity when it came to women, but no one knew about it until you gave the tag number of his red Corvette to the Bloomington police. His twenty year prison sentence for rape and manslaughter delayed his completing his work on the vaccine. You see those rapes were never solved until you went back and changed things and the poor guy was punished for a murder that you committed. Bottom line is, Norman, if you hadn't given the cops that lead, the vaccine would have been developed in time for me to have received it before I became symptomatic and the person standing before would look like the Kasam *you* remember."

"So, are you going to go back and make everything right for the good doctor so he can develop the vaccine in time for you to benefit?"

"Oh no, that would be much too complicated. I'm simply going to go back with a vial of vaccine and inject my young self before the symptoms showed up. It's rather ironic, don't you think; I sent you back to make some changes in the past just to test a theory. You thought you were being sent back to kill me. Instead, you made me into a bent, withering cripple. Now to pay back your effort, once I'm rejuvenated, I'm going to kill you with my bare hands."

Kasam ambled back to the time machine console and picked up a small black leather bag. "I'm not going to kill you yet, though. That won't happen until I return. Then it will be much more fun."

Kasam nodded toward the console of the machine. I was so focused on Kasam that I hadn't even noticed the man standing next to it; it was Bill Blake.

"You know what to do." Kasam said to Blake. "I'll be back in a few minutes."

He turned toward me, smiling. His dull eyes seemed to flash at the thought of my demise at his hands. Then he turned and pushed through the filmy wall of the bubble. Kasam nodded toward Blake and said something, but his voice could not escape the thin walls that encapsulated him.

As Blake reached toward the console, he spoke to me for the first time. "Don't worry, Norman. He'll not be back."

Kasam could not have seen Blake's finger press a key on the number pad, but from my vantage point, I could see that he was changing something . . . something very important.

"But you said you work for Kasam," I protested.

Bill Blake's lips curled into a sheepish smile. "What can I say, I lied. The truth is, Kasam really did kill my father, but when you're responsible for the deaths of millions, I guess you lose track. Kasam was totally unaware of any reason why I should hate him. I only pretended to cooperate to get close enough to kill him. But as you can see, his security is too tight even for his closest associates to do anything of the sort. Your successful mission and the change you made provided the opportunity I had been waiting for. I convinced him to go back and vaccinate himself against his debilitating disease."

"Why take such a risk?" I asked. "Why didn't he send someone else with the vaccine?"

"Think about it. He's paranoid; who could he trust?"

"Now brace yourself," Blake warned as he began the initiation sequence of the great machine. "Unless I miss my guess, everything is going to change in a few seconds. I sent him back to the right year—not the beginning of the year, but the end, after he became symptomatic. He'll inject a ten-year-old Kasam, who is already displaying symptoms of the disease, and as we heard from Kasam himself, at that point, the vaccine becomes deadly." A perverse smile broadened on Bill's face. "I believe our beloved leader is about to commit suicide."

———

Sitting at the breakfast table and sipping the whole bean black coffee with Liz is always the best way to start my day. Today seems even better. Yesterday, Kasam was very real; today he seems like a figment of some bizarre nightmare; tomorrow he may fade completely from my memory.

I rise from my chair to refill Liz's cup, kissing her gently on her soft shoulder as I do. The warm sun bathes our large kitchen in color as it filters through the prismatic glass surrounding the windows and the bright blue cloudless sky tells me it's going to be another beautiful day.

Liz reaches up to touch my hand. "Are you happy?" she asks.

"Oh yes," was all I could say as a fading glimmer of another world choked off my words.

The Disintegration of Terry Blanchard

Terry Blanchard selected his best Dacron trousers from the closet rod, nearly tripping over the pig that was rooting around the bedroom, its nose to the floor, sniffing for an elusive morsel.

"Frank," Terry addressed the pig crossly. "It's rude to enter the bedroom without knocking. Remember the rules: I'll knock when I come into your room and you'll knock when you come into mine. OK?"

The pig, unaffected by the scolding, followed his truncated snout into the hallway.

"Sometimes I wonder if you pigs really are as smart as the Association for Animal Equality says you are," Terry chided. "You could be replaced by a mule, you know," he said, thankful that his apartment was too small for a mule.

"Molly," Terry shouted to his wife, exasperation still coloring his tone. "Where's my cotton shirt?"

Molly, who had been sweeping the living room rug with a natural bristle broom answered without missing a stroke. "You mean your white one?"

They both knew he had only one cotton shirt and it was white, but Terry answered as if he thought Molly's question was pertinent. "Yeah, the white one."

"It's still drying on the stretcher in the kitchen, honey. Why don't you wear your Dacron shirt?"

Terry stepped into the efficiency kitchen and removed his best shirt from the anti-wrinkle rack. It was nearly dry. "One less power plant," he said, recalling the slogan the Fresh Air Coalition coined during their battle to ban electric irons. A shiver of pride, like electricity, coursed through him as he viewed himself in the mirror. The white tee shirt with its colorful Vegans-for-the-Environment logo on the breast pocket had been a well-deserved reward for his contributions to the VFE cause.

"I want to look my best, sweetheart," he said, entering the living room and quickly becoming mesmerized by the sensual sway of his pretty wife's hips as she swept the last crumbs of Frank's lunch from the tattered rug. "I'm giving my report on the Free Our Planet project at the VFE meeting this evening. It should seal my nomination for chapter president."

He placed his hands gently on the curve of Molly's lovely hips, and kissed her neck. "Damn I hate to leave, he whispered, but if I'm going to make it to the Ecology Pavilion on time, I'll have to run."

It's finally finished, he thought as he jogged slowly past the dark, abandoned high rise office buildings. Seeing the result of his work in the warm moistness of the failing twilight was a rush that rivaled sex. A flock of chickens scurried ahead. Except for them and a few cows, the traffic was pretty light. As two turkey buzzards watched from a broken window forty stories above, Terry rehearsed his presentation aloud, his speech assuming the staccato rhythm of his footfalls and choppy breaths. He visualized his audience hanging on his every word as he recounted their great victory.

"My brothers and sisters," he began as he jogged along the empty street. "As I traversed the streets to this meeting place, the success of our struggle was apparent. We can feel pride in our accomplishment, for it was from our organization that sprang the many groups, associations, and coalitions that have molded our new society. We started with one goal, to free America from the evil of eating animal flesh. Then from within our ranks new groups formed, taking our original concept further than we ever imagined. Thus divided, we attacked on several fronts and simply wore the enemy into submission."

Terry interrupted his concentration long enough to dodge a large pile of cow manure in the center of the street. "Praise the cows," he chuckled aloud; "and pass the fertilizer." *I'll have to put that in*, he thought. *Might get a laugh.*

OK, where was I? "While the VFE fought to ban the slaughter of farm animals, the Association for Animal Equality worked successfully to ensure their rights. With animal flesh banned at the dinner table, The Power to the People Committee had a much easier job of eliminating the electrical appliances used to cook it. This, plus the anti-television and computer provisions of the bill sponsored by People for Responsible Entertainment, eliminated the need for most of the nation's power plants. Then when the Fresh Air Coalition spun off from the PPC, they leveraged their strong Washington lobby to eliminate all small appliances. The one event, however, that did most to turn the tide was the recent passage of the fuel tax bill, co-sponsored by Senator Macklin of People for a Pristine Planet and Representative Williams, of Protectors of the Ozone dot com. The bill's twenty-eight dollar per gallon tax, removed virtually all automobiles from our streets and roads . . ."

Terry noticed a large man in a gray and day-glow orange uniform moving quickly toward him, his raised hand seemingly pushing the air before a rigid arm.

"Hold it right there, buddy," the policeman shouted. "You goin' to a fire?"

"No sir," Terry mumbled, trying to look innocent.

"You know there's no runnin' after sundown. It agitates our friends here." The officer nodded toward two dappled mares standing in the alley. "It's their bedtime, ya know."

"Sorry, amongst these buildings, I was unaware that the sun had set."

"No excuse. I'm gonna hafta write ya up." The officer began writing. "Uh, what kind of shoes are those?"

Terry looked down not remembering which pair he had put on. "Tennis shoes?" He shrugged.

"I'll have to cite ya for that too. Law clearly states, runners must wear runnin' shoes. I know, 'cause I'm chapter president of the Healthy Exercise coalition."

"The what?"

"The HEC. We just started last month. Already got our own law too," he said proudly while continuing to write.

"I'm sorry officer, but I didn't know about the law and I didn't have time to change my shoes when I got home from work. I . . ."

"Where do you work?" the officer interrupted.

"Moss Paper mill over on Juniper Street."

"Not anymore," the officer said

"What?"

"No more paper gonna be made 'less they can figure a new way to make it. Friends of the Trees just got their law passed." The man in gray and orange handed Terry the ticket and made a fanning gesture with the back of his hand. "Now git on your way . . . and no runnin'."

Outgoing VFE president Joe Hopper was vamping for time when Terry finally arrived to take his place on the dais. At least the encounter with the officer had cooled him enough to halt the perspiration that could have stained his good shirt.

Terry stood behind the lectern, and began. "My brothers and sisters . . ."

Suddenly a man stood up, and pointed toward Terry. "Is that a cotton shirt?"

"Why yes it is, thank you," Terry beamed.

"What kind of a beast are you?" A young woman shouted from the back of the room.

Terry turned in confusion to his colleagues on the dais.

President Hopper motioned for Terry to lean down within earshot. "You missed the meeting last week. Vegans for the Environment merged with the Rootenites. We figured we'd have more clout that way. Under our combined constitution, only root crops are acceptable for food and clothing. Cotton isn't a root crop. Sorry.

"Wait," Terry pleaded to the audience. "Listen to my report. We don't need to go any further. Our environment is safe our brother animals are safe . . ."

"How about our sister tomatoes and beans?" someone shouted. "Are they safe?"

"Yeah, and our cotton." Someone else added.

"Kick the son of a bitch out," someone screamed. Four large Vegan/Rootenites carried Terry roughly out to the street, tearing his cotton shirt. Someone pulled Terry's wallet out of his hip pocket, extracted his VFE membership card and tore it to pieces.

Dazed, Terry staggered between the empty buildings that once housed thousands of office-workers, but were now just towering black shadows against the slate sky. The derelict structures provided a stark backdrop for the bull antelope grazing on the weeds that garnished the sidewalk cracks. Terry's mind should have warned him to keep his distance, but it was numb from a flood of disturbing thoughts. He no longer held a job. He would never be VFE president. The cause for which he had devoted his life had turned into a monster, becoming lord over its creators and now creating monsters of its own. The derision of the fist-shaking mob drove shafts of cold, lonely terror through Terry's heart. The gaping streets that earlier had seemed so inviting, were now reverberating with a threat that he would never see his home or Molly again.

When the antelope began its deadly charge, Terry was thinking about Molly sensually sweeping the living room rug with her straw broom, and in the moment before the impact shattered his spine, he wondered what Molly would sweep the rug with tomorrow?

Signs of the Time

The two old friends sat at one of the tables in the Coffee-Talk diner in Cabbage Town, drinking their usual bourbon on the rocks as they had been doing almost daily since Jim Morgan opened the place back in the late seventies. Bourbon wasn't on the menu, but it was in the cabinet to celebrate quitting time. Neither said much; it was just a way to wind down after a day of slinging hash for Jim and a day of spot welding for Willie Robinson. The television was providing background noise and every now and then one of the two men would comment on a story that was being covered on the six o'clock news.

"Damned shame about that kid being killed like that," Jim said as he stared into his bourbon glass.

"Bigger shame is what the TV folks are doin' with it," Willie replied. Kid attacks a cop; cop shoots the kid to protect himself and everybody blames the cop. A couple of agitators from outta state show up and get everybody stirred up and they burn down their own neighborhoods. Don't make no sense."

Jim took a sip of Bourbon. "If I didn't know you better, I'd say that sounds funny coming from you, Willie. I mean you were the victim of a lot of discrimination growing up, weren't you—being black and all?"

"Oh yeah, I remember the bad old days, the separate drinking fountains, substandard segregated schools. Yeah, I lived through that, but I never considered myself a victim, and I never tried to attack a cop, no matter what they did or said. I had better sense than that. Kids now-a-days ain't got no brains. Truth is, if they just stopped to think about it, they'd realize they got the same rights as the white folks; they just gotta learn the right way to exercise 'em."

"Right on," Jim said, giving Willie an automatic high five. "And if a white guy attacked a cop, he'd get shot too, but nobody would ever know about it . . . media would never cover it."

"Yeah s'pose you're right. Used to be when something happened, it was always the black guys fault. Now it's always the white guys fault.

"But what really bugs me," Willie continued, "are those damned agitators—you know the ones who do that for a living—well they feed off of preconceived notions and fear, pitting whites and blacks against each other, and they make black folks look like helpless 'victims' . . . like we're still a bunch of slaves or somethin'. Oh well," Willie said resignedly, "guess we have to live with it; nothin' we can do."

"Yeah, maybe not," Jim said. "Then maybe," he added, as if suddenly inspired, "There might be something we *could* do."

———

The sign went up at five a.m., about an hour before opening time at the Coffee-Talk. It was a large sign—yellow with big bold face letters—that covered half of the glass in the weathered wood frame door. Jim Morgan eyed his handy work with a satisfactory grin.

"Let's see what they say about that," he said, twirling his staple gun like a Wild West six shooter.

As usual, Willie Robinson was Jim's first customer of the morning. Like clockwork, Willie was always the first customer and had been for the nearly forty years that Jim had been in business. The two men met while serving in Viet Nam. They became friends during a fire fight, and over the next ten months saved each other's butts on more than one occasion. Jim was surprised when Willie revealed that he was from the same town in Georgia as Jim, but with Jim being white and Willie being black, they had gone to different schools and had never met. Returning from the war, they both got jobs at the GM plant. Five years later, Jim started his diner and Willie stayed on as a welder, and remained Jim's best friend and customer.

"Hey, Willie," Jim said. "What's up?"

"Might ask you the same thing, Jim," Willie replied, nodding toward the sign.

"Oh that. Just a li'l experiment; I want to see who notices it and what kind of comments I get."

"Kinda dangerous ain't it? I mean you're gonna lose some customers over it.

"I doubt it," Jim said, plopping two cups of black coffee down on the counter.

"You kidding? That sign's gonna offend half of your regulars if not more. You'll be lucky if you don't get a rock through your winda."

"Nah; nobody's gonna break my window just because of that li'l ol' sign."

"Well, I say they will, and you are gonna get run out of business; the TV guys will see to that."

"Bet you're wrong about that," Jim said resting his elbows on the Formica counter top and sipping the coffee steaming in his white Buffalo-China cup.

"You're on," Willie said with a grin. "I bet you ten bucks that by the end of the week your business will have dropped off by twenty-five percent compared to your average and that at least one TV reporter will be demanding your scalp."

"I'll take that bet and I'll give you two-to-one odds," Jim said, pulling a twenty out of the cash drawer and sticking it under a stack of saucers. "Gimme your ten and I'll put that here too. Whoever wins gets the whole thing."

"Look, Jim," Willie said, leaning further over the counter to make his point, "we've been friends for what, forty-five years? I just don't want you to get hurt over that stupid sign. If some redneck doesn't come in here and blow you away, the government will probably shut you down. Regardless you're gonna ruin your business. Besides, you're talking about your own people."

"Ok, Willie, calm down. Just what do you think that sign says, anyway?"

"I know what it says, fool. "It says plain as day, NO HONKIES SERVED HERE."

"What d'ya know, y'all *can* read."

"Yeah, I can read. What the hell man; *you're* a honky."

"No I'm not."

"Well, you're white ain't ya?"

Jim smiled. "What d'ya think a Honky is anyway?"

"A white guy . . . like you."

"No it's not . . . any more than a nigger is a black guy like you."

Willie cringed at Jim's use of the word. "I hate that word, man. It hurts."

"Yeah, well it's a hurtful word," Jim said, "especially when an entire race is lumped together like that. But you know as well as I do that there are some instances where that particular word fits, just like there are some white folks who deserve to be called honkies.

"Yeah, well some of them white folks gonna be bustin' your windas for callin' them that."

During their conversation a few more regulars came in and Jim filled a few more coffee cups and sat them on the counter in front of the patrons. Big Bill Ferguson plopped his large butt down on the swivel stool next to Willie.

"What say, Willie . . . Jim?"

"Oh, not much, Bill," replied Willie. "What'd ya think of the sign on the door?"

"I dunno . . . didn't read it; colorful though."

"Well, it says 'No honkies served here.'"

"'Bout time. Don't care to drink coffee with no honkies."

"What the hell you talkin' about, Bill; *you're* a honky," Willie said, his voice rising to a shrill squeak.

"No I ain't," Bill said in his quiet, matter-of-fact tone.

The restaurant started to fill with third trick workers from the GM plant seeking dinner and first trick workers seeking breakfast. It didn't really matter which shift a person was working, the menu was the same all day—breakfast. Jim got busy serving it.

Suddenly, a large lady appeared at the counter, her reddened face exuding emotion.

"So," she shouted. "So, you're not going to serve me, huh. Well, we'll see about that."

Jim turned from the urn where he was filling five or six cups with his wonderful personally blended coffee. "Of course, I'll serve you, ma'am. Why wouldn't I?"

"Well the sign on the door says you don't serve white people."

"No ma'am, it says I don't serve honkies. You're not a honky, are you?"

"Of course not, but I am white."

"I see that. Now what can I get y'all?"

"Coffee, I guess, but you better take down that sign, or you're going to lose a lot of business."

"No ma'am; sign stays."

With that, Willie mouthed the words, *I told you so.*

Jim just smiled and winked back.

Three days later as Jim was serving breakfast to the lunch crowd, he noticed a white van parked illegally on the sidewalk in front of his diner. The call letters of the local TV station were emblazoned on the side along with the slogan, *Get the News Before it's News.* Out of the van's passenger seat came a young coffee-complexioned woman with a microphone. The side door slid open and a shaggy haired young man jumped down. He already had a camera positioned on his shoulder and was shooting 'b' footage before he hit the ground. The girl posed beside the door for a two shot of her and the sign, then she turned and entered the Coffee-Talk. Walking up to the counter she announced, "I'm Gloria Washington from Nine News. I'd like to speak with the owner."

"Yes ma'am, you're lookin' at him, Jim said."

"No, the owner," she demanded. "He would be a black gentleman?"

"Uh no, I'm the owner . . . have been for 40 years."

"But you're a honk . . . I mean, you're a white person," the reporter said.

"Yes ma'am; nothin' wrong with your pretty eyes. Been white all my life. Now what can I do for y'all?" Jim asked, his broad smile exuding southern charm.

Somewhat taken aback, Ms. Washington said, "Well we got a call from a viewer about that sign on your door and my producer sent me over to interview you about it."

The interview took five minutes. As the reporter started to leave, Jim asked when the interview would air.

"Tonight at six, if the producer decides to run it," she told him. "If not, it might be on at eleven."

That night, Jim watched the six o'clock news, and although the news producer included a ninety second segment about a chicken crossing a road, Jim's interview never made it. Nor did it air at eleven.

The next morning Willie sat at the counter as Jim poured the first cup of the morning.

"Got a visit from a reporter from Nine News yesterday," Jim said, not turning around.

"Told ya so. I knew it was only a matter of time before the TV folks got hold of it."

"Yeah, well I got tired of waiting, so I called 'em myself—gave 'em a fictitious name. It was supposed to be on last night's news, but I got preempted by a chicken."

"Preempted by a chicken; now ain't that somethin'." Willie paused and stared thoughtfully into his coffee cup. "So how's your business been?"

"Never been better."

"OK, I guess you got me," Willie said, shaking his head in amused acquiescence. I'll concede the bet one day early if you will just take down that stupid sign before some nutcase comes in here and kills you."

"Well if you insist," Jim said, then added, "I have to take it down anyway."

"Ah hah! And who's forcing you to take it down? Some government agency I bet."

"Oh no; no one's forcing me to take it down. You see, I've always wanted to try this little experiment, but I knew it would ruin my business if I did. Well, last month I signed an agreement for the state to buy my property for the new ramp to the Interstate, so I don't have to worry about that anymore. Made enough money to retire in style. In two weeks Coffee-Talk will be bulldozed.

Jim continued, "The first sign was only half of the experiment. I need to take that sign down to make room for the new sign that will be in my door for the final two weeks; the one that will show the great disparity in how so-called discrimination issues are spun by the media and how that spin is blindly accepted by unthinking people. No one cared that my first sign discriminated against honkies, but I imagine they'll care about the new one. I'm pretty sure it will kill the Coffee-Talk before the state can demolish it. But it will be worth it if it makes people think." Jim slid the thirty dollars out from under the stack of saucers and handed the cash to Willie. "So my friend, I believe that by the end of the day tomorrow you will have won the bet."

With that Jim pulled out the other bright yellow sign from behind the counter. "What d'ya think of this?"

With the exception of one word, the sign was almost identical to the first sign that Jim had posted on his door. When Willie read the one word that was changed, he cringed, then he managed a half smile and shook his head.

"You damned fool," he said, "you gonna get yourself killed yet." Then with a humorless chuckle he added, "But then, ain't no chicken gonna preempt you on this one."

The Indispensable Component

With a Bachelor of Science in mechanical engineering from Purdue, an MBA from Indiana University, and five years of experience working for a Fortune 100 company, Mark Goodman was the ideal candidate to head up the Servo-Actuator Assembly Division at Amalgamated Machinery Products, Inc. of Waukesha, Wisconsin.

He actually would replace three sub-assembly managers since the company had decided to merge some of its vertical manufacturing processes as part of its productivity and austerity program. Mark had enjoyed a great deal of success with his previous employer and he was confident that he could be even more successful at Amalgamated. He had already worked out his day-by-day plan that he hoped would put him on that road by the end of the first week.

After introducing himself to his office staff, Mark keyed his assistant. "Cathy, would you bring me the design drawings for the servo-actuator assembly, please . . . Oh, and bring me the drawings for each of the three sub-assemblies too. Thanks."

His first task was to thoroughly understand the design of the product for which his division was responsible. The servo-actuator was a key component in every product found in Amalgamated's voluminous catalog. The proprietary device was also being marketed to dozens of manufacturers throughout the U.S., and the company was about to take the next step into the international marketplace. For Amalgamated that meant tens of millions in new revenue. For Mark Goodman it meant that during his first year and a half he would have to expand his production quota from 500 units per day to 3,000 units per day. In the process, he would have to make sure that the production costs decreased, not just from shear volume, but organically as well. That could prove as difficult as squeezing water out of a rock.

As Mark became familiar with the engineering drawings he also looked for quick and simple ways to improve production without reducing quality. The drawings were of a fairly simple device that could have been duplicated by anyone had it not been for the 63 patents that protected nearly every component mounted on the assembly base. With the exception of one spring, a handful of screws and rivets and something called an Engerstad Pin-Clip every part was manufactured exclusively by one or more of the Amalgamated divisions. So if anyone attempted to copy the device, they would still have to buy most of the parts from Mark Goodman's employer.

"Sweet," Mark said to no one in particular. "A nice tight package, no supplier problems and no competition." There also didn't appear from the drawings to be any obvious way to cut costs by further simplifying the device. Cost cutting would have to be in the manufacturing process.

"Cathy, I want to talk with everyone on the assembly line individually. Get a schedule together and let's start a parade of assembly workers through here starting first thing tomorrow."

"All of 'em?"

"Yeah, I don't want to miss anything. I'll only need 15-20 minutes with each one. Go for a schedule that won't slow down the line though."

"Yah, you got it, Mr. Goodman," Cathy said, her thick Wisconsin accent eliciting a broad smile from her Hoosier boss.

The first several interviews the following morning were with component assemblers, line supervisors and parts runners. Mark listened intently as the workers told him what they did on the line and how they did it. When he asked each of them what they could do to make the operation more efficient, the answer invariably was "Nah! It's pretty cut 'n dried. We just put 'em together fast as we can."

That pattern continued until mid-afternoon and Mark's interview with Arvid Jensen, whose job title was pin-clip sorter.

"What exactly is a pin-clip sorter," Mark asked.

"Well," Arvid began, "We got two bins over by the line dere. One bin is fer da clips and da udder is fer da pins. Sometimes dey get mixed up. So my job is ta sort da pins outta da clip bin and put 'em back in the pin bin."

"Is that a big problem?"

"Oh yah! If da assembler reaches inta the pin bin ta get a pin and comes out wid a clip, it slows down production. So I sort 'em so dat won't happen."

"Ok," Mark said as he made a note of Arvid's explanation. "Thanks Arvid. On your way out, send the next guy in."

The next worker was Frankie Butler.

"What do you do on the line, Frankie?" Mark asked.

"I'm a clip-pin sorter," he said, smiling broadly.

Mark straightened, "I just talked with Mr. Jensen and he said he did the same thing. How many . . ."

"Oh no," Frankie interrupted. No, Arvid's a pin-clip sorter. He sorts the pins from the clips. I sort the clips from the pins." Frankie went on for the next ten minutes differentiating between the two jobs. ". . . So you see the bins are about ten feet apart, so we don't get in each other's way when we're sortin'.

Mark suppressed his amusement. "OK. So there are just the two of you."

"Oh, yeah. You wouldn't want more than the two of us. Joe wouldn't be able to fill the bins fast enough if we had more sorters."

"Joe? Who's Joe?" Mark asked.

"Joe Barstow!" Frankie said as if Mark should have known. "Joe is the pin-clip gatherer."

"I see. Frankie, would you get Joe and send him in. I think you need to get back to the line."

"Yeah, I wouldn't want to get behind."

As Joe settled into the chair in front of the large wooden desk, Mark asked, "Joe, what does a Pin-Clip Gatherer do?"

Looking as if he'd seen a man with two heads, Joe replied. "Well, I gather the pins and the clips and I put 'em in the bins so Frankie and Arvid can sort 'em."

"And where do you gather these pins and clips?"

"Joe gave a derisive chuckle, "Why off the floor under the line, of course."

"How do they get on the floor?"

"I don't know, I guess the assembler drops 'em when he's putin' the subassembly together."

"Which one of the assemblers would that be?"

"Well, on the day shift, it's Bennie and then Jose on second trick and Mike on third. I don't know their last names."

Resisting the attempt to launch into an Abbot and Costello routine, Mark finished the interview then asked Cathy to bring Bennie in off the line.

"Ok, Bennie," Mark began. "Apparently there are so many pin-clips dropped during your shift, that we have a special process for gathering and sorting them. Can you tell me why?"

"Sure—and it's on all the shifts," Benny said. "You see, all three of the sub-assemblies are made about the same, except for the one me, Jose and Mike work on. That one has that stupid pin-clip where the other two have a simple rivet. The pin-clip is bulky and hard to install. Besides that, it looks sloppy. So I just drop the pin and clip on the floor and pop in a little rivet. Looks better, works better and doesn't cost as much. Oh sure, I try to use the clip, but if it hangs up when I'm installing it I just drop it and pop in the rivet. I don't want to slow down the line, ya know."

"But the design engineer must have had a reason for including the pin-clip. You could be jeopardizing the integrity of the unit by not using it," Mark protested.

"Ain't had no complaints yet and we've been doing it for more than a year now."

"We?"

"Yeah, Jose and Mike and me – we all agreed that we'd do it that way."

"Have you told anyone about the problem with the pin-clip?"

"Sure, but no one will listen. They just say 'use the clip the way it was designed.' So we use it when we can and drop it when we can't. Don't want to slow down the line."

When Bennie left the office, Mark keyed his assistant's desk. "Cathy, cancel the rest of today's interviews and get me Phil Potts, the design engineer on the servo-actuator program."

Cathy hesitated a moment then replied. "Uh, boss, Mr. Potts took early retirement right after that project was completed. I think he moved to Costa Rica or someplace like that. He didn't leave any number where he could be reached."

"Well, do a little detective work and see if you can locate him. In the meantime, I want to see the chief line supervisor, a Bob Hartberg, ASAP.

Bob Hartberg was a fireplug of a man who obviously never missed a meal in his life. Despite his sloppy appearance, he seemed to be capable of doing a good job and the workers seemed to like him.

"You wanted to see me, Mr. Goodman?"

"Yes, Bob. What do you know about the Engerstad Pin-Clip on the actuator rod sub-assembly for the servo actuator?"

"I know it's made out of stainless steel, costs about four dollars apiece and it's a pain in the ass to install."

"What does it do . . . exactly?"

Hartberg grimaced. "It pins the actuator rod bracket to the sub-assembly frame. Other than that, not much."

"Bennie says he sometimes uses a rivet instead; it seems to work better and it doesn't slow the line. So from now on, we're changing the design to use the rivet and we'll stop using the pin-clip."

Hartberg shook his head. "I don't think you want to do that, Mr. Goodman. You might want to check that out with engineering first."

Goodman focused on the design drawings on his desk then looked up at Hartberg. "The original designer has made himself scarce, and since I'm a qualified engineer and head of this division, I'm making the decision to discontinue using the pin-clip. Make sure that Bennie, Jose and Mike get the word."

"All due respects Mr. Goodman, I think that would be a big mistake."

"Well, that's my decision, and since we won't be using the pin-clip, I don't believe we'll be needing any Pin-Clip Gatherers or Sorters any longer, so those jobs will be eliminated. I will get with HR on that."

"You can't do that, Mr. Goodman. Bob Hartberg said. Those are union jobs and it won't be easy to get rid of them."

"Well, I've got to cut costs and that's a good start. Your job is to let them know that they need to start looking elsewhere for employment. HR will arrange for severance and whatever it is that they get in addition."

"Ok, Mr. Goodman, but I'm just sayin'. . ."

"Yeah, I know," Mark said, dismissing Bob's warning.

"Purchasing! Frank Bradley," came the response on Mark's next call.

"Frank, this is Mark Goodman in the Servo Actuator division."

"Yeah, the new guy—congratulations, that's a good division."

"Thanks. Listen Frank, does any other division at Amalgamated use the Engerstad Pin-Clip?"

"Ahh, the Engerstad Pin-Clip. Let me check." There was a pause as Frank scrolled through his records. Ahh, no, you are it, and you have a standing automatic repurchase order for 15,000 per month."

Mark did a quick calculation. "Are you kidding me? That's 60 grand a month, almost three quarters of a million a year. Frank, I want you to immediately cancel that standing order. Check the contract with the supplier and see if we can send our unused ones back."

"I don't think we can do that, Mark."

"OK if they won't take them back . . ."

Frank interrupted, "No, that's not it. I don't think we can cancel the order."

"Why not?"

"Well, it might be . . . it could just be one of those things that are . . . indispensable."

Mark tried not to let his frustration get the best of him. "Just cancel the order, Frank. This division will no longer be needing the Engerstad Pin-Clip.

Extra heavy morning traffic the next day made Mark 15 minutes late getting to work. Cathy was sitting in his office when he arrived.

"Mr. Foster wants to see you in his office right now," she said. "I think he's pissed.

Brandon Foster, the 52 year old Chairman and CEO of Amalgamated, was not known for his patience or mercy. He had built his corporation from a startup in Detroit where his innovative company served the thriving auto industry. As Detroit went from riches to rags, Foster began to diversify his portfolio of proprietary products and ultimately extended his reach to nearly every type of heavy industry. The business community was shocked when he pulled up stakes and moved the entire corporation to Waukesha, a dozen years ago, but as with most of Foster's decisions, it was a good move at just the right time. And it was in Wisconsin where he met his 33-year-old trophy wife, Zoe, a former cheerleader for Green Bay. Talk around the water cooler was that she could still bring out his softer side even after four years of marriage . . . that is if he had a softer side.

As tough businessmen went, Foster was the toughest. It was said that no one ever got the best of Brandon Foster—no one. Mark Goodman had met the man only once during the job interview process that took place the previous month. Foster was very scary then, but now as Mark entered his office, he seemed even scarier.

"Sit down," Foster said, more a demand than an offer.

Foster began. "Goodman, you're new, so let me explain something to you. You are a division head. You are not a design engineer. You do not have the authority to redesign anything, especially something that is used in every one of our products and is a major purchase for our manufacturing customers."

"Sir, I am an engineer and I saw where I could save the company nearly a million dollars a year and make a better product more efficiently."

"You thought you could do that by removing a key component from the Servo-Actuator Assembly?"

"Key component? No! I just replaced an expensive pin-clip that served no apparent use with an inexpensive little rivet. It holds up better, looks better, is easier to manufacture and saves thousands of dollars."

"Mr. Goodman, the Engerstad Pin-Clip is an indispensable part of the servo-actuator assembly and we will not sell one of those products without it."

"Indispensable? With all due respect sir, what can it do that a simple rivet can't do?"

Foster settled back into his oversized leather swivel desk chair. "You have two degrees from two fine universities and you have to ask me that?"

"My friend," Foster continued, looking down at his folded hands. "I'm beginning to think that you might not be the right man for the job after all. You've been here three days and during that time, you have redesigned a product without authorization. You have laid off three long-term employees, potentially costing the company several million in severance, continued benefits and retirement over the next several years. You've thoroughly pissed off the union and have discontinued a long-standing contract with a valuable supplier."

"Mr. Goodman, I have no choice but to fire you. We will mail you a check for one week's pay and two week's severance. Please wait in the outer office and I will have a security guard escort you out." Foster turned his focus to a file folder lying in front of him on the desk. Realizing that Mark was still sitting there, he said, "That's all . . . leave."

Stunned, Mark took a seat in the outer office. As he waited, he began to pick up snippets of a phone conversation between Foster's gum-chewing secretary and someone in another part of the building. Mark clearly was not supposed to hear what she was saying, but the acoustics of the room allowed sound to carry better than normal.

" . . . I couldn't believe it," the secretary whispered. "Yeah, they both were in there screaming at Mr. Foster. I felt so sorry for him. First his wife would scream at him, and before he could even say anything, the other guy would chime in about some . . . pin clippy thing. I heard Mrs. Foster say that if Mr. Foster didn't reinstate some contract and fire the guy who cancelled it that it would be a cold day in hell before he ever slept in her bed again." When the secretary stopped giggling, there was a pause, then she said, "The guy with Mrs. Foster? I'd never seen him before, but the security guard told me that it was her brother. Funny name though, a Mr. Engerstad or something like that."

For the first time this morning a slight smile appeared on Mark's lips. It was a smile of realization. Yes, he thought; the Engerstad Pin-Clip was truly indispensable . . . at least for Mr. Foster.

The Check is in the Mail

John Mason had done everything he could think of to get his new landscaping business off the ground, flyers, ads, postcards, robocalls—everything. After having studied horticulture and landscaping at the community college and receiving a degree, he bit the bullet and made a healthy investment in tools and a truck. He had enough money saved up to keep him going for about six months, but if he were to survive any longer than that, he needed to get a client or two.

Then it happened, the phone rang—a prospect. It was a man who said he wanted to see him a.s.a.p. The address was in a swanky Atlanta suburb, which was home to some of the South's biggest hitters.

As John drove up the winding driveway he could see that someone had already taken care of the landscaping in the neighborhood. Every yard was manicured, every bush placed perfectly and pruned to a fare-thee-well. The prospect was Franklin

B. Chesterton, Esq., an attorney of some notoriety throughout the Southeast. He asked John to follow him into the Indiana-limestone mega-mansion and up the stairs to a huge balcony that overhung the multi-acre back yard. There was an Olympic-size pool and a tennis court separated by a half acre of well-mowed Zoysia grass. Chesterton pointed to the grassy area.

"See that spot there?" he said. "That's where I want it."

"Want what?" John asked.

"The logo of my Alma Mater," replied Chesterton. "I want a large red and black logo right there . . . on that spot."

"You want me to paint the grass?"

"Hell no, I want you to dig up the grass and use the kind of material that you landscape guys use for that kind of thing—he spat the words " landscape guys" as if it were a pejorative term. "You know, like you see in front of some corporate offices or government buildings."

"How about an attractive ground cover and some flowers?" John asked.

"No, no. That stuff would be too much trouble to maintain."

"Well, we could augment it with some nice colored mulch."

"That's it," Chesterton cut in. "Do it all in mulch, and I want it big; I mean really big. Big enough so that asshole neighbor has to look at it every time he comes out on his balcony." Chesterton pointed over toward another large home that overshadowed his backyard.

"That's gonna have to be pretty big . . . twenty by thirty, maybe?"

"Bigger," Chesterton bellowed. "That guy over there is some kind of an egghead. Graduated from that other school. Blue and gold this and blue and gold that; that's all he ever talks about. *Go Yellow Jackets*," he said derisively. "I think he craps blue and gold. Red and black, that's what I want him to see—lots of it—and I want to remind him of that every time he opens his curtains."

"I take it you don't like him."

"I hate the arrogant S.O.B. Every weekend during football season, he sits up there on his balcony and watches his school on that oversized TV screen of his, and then when they win, he blasts that stupid school song from his outdoor speakers for the rest of the weekend." Chesterton stared viciously at his neighbor's house. "I don't care what it costs; I want to jam red and black down his throat 'til he chokes." Chesterton extended his hand. "Deal?" he ask.

"Deal!" John replied, shaking the attorney's hand, grateful to have his first client.

John worked on the project for two solid weeks; cutting out the sod, leveling, putting down a weed barrier and finally laying the mulch. When he finished, he surveyed his work of art. It was a thirty by fifty foot rectangle. The background was done in red, rubber mulch that would not rot as would natural mulch. In the center was an oval composed of white marble chips, with two thin lines of black, rubber mulch outlining the edges. The school's initials, also done in black, rubber mulch, were in the middle of the oval. Below the oval were the words, Go Dawgs, in black letters highlighted with white marble chips and red mulch. Best of all, it was facing directly toward the hated neighbor's balcony.

"Perfect!" Chesterton said, as he wrote the check for John's two weeks of work.

The check bounced.

When John called him about it, Chesterton Skirted an apology, and said innocently, "I accidently wrote it out of the wrong account. I'll send you another one."

The check never came. Numerous calls later, the money still hadn't been paid. The college football season came and went, and John still had not heard from Chesterton. In fact it seemed that the attorney had stopped answering his phone. John finally decided to see if an in-person visit would be any more effective. Receiving no answer after ringing the doorbell several times, John walked around to the back of the large house, and there were Mr. and Mrs.

Chesterton on the tennis court on the far side of the huge mulch display. John approached the tall fence surrounding the court and called over to Mr. Chesterton who flipped his racket into the air in a fit of anger and stomped over to the fence toward John.

"What the hell are you doing here?" he said.

"I came for my money."

"There will be no money," Chesterton said. "I'm not satisfied with the work you did, so I'm not paying."

"Mr. Chesterton," John said, "Our arrangement was for five thousand dollars; the materials alone cost nearly half that."

"Well, I'm not satisfied."

"You said it was perfect. What's wrong with it?"

Chesterton walked closer to the fence and pointed to the colorful mulch bed. "Well look at it. It's fine during the football season, but out of season, it's kind of ridiculous, don't you think?"

"But that's what you asked for and that's what I gave you."

"Look sonny," Chesterton snapped. "Are you a landscape consultant or not? You should have known that I would need something different for the spring. Your advice was non-existent. You're nothing but a landscape hack. So if you want your money, you are just going to have to sue me. But before you entertain such a thought, bear in mind that I *am* the premiere trial lawyer in the state."

The thought to sue *had* crossed John's mind, but in the final analysis, he knew he could never afford an attorney as good as the renowned Franklin B. Chesterton, and would probably lose.

"I won't bother suing you, Mr. Chesterton, but I will put a lien on your property for the entire amount," John threatened.

"Good try, but we never had a written contract—kind of stupid on your part—so I doubt you can secure a lien." Chesterton smiled contemptuously, "Think of this as a lesson in good business."

Since John's business had grown rapidly over the past nine months, the bad debt had become less of a problem and John busied himself with much more important projects. Chesterton was just a jerk, and he didn't want to waste any more time on him. Still, being stiffed by his very first customer stung, and John felt strongly that someday he would get his opportunity to turn the tables on Mr. Chesterton.

The opportunity came the following August when Chesterton called John's cell phone.

"Look, Mason," Chesterton began, "We probably got off on the wrong foot this past year, and I'd like to give you the opportunity to make it right"

The man's more arrogant than I ever imagined, John thought, but he agreed to a meeting the next day at Chesterton's house.

The two men stood in front of the slightly faded mulch bed as Chesterton pointed out some of the areas that needed to be refurbished. "I'll be happy to pay you the money for the original work plus a reasonable amount for sprucing this up in time for football season," he said.

John stared at the red, black and white display thoughtfully. "I can do that," he said, "but you understand that any work I do for you will require cash payment up front for the original work and the refurbishment. No checks."

"Of course, but is there anything you can do to make this less . . . uh . . . obtrusive after football season?" he asked. "My wife said she could tolerate it for a few months, but she doesn't want it year round, and she can be very insistent, if you know what I mean."

"Well, yeah. Beneath the mulch, we could plant some bulbs that would be dormant during the football season and bloom in the spring. I suggest using different colors and textures and blending them into a very attractive floral design. It would be pretty expensive, because the type of premium bulbs I plan to use don't come cheap and we'll need a lot of them."

"How expensive?"

"Oh, off the top of my head, I'd say eighteen to twenty thousand, if you want to do it right." Then John added, "and I'm sure your wife would want you to do it right. Combined with what you already owe me, I'd say twenty-four grand would probably cover it."

"Ok, do it," Chesterton commanded in his usual self-important manner, "but I will only pay half up front and half when the job is finished."

John agreed, happy that he had more than tripled the price in anticipation of the attorney pulling some sort of shenanigans.

After receiving the $12,000 up-front cash, John began work on the project, removing the mulch, and planting several thousand bulbs of different types and colors. Then he replaced the mulch, carefully recreating the school logo and spelling out "Go Dawgs." It looked even better than before. But, as John had expected, when he presented the bill for the remaining $12,000, Chesterton shouted, "I won't pay it," And slammed the door in John's face.

As John's business continued to grow, he had little time to think about Chesterton. John had been paid, and was content knowing that very soon, Mr. Chesterton would receive his payment as well. Then on a nice, warm, sunny March day, the phone call he'd been expecting came.

An out-of-control Franklin B. Chesterton was standing on his balcony, shouting over the phone, "You son of a bitch, you get your ass over here and dig this thing up." His diatribe became more incoherent as he looked down on the beautiful display of tulips, crocus and other early spring flowers that seemed to have sprung up over night, and now adorned the area between the pool and the tennis court. The red and black mulch display was completely hidden by a lovely blue background of crocus that covered the entire thirty by fifty foot rectangle. In the center, brilliant golden-yellow tulips formed the logo of Chesterton's nemesis, and below that the words in dazzling white flowers, "Go Jackets." John imagined he could hear rounds of laughter coming from Chesterton's neighbor.

"I want my money back," Chesterton screamed.

"Of course, Franklin," John said, a mocking chuckle in his voice, "The Check is in the mail."

"The definition of a good story is one that remains with you long after you've turned that last page."
— T.A. Uner

Acknowledgements

First of all I would be completely remiss if I didn't thank my wonderful wife Mary Ann, for putting up with me when I would disappear for hours at a time to pursue tantalizing plot lines as they bounced about in my mind. Her critiques were invaluable. Thanks also to my son Thomas, whose quick wit provided inspiration, and to my daughter-in-law Ann, and my grandkids, Madelyn and Matthew whose personalities I wove into some of my characters. To my good friend and mentor, Dick Dowis, who offered his editor's eye to my work and ultimately made me look smarter than I am, a big thanks. Finally, thank you to Father Nugent, who, many years ago, at Central Catholic High School in Fort Wayne, Indiana, told me that I was a good writer.

Made in the USA
Charleston, SC
27 October 2015